THE GOLDEN HUSTLA 2

WAHIDA CLARK

WAHIDA CLARK
PRESENTS
INNOVATIVE PUBLISHING

Wahida Clark Presents Innovative Publishing
PO Box 383
Fairburn, Georgia 30213
1-866-910-6920

Paperback ISBN: 978-1-954161-98-6
Hardback ISBN: 978-1-954161-99-3
Ebook ISBN: 978-1-954161-97-9
Audiobook ISBN: 978-1-957954-00-4
LCCN: 2022904378

Creative direction by Nuance Art
Cover design by Tina Shivers
Printed in United States

ACKNOWLEDGMENTS

To all of my readers, thank you so much for your patience and for rocking with me year after year. I am so excited to have delivered this book to you. But STOP if you have not read Part 1 lol. Special thanks to all of my proofreaders and editors. Chase, Kwame, Tashiyanna, Caroline, Alanna and Khloe.

Peace and Love
Wahida Clark
The Official Queen of Street Lit

PROLOGUE

*H*ow *did it come to this? How did I get here? Some stories only make sense when they end at the beginning.*

The muzzle flash ignited the darkness of the chrome Desert Eagle's barrel like a flare in the night. *BOOM!*

Nina was so very confused. Time stretched as things completely stopped making sense. This shouldn't have been happening. *Couldn't be happening.* She had to be dreaming, trapped in a nightmare that she desperately needed to end. A thousand questions, starting with *why*, began flying through her mind as the bullet made its inexorable way from the barrel. As it cut the air, Nina's heart thudded in her chest, threatening to burst. Her brain struggled to make sense of it.

But how?

Even with seconds stretching like years, the thunder of the first shot rang out, forcibly reconciling Nina with reality. The hand of an angry god slapped her as the first bullet hit. Fear, panic, pain, and a curious feeling of weightlessness took over as the large-caliber weapon tore her from gravity's grip. Being behind the gun was a viscerally different experience than being on its business end. Nina lived with fear before, but this was something altogether different as tears flowed to join her blood. She thought of Darlene, once a good friend and her first kill. *Was this how* she *felt as she journeyed to the beyond?*

Nina sentenced her to death for betrayal. But how many people had Nina herself betrayed? The escape to Georgia, the robberies, the constant running?

BOOM!

Another sound joined the first, flinging Nina back like a rag doll. Her dark eyes widened with shock; her full lips locked in an "O" of surprise as her caramel skin paled in disbelief. She screamed as her eyes were forcibly torn from the stricken glower of her killer, and her vision filled with blue sky. *So beautiful*, Nina thought, feeling like a leaf in the wind.

BOOM!

The third bullet struck Nina low, throwing her body forward to reacquaint her with gravity. With bloody fingers, she grasped desperately on the hood of the black Town Car the strange men had forced her and Rick into. They were dead now too. Her hands spasmed, trying to grip the hood of the car as if it were the only thing holding her to this world and maybe it was. But like everything else she wanted in life, it slipped away from her, leaving behind only dark streaks on the even darker paint. Then Nina slid to the ground.

As she lay in a puddle of blood spreading faster than she could ever imagine, it all unfolded before Nina like the petals of some terrible flower. A trail of bodies. A chain of so many ghosts. Her brother, D-Rock, and her best friend, Michelle, both gunned down as collateral damage in Nina's scheme. Customers from her old job. She saw the faces of the men she had loved, hated, and used. Nina thought about how she put her brother, Peedie, in a wheelchair. How many lives she played with, and for what?

Rinaldo, her old boss at We Make Millionaires, or WMM, elevated greed to an art form with his less-than-legal operation, eventually getting them all netted by the Feds. Oh, how she hated Rinaldo. His avarice and the way he used people disgusted her. But was Nina really any different? Nobody got filthy rich with clean hands, and as the curtain closed for her final act, Nina couldn't deny the truth. So, she lay there.

The sound of her own heart filled her with thunder. The pain was a living thing, tearing her sanity away layer by layer until death was a lover whose embrace she longed for. She opened her eyes, not to the white light of the loving embrace of her departed, but to cold steel and the stricken eyes of her killer.

"Nina!" She heard the familiar voice call out her name, and then one last gunshot sent her into darkness.

Where did it start? Why am I here?

Three Months Earlier

After snatching her from her father's family, Nina's youngest child, six-year-old Jatana, sat by the pool, soaking in the Florida sun. She had thought her mommy said that they were going to live in Georgia, but they didn't stop there. She didn't mind, though. Things felt like an adventure, and she liked their new destination. Rick was like a mysterious super-hero. Daysha, her eight-year-old sister, was convinced that Rick was one since he'd saved her from the bishop who was touching her.

Her seven-year-old brother, Jermichael, and Daysha played in the water. It had been what seemed like forever, and Jatana was enjoying reconnecting with her mom and her siblings. She had been living with her father's people. She knew her father adored her, and that was cool and all, but she would rather feel less like some sort of golden child and more like a kid again. To Jatana, her daddy was a mythical force, even though he was in prison, and his devotion made her feel special, but she was happy to be somewhere she felt like she belonged, instead of a spoil of war.

Her mother, Nina, lay back in one of the deck chairs, listening to her iPad. She had rubbed shea butter into her creamy caramel skin, and it shone in the warm sun. A pair of Ray-Ban shades hid her Egyptian eyes, and her full lips were pursed in contentment.

Nina's hand glided across her stomach, her mind turning to the new life she lived and the man she shared it with. Rick was tall with broad, well-muscled shoulders and a V-shaped frame that made her core quiver. His dark eyes and juicy lips worked like hypnosis and made her throb. The way he moved and occupied space radiated intellect and strength. His shoulder-length dreads were always tight, neat, smelling of frankincense and myrrh, and reminding her of some sort of Nubian king. Something about him made her want to risk it all, and together, they had scored a fifty-million-dollar lick. Her type of nigga.

Nina had been part of the Platinum Sales team at WMM working for Rinaldo, a ruthless genius. There were bums with feet cleaner than that man's hands. He was as dirty as he was brilliant. They were all making money, with an organizational culture that thrived on opulence. Her ex, Cream, had gotten her the job and while Nina had always known it was shady, the money was too good to pass up. As the organization started to slip, she and Rick had discovered a few things. For instance, her coworker, Shawn, was fucking Rinaldo's wife, Rochelle, and together, they had devised a plan to hit Rinaldo's stash with her ex. Rick had figured it out, stalked them like prey, then paid them with their own coin.

Things were finally beginning to come together, and her life was starting to look like she always imagined it would. She had her children with her, the drama and Trenton, NJ, were behind her, and she had a good man that not only loved her but had her back. Every time she thought of Rick, her pussy tingled, and her heart skipped a beat. Loving, strong, protective, fine, and good dick for days. He was just what the doctor ordered. Now pregnant, her libido was on fire, and Rick was the perfect fuel. But the fifty million dollars. *Fifty. Million. Dollars.* Nina didn't know what aroused her more—the cash or Rick. She knew money didn't buy happiness, but it sure made for one hell of an aphrodisiac. And the freedom it provided would allow her to focus on the finer things in life, like her kids and Rick.

"Mommy, you wanna play *Angry Birds*?" Jatana asked as she pulled out her iPhone and began playing the video game.

"Not right now, baby. Maybe later," Nina replied dreamily. Their rented house in Key Biscayne offered almost always-perfect Florida weather, and the sunshine and contentment had lulled her into a pleasant half sleep.

Rick walked poolside, talking on his cell. As he approached Nina, he hung up and sat on the outer edge of her chair, looking into her napping face with a smile. Even though he still saw Kyra when he looked at her, he was beginning to see Nina more vividly. She shared his dead lover's eyes and smile, and their mannerisms and sense of style were almost like twins, but Nina was solidifying her unique presence more, and the sensation of déjà vu was fading. Years after her death, the memory of his slain lover still haunted him. Rick's heart belonged to Kyra, but Kyra had belonged to another man, and her junkie husband had gotten her killed. The truth of it still pained Rick to this day, but the ghost was finally fading away, thanks to Nina.

Focusing on the living, he leaned down and kissed Nina's soft lips. She smiled as her eyes fluttered open.

"Sleeping Beauty awakes." Rick smiled.

"Only for the kiss of the prince," she replied playfully.

"You mean king." He winked. "We all packed?"

"Yep. All the loose ends tied up?"

"Of course."

"Then Arizona, here we come!"

They laughed. Rick glanced over at Jatana. She had finally warmed to him, the last of Nina's children to do so. It was bound to be like that, considering she was the child closest to her birth father.

"Hey, Jay, what you playin'?"

"*Angry Birds,*" she replied without looking up.

He smiled to himself and started to turn away until a thought hit him, leaving him shocked at his oversight. He got up quickly.

"Rick, what's wrong?" Nina asked, sensing his anxiety.

He didn't respond. He knelt next to Jatana as she instinctively inched away.

"No, Jay, it's okay, but...your phone. Can I see it?" Rick asked intently.

Jatana shook her head, then got up and moved to Nina's chair. Nina sat up.

"Rick, what—"

"The GPS, Nina! Jatana, baby, I promise we'll get you another phone," Rick vowed.

The word "GPS" hit Nina like a cold shock. Realization dawned, reminding her of the movie *Enemy of the State.* Yes, the movie was fiction, but GPS tracking was very real. *If ordinary people could track an iPhone, so could everyone else looking for them. Hadn't she hired a private detective?* She had already discarded her phone, but they had forgotten about the kids' phones all attached to the same line, the same bill. Nina turned to Jatana.

"Baby, Rick's right. We have to get rid of your phone, so nobody bad can find us, okay?"

"I can have another one?" Jatana pleaded, on the brink of having a fit.

"We promise," Rick assured her.

Reluctantly, she handed the phone to Rick, and he quickly

snatched the chip and the battery out of the phone, then stomped the phone, crushing it under his heel.

"What about Daysha and Jermichael's phones?" Jatana asked, unwilling to go down alone, in typical sibling fashion.

"Get 'em."

After destroying all three phones, he could finally breathe easily. Supreme would almost certainly be using Jatana's phone to track her. But for Rick and Nina's plan to work smoothly, anonymity was required as they slipped off the grid. Only once they had disappeared could they start spending the fifty million they'd stolen from Cream and Shawn, who'd stolen it from Rinaldo.

"Baby, don't worry. We're in Florida, but not for long. It was just good we caught it before we got to Arizona," Nina remarked.

"Yeah...Yeah, I hope you're right," he replied, but his cop's instinct was screaming she was wrong.

Dead wrong.

∼

"FLORIDA, YO...THEY IN FLORIDA," Charlese told Nina's ex and baby daddy, Supreme, as she sat with her laptop on her lap and her cell phone in her hand.

On the other end, Supreme paced the floor of his cell at FCI Fort Dix, with his cell phone glued to his ear.

"What part?" he growled.

"The Florida Keys area," Charlese replied. "Li'l cuz, don't worry. As long as Jatana has that phone, we can track 'em."

"Fuck that! Nina ain't stupid, Lala. Sooner or later, she gonna dump that fuckin' phone just like she dumped hers," Supreme ranted.

Charlese sighed. "Well, what you want me to do, Supreme? And stop calling me Lala. We are not ten anymore."

"I want you to go down there and get my goddamn daughter, Lala!" Supreme barked, ignoring her tirade about her childhood family name.

He tried to hold down his voice, but he was like a raging bull. He already looked like a boxer ready to rumble. Now, he was ready to fight like one. Prison buff, muscles bulging, and his nostrils flaring, he was prepared to spaz on anyone just to get rid of the tension he was feeling from losing his daughter. When his aunt told him that Nina had kidnapped Jatana, he had knocked out his cellie on G.P. Now, his new cellie, having heard about the last cellie, put his hand under his pillow and gripped his knife. Nina was Supreme's ex, but in his mind, she would *always* be his, and Supreme wasn't the type of man who let go of anything he thought was his. They hadn't been together for years, as he'd been in prison, but that didn't change anything. He figured as long as he had Jatana, he had power over Nina. So, the sooner he got her back, the better.

"Look, 'Preme, you'll be home in a coupla weeks, okay?" Charlese said in a reassuring tone. "I promise you, this bitch won't get away, phone or no phone. Trust me on that!"

"Whateva, yo. But, Charlese, seriously, I'ma hold you to that," Supreme answered, then hung up.

～

DIAMOND FRETTED OVER HER MAN. His light brown curls were plastered to his pale forehead. He looked like the death he had narrowly escaped. Cream's eyes opened up, and he fought to focus. At first, he didn't know where he was. The last thing he remembered before blacking out was the explosion.

"Oh my God, baby, oh my God! Nurse! Nurse!"

He heard the familiar voice and couldn't help but smile. *Diamond.*

She was definitely his ride-or-die chick. He looked into her brown, cheeky face, which always reminded him of a baby Jill Scott. She kissed him gently as tears streamed down her face. She was pregnant with this man's baby, and when she looked into his eyes, she saw a future. Cream might not have been worthy of her devotion, but devotion was never a thing of reason.

"Oh, baby, I love you! I love you! I *knew* you would make it!" she sobbed. The happiness was more for the bag. Where was the bag of money? She had been sitting by his side night and day since the shooting. His FBI handler, Federal Agent Rhodes, was the one who had informed her that Cream had been shot. She jumped on the first thing smoking to Florida and had been there ever since, never questioning how he knew to call her.

The nurse walked in and smiled with relief.

"Well, well, Mr. Davis, welcome back to the land of the living."

"My...My head is killin' me," Cream croaked, his voice weak from almost six days of nonuse.

"Which is to be expected," the nurse nodded. "You're lucky even to *have* pain. The gunshot could've ended everything."

"I was...shot?" Cream questioned.

Diamond squeezed his hand. "Yes, baby, you and your friend, Shawn. Unfortunately, Shawn didn't make it."

What? Shawn? His partner in crime? Gone?

It all came back to Cream—the fifty million. Shawn getting pulled over. The cop with the dreads. He remembered reaching over to get the registration and then, nothing. Cream should never have been here. His and Shawn's plan was flawless. Cream had used Nina as a spy inside WMM, and Shawn had been sleeping with Rinaldo's wife. They had the inside track for a move nobody but the Feds could have known about.

"A cop shot me," he said.

"A cop?" Diamond echoed. "Are you sure?"

He struggled to nod. "I'm positive. It was a cop with...

dreads," he snitched. Fear dominated his senses. "Can I get something for my head? It's throbbing," he asked the nurse.

"I'll see what I can do." She winked, then walked out.

Diamond looked to make sure the nurse was gone and then asked, "If a cop shot you, then he must've taken the money because the police didn't find anything, and the agent named Rhodes has been calling day and night to check on your progress."

"What did you tell him?" he asked, looking her in the eyes.

"Nothing. But, Akil...Are you working with the Feds?"

He shook his head. "It ain't like it seems. Trust me. Now call Rhodes and tell him I'm alive."

Diamond nodded. "What about the money?"

Cream remembered his brush with death. The swinging locs caught his eye in the side-view mirror. The barrel, the muzzle flash, and waking up in the hospital. It was simple.

"I guess we gotta find a cop with dreads and a big-ass smile on his face."

"Dead?"

"Dead," Rochelle said, void of any emotion.

"Who the fuck—how the fuck? Goddamn! I told you, Shawn was the wrong son of a bitch to use!" Rinaldo ranted, holding the visitation phone to his ear with one hand and running the other through his sandy-blond hair. His hawkish blue eyes were blazing indignantly. For a white boy who grew up in a trailer park, he felt that he had done really good for himself. His longer hair might've looked playful on others, but combined with the blue undertones of his skin, it made him look especially intense and ruthless. He had been the boss of WMM, where he made millions off his Platinum Sales Team, selling gaudy office products and hooking high-rolling customers into a high-stakes buy-in, gambling their wealth on a massive payout in gold coins. His business activities, which he swore were legal, had landed him in federal prison on conspiracy, money laundering, mail fraud, and wire fraud charges.

Rochelle had soulful, dark eyes and full, bee-stung lips. She was his chocolate goddess, Nubian queen. She sat on the other side of the Plexiglas, holding an identical phone.

"*No!* You said he was the best son of a bitch to use. Why the fuck do you think I seduced him?" Rochelle shot back.

"Since when did you start listening to me?" Rinaldo's tone dripped with sarcasm.

"Since our money was on the line," Rochelle retorted with a sexy wink.

Rinaldo chuckled. "Nothing beats the cross but the double cross, huh? Who do you think found out? Ole Charley Adams, our very own?"

"I doubt it."

"Why?"

"We're still breathing."

"Good point," Rinaldo admitted.

He knew his partner and mentor in WMM, Charley Adams, was an old-school gangsta with strong mob ties. He was in charge of the telemarketing scheme in Vegas. Nothing came in or out without his name on it. He made sure he had a piece of all the action. If he even thought for one second Rinaldo had orchestrated the robbery of the stash, no prison in America could keep him alive.

"So, what do we do now?" Rochelle asked anxiously.

Rinaldo shrugged. "What *can* we do?"

"Baby, we can't just let fifty—" she began to say, but Rinaldo cut her off.

"Watch your fuckin' mouth. Remember where we are. That's all I need is another charge." *Tax evasion, wire fraud, mail fraud, and prostitution are enough.*

"I'm sorry, baby. It's just...That's a lot of money."

"*All* our fuckin' money," he added with a growl.

"Exactly. So, what do we do? Just let it go?"

"Hell no! The first thing we gotta do is get me out of here."

"And how do we do that?"

Rinaldo smiled, thinking about his inside man from the GBI, *Detective Houser*, who intentionally botched the investigation by prematurely arresting Nina. They had been forced to let her go because the evidence didn't pan out. They couldn't prove she knew anything. All it did was provide him some warning.

∽

"*THE NUMBER you have called is no longer in service. Please check the number and dial again,*" the automated recording said for the second time. Reese started to dial a third time, but he knew it was useless. He was positive now that Nina had cut off her phone. He had gone to Atlanta but couldn't find her in any of her usual haunts. Dejected, he returned to Jersey. He remembered helping her unload the stolen dope and their escape from Jersey. The way his body responded when he thought of her. Reese couldn't deny the feelings he had for Nina, and now she was gone. He fought the impulse to smash his phone against the wall, barely holding himself in check. He knew he only had himself to blame. He ran his hands over his smooth, bald head. His high cheekbones, full lips, and expressive eyes usually helped with the ladies, but it was Nina he wanted.

Why couldn't he have told her the truth? He had a baby by Canada and was also a member of the Kings. Although he'd come close to being honest with her, he had covered it up with the "I have a family" line. The truth was, if the Kings found out he had helped Nina get away, he'd be a dead man. The gang was as dangerous to its own members as it was to outsiders, and his betrayal would earn him a special death.

But when he saw her sitting on the porch looking so gorgeous and gangsta at the same time, he knew he had to have her. Then, Canada's mom got killed, and all fingers pointed to Nina, which was when he'd decided to help her. He didn't regret it. That pussy was the best, but on top of that, he had fallen head over heels for her.

"Baby, you okay?"

Reese heard Canada's voice and came back to reality. She had just gotten out of the shower and stood in front of him butt naked, drying her hair with a towel. He eyed her delicious, Egyptian-brown skin tone, small but perky breasts, and thick, *ass-so-phat-I-can-see-it-from-the-front*-type hips. She may've been one helluva gangsta, but she had a baby face that made her look like she was forever eighteen, even though she was twenty-eight.

"Yeah, yeah, ma, I'm good," he assured her, putting the phone down and wrapping his arms around her waist.

Reese leaned down and kissed her lips, sliding his tongue into her mouth. Canada wrapped her legs around his waist as he walked her over to the bed and laid her down.

"You gonna make me have to take another shower," she giggled.

"Not if I lick you clean," he replied, then spread her luscious thighs and ran his tongue along the inside all the way up to her pussy. Finally, he took her clit in his mouth and began to suck on it as he slid two fingers inside her.

"Mmmm," Canada moaned, throwing her hips into his finger fuck as if it were a dick.

Reese bit down gently on Canada's clit, making her whole body tense up and her back arch. Electric waves of pleasure shot through her senses. Her pussy was soaked, and Reese couldn't wait to slide up in her.

"Gimme that dick, daddy," she begged, her pussy on fire.

Reese put Canada's legs over his shoulders and began long-stroking her hard and fast. The room filled with the sound of Canada's squeals, moans, and their bodies clapping together. Reese gripped her under the ass and spread her pussy lips, pushing himself in deeper until he exploded inside her, coating her walls.

"Nina," he mumbled under his breath absentmindedly.

Canada, swimming after sex's bliss, didn't know if she had heard right, but once she decided that she had, she didn't flip. She held her tongue. If he had said her name, she knew he'd lead her to Nina. Then she could kill two birds with one stone —literally.

Nina had helped orchestrate a robbery that left Canada's mother, Serita, dead, and a price had been put on Nina's head thanks to Canada's brother, B-Murder. Nothing would bring their mother back, but life would be much sweeter with Nina dead.

It was just another afternoon in Trenton, New Jersey. The weather was nice, and the women were nicer. Systems bumped, and the hood did what it did on a good day. A case of too much ass and not enough shorts caught Mo's eye as she sashayed past. Mo tried not to break his neck, but with an ass like that, it was a sin not to stare. He wasn't the finest nigga, but he was chocolate with a broad-shouldered, husky build and a full beard that did nothing to his full lips that ladies loved. He might have a shot and imagined sliding on her and bringing her to a spot to fuck.

He was slipping when the shots shattered the windshield and shredded the driver's headrest. It would've been Mo's head if shorty's trajectory hadn't had his head turned the right way. It was the only reason he'd seen the van swing into the intersection. The sliding door flew open, and a Dread with an automatic rifle leaned out, aiming at Mo. It had him ducking and, at the same time, throwing the car into reverse. The gunshots continued to pepper his car and whiz over his head. He couldn't see, but he mashed the gas, driving in reverse, just trying to put some distance between him and the shooters.

He didn't get far.

He backed right into an oncoming car, the momentum throwing him forward and into the line of fire. One of the bullets sank into the flesh of his shoulder.

"Aarrrghh, fuck!" he bellowed.

He grabbed the gun off his waist, squeezed off a few shots, and then dived out, leaving the door open for cover. The gunshots hit the door with such force they almost closed the door and left him exposed. Mo stayed low, trying to make his getaway when he felt the shotgun barrel pressed to his neck.

"Don't move," the gunman growled.

The car he had reversed into was part of the attack.

They had come around to box him in. Mo braced himself for the head shot, but instead, they snatched him up, threw a bag over his head, and dumped him in the backseat of the car. He had feared something like this would come ever since he and Cream had robbed Wicked, leaving Nina as his prisoner.

Unbeknownst to Mo, they drove him out to Hightstown, a small rural town about half an hour outside of Trenton, New Jersey. Cutting off the main road, they drove down into the woods to a farmhouse, the ass-end of nowhere deep. Behind the main building was a large barn and standing outside the barn was a man with long, matted dreads that looked like the roots of a tree. They hung down almost to his knees. He was dark-skinned and fit; his wiry frame was just a shade under what people would call tall.

One of his eyes was missing, and in its place, he wore a jet-black glass eye that made him look like Screwface and definitely helped him live up to his name.

Wicked.

Wicked held a long, wooden staff with snakes carved all around it.

The car pulled up in front of Wicked. The three dread-headed killers from Wicked's crew got out and dragged Mo between them. Straight from the "Yard," as the old-timers called Jamaica, just like their boss, there wasn't an ounce of pity between them. One of them snatched the bag off his head, and he came face-to-face with the hood legend and myth himself.

"'Member me? Mi youth," Wicked leered at him, his mouth full of a platinum grill.

Mo now knew he was a dead man. It was only a matter of time. He and Cream had robbed Wicked of mad weed and coke and had left Nina as payment. He thought they had got away, but it was never enough. He could pull Nina out of his back pocket, and Wicked might still kill him for spite.

Wicked took the staff, placed it under Mo's chin, and jacked his head back into a painful angle.

"You are going to die...but how is up to you. Me wan' know where is Cream and the gal?" Wicked hissed.

"Man, fuck you," Mo gritted. The pain in his shoulder burned into his brain. "I ain't tellin' you a goddamn thing!"

Mo knew he was about to die anyway, so why get his man fucked up too?

Wicked smiled. "You nah talk now, but you will soon. You'll see."

Wicked jerked his head toward the barn. His killers dragged Mo to the door and opened it. The stench hit him full in the face, but when his eyes finally focused, what he saw made him truly believe in hell.

Because he was looking at it.

"Soon come," Wicked snickered. "Soon come."

∾

Phoenix, Arizona

NINA HAD EXPECTED the place to be all desert and cactuses, but it was more than that. She fell in love with its warm, yellow-tinted paint colors, stone walkways, arches, plenty of terra-cotta accents, and the extreme dry heat that was good for her son's asthma.

The Airbnb they were renting was beautiful. It had a south-western adobe flavor with an attached garage, four bedrooms, and an in-ground pool in the backyard, sporting an eight-foot wooden privacy fence.

"Oh my God, it's beautiful, Rick! I love it!" Nina exclaimed. But to a woman in love, everything was beautiful. Even if she was a little nauseated from time to time, she knew it was the pregnancy, so she tried not to pay it much mind. Her dreams were coming true, and nausea was a minor inconvenience, especially since she always seemed horny, and Rick was always ready for her.

Rick smiled, satisfied that he was able to please her.

"I knew you would. I picked it out especially for you until the house is finished. Monday, you can start shopping for furniture."

"Now, you know I *love* that," Nina snickered and gave Rick a thank-you kiss.

"Mommy, look! We got a pool!" Jermichael yelled, taking Nina by the hand and leading her out the patio door. "Can I get in now, Mommy? Pleeeease?'"

"Wait until we unpack."

It took them a couple of hours to unpack their belongings. So, after dinner, the kids went straight to sleep, too tired to even think about swimming. Finally, Nina and Rick went out onto the patio hand in hand and looked up at the almost-full moon.

"It looks so close like I can reach out and touch it," Nina remarked.

"Go 'head, baby. Reach for the moon, and even if you miss, you'll still be among the stars."

Nina smiled and squeezed his hand. "I love the fact that you're so corny, Rick," she said, smiling. "Thank you."

"Thank me? For what?"

"For loving me. I know I come with my share of baggage and...Well, I just thank you for being able to see past all that," she explained. A tear sparkled in the moonlight as it traced her cheek.

Rick gently wiped it away, then put his tear-stained finger in his mouth.

"It's that flame you have for life that is why I love you the most. Flames, we both have our issues, but that's what love's all about, you know?"

She nodded. "I know, baby. I know. I love you."

"I'ma take care of you, Flames. I'll always have your back."

He kissed her gently at first, but the passion engulfed them both on the second contact. Rick thought of the poem that had sparked the nickname. He had been igniting the flames that night he brought Nina to New York. That was then. Now, he let himself be consumed by the very flames he ignited. Nina put her arms around his neck, drawing him into her kiss. Rick laid her down poolside, pulling up her shirt and bra simultaneously, running his tongue over her nipples. She arched her back and moaned deliciously, "Mmm...Rick, that feels good."

He slid off her shorts and dropped his to his ankles, then slid his hard dick inside her tight, wet pussy. Nina gasped and wrapped her legs around his waist, taking him deeper and meeting his every thrust.

"Right...there, baby, fuck me right—" Nina moaned in Rick's ear, nibbling on his earlobe.

Her pussy muscles gripped his dick tightly, making Rick want to long stroke her faster and faster, pounding her into submission as her pussy creamed all over his dick. Rick, unable to hold it, exploded inside of her with force.

"I love you, baby. You better not ever leave me," Nina huffed.

"I ain't goin' nowhere," Rick vowed.

～

SEVERAL HOURS LATER, Rick took the suitcases full of money to the storage spot he and Nina discussed. On his way, his phone rang. He already knew who it was.

"So, we good?" his connect questioned.

"Of course," Rick assured the connect. "When can we meet?"

"Hopefully, in a few days. In the meantime, I hope you have a safe place for our little nest egg."

"I'm takin' it there now."

"Does Nina know about it?"

Rick sighed. "Ay, yo, we talked about this. She's good. I trust her."

"Yeah, well, I don't, and if you trust her, maybe I shouldn't trust you," the connect grunted.

"Look, I—"

"No, *you* look! I put my ass on the line for that unmarked vehicle and that uniform. We're both in this thing up to our ears. Fifty million is a dream, but it'll stay one if that murder comes back to bite us in the ass!"

Rick frowned. "Murder? It was two, remember?"

The connect chuckled. "No, my friend. You fucked up. One of 'em lived."

"Fuck!" Rick spat and slapped the steering wheel.

"I hope for your sake he can't identify you."

"He can't," Rick lied.

"We'll see. In the meantime, take the money and stash it somewhere the bitch doesn't know."

"Ay, yo, watch your fuckin' mouth. That's my lady you're talking about."

"Fifty million says she ain't who you think she is," the connect laughed, then hung up.

Rick turned around and googled another storage company just in case his connect was right. Nina might not like him switching the stash, but she would understand the need to cover their tracks and create a layer of insulation. She didn't have to like it.

〜

He knew he was dreaming, but the dream seemed so real. It was like he could feel the California breeze, smell the smog, and hear the crash of the ocean.

In his mind, Rick saw all the familiar faces. Trae, Tasha, Kaylin, Marvin, and finally Kyra. Her eyes peered into his, almost as if they were beckoning him.

Come back. Come back. Come back.

Rick opened his eyes. It took him a minute to realize the woman with her head on his chest wasn't Kyra. It was Nina.

Damn, why does it feel like I'm trippin'? he thought to himself.

It was the fifth night in the row he'd had that same dream. Now, it was beginning to spook him. California. Something was calling him, pulling him back. He couldn't pinpoint what or how, but he knew he had to go.

Rick slipped out from under Nina and went to take his morning piss. As he relieved himself, he closed his eyes and saw Kyra's face. He knew he had to let her go, but it was hard. Damn hard. He washed his face and hands, then went back into the bedroom. Nina was awake.

"Did you take care of that?" she questioned.

"Yeah, good morning to you too," he chuckled and sat on the bed.

Nina smiled self-consciously. "Good morning, baby. Did you take care of that?"

"Yeah," he nodded.

"You put it in the storage spot we talked about?" she probed.

"Yeah," he lied, then caressed her cheek. "Relax, baby. Everything's good."

Nina took a deep breath. "I know, baby, but fifty million is a lot of money. I mean, I can't *believe* it! It's like we hit the freakin' lottery," she laughed.

"I know. We set for fuckin' life."

"So, when can we start ballin'?" Nina cracked, doing a little dance in the bed.

"Soon. We just gotta tie up some loose ends...which reminds me. I need to take a trip."

"A trip? Where to? We just got here."

Rick looked her in the eyes. "California."

"California? But I thought you said you could never go back? You would *never* go back," she reminded him. Her woman's intuition started to twitch.

"I know, but...I have to. Something's telling me I need to go. It won't be but a few days, okay? I promise," he assured her.

"What can I say to stop you?"

"I'm good, Nina. No need to worry."

"O-okay," she agreed reluctantly.

She leaned over and hugged him, but deep down, an uneasy feeling began to form, and it even seemed to have a name. One she questioned, but no matter how hard she tried, she couldn't shake.

Kyra.

1

Kyra stood in the mirror in her room and stared at
herself. "Who am I?" She looked into her face, high
cheekbones, skin the color of toasted almonds, and her exoti-
cally shaped eyes stared back. She waited for the bee-stung lips
to speak as if the mirror image would somehow talk back and
answer the question she posed again. "Who am I?"

Was she Kyra Brown, the name Nurse Wright called her, or
was she Kyra Blackshear like the white girl Keli had called her?

*"The name you're going by, that is not your name. Your name is
Kyra Blackshear. You were a medical student at UCLA. You are
married. I don't remember his name...Michael, Marvin, or something.
But if I saw him, I would know him, and you guys have a daughter.
Her name is Aisha, and a couple of times, you even brought her up to
campus," the white girl had told her.*

"Kyra, do you remember anything she just said? Any famil-
iarities at all?" Mrs. Bankston inquired.

Kyra looked at Mrs. Bankston and shook her head. She had
come to really like Mrs. Bankston, who was the director of the
group home she had been staying in ever since she came out of
her coma. Besides Nurse Wright, she was the only person she

could trust because everything else was a total blank. She still couldn't answer the question.

"Who am I? Do I live here in Arizona, or do I live next to UCLA? Do I really have a husband? A daughter? Are they looking for me? Do they miss me?" she said aloud to nobody but herself, or maybe her guardian angels, if they were listening.

The questions flooded her mind until she broke down and began to cry. She sat on the edge of the toilet, put her face in her hands, and let it all out.

Nurse Wright heard her sobbing through the door and knocked.

"Kyra, can I come in? It's me, Nurse Wright," she inquired.

Kyra jumped up and rushed to the door. Nurse Wright stepped in, and Kyra hugged her, crying into her chest.

"Why can't I remember anything, Nurse Wright? Where is my daughter now? And if I have a husband, why didn't he come looking for me?"

Nurse Wright hugged her tight.

"Baby, it's going to be all right. Now, get yourself together and don't shed any more tears. The only tears I want to see are tears of joy. Don't worry because, as Dr. Shalala said, you will wake up one day and may remember everything in bits and pieces or all at once," she explained.

Kyra nodded her head and hugged her arms around herself.

"This is all too much, Nurse Wright. I'm thinking all kinds of things," Kyra said, wanting to tell her about the dreams she'd been having but scared she'd have her committed or something. "My imagination is running wild." Anxiety took her, and she wondered if she looked as crazy as she felt right now. Kyra's hands trembled, and her heart ran laps in her chest.

"Baby, it's all right. Relax. Your imagination is supposed to run wild, but once you relax, we can get to the next step."

Kyra took a few deep breaths. "I'm relaxed."

Nurse Wright giggled. "That was fast. You are serious, aren't you?"

"I'm ready. What's next?"

"We have to go down to the police station and file a report. They will follow up with Keli's story, contact the college and your husband, you know, to let them know where you are. It'll be fine. I'll be there for you, all right?"

"All right."

"Then let's do this."

~

Nina's brother, Peedie, sat in his wheelchair smoking a blunt and watching the NBA Playoffs. In the back of his mind, he envied the men on the court. Not because they had million-dollar contracts, endorsement deals, and women galore, but simply because they could play the game. He loved basketball, which was a major reason why being paralyzed really ate at him. He thought about his sister, Nina, and even if he could do it all over, he would still be there for her. Still, he resented her for getting him mixed up in her bullshit. Here he was, para-lyzed for life, broke, and living with a trifling-ass broad. And for what? Because of Nina's scheming and lackluster shenanigans.

Behind him, Charlese, a.k.a. Lala the Hood Hacker, was silent as she crept in through the back door. Her smooth choco-late skin, diminutive size, large brown eyes, and full lips made her look like she should be in the top five percent on OnlyFans. Her body caused people to discount her abilities. But tonight, that didn't matter. Stealth and surprise were all she needed. That, and a lifetime of skill. When she was little, she had fallen in love with computers. They were simple and less messy than people. Numbers were numbers; they didn't change, but murder was simpler still.

The game was up loud, and Peedie was fully engrossed. He

let the game take him away to a place where he was a star on the court in his head. He was completely lost in the fantasy.

Lala ghosted through the kitchen like a shadow, and before Peedie's girl, Natalie, could scream, Lala had her hand over her mouth and a gun to her head. Supreme stormed past them, flipping Peedie's chair with his trademark aggression. Peedie squawked. His face morphed from fury to fear as Supreme filled his vision. *Jail put muscle on this nigga's muscles,* Peedie thought grimly.

"Where the fuck is Nina?" Supreme roared in his face.

Peedie's fear turned back to anger. *Once again, Nina's bullshit is coming back to haunt me!*

Peedie was easy to track down. Lala had simply uncovered where his disability check was being mailed. People at the post office loved to talk, and Lala hadn't met a mailman that wasn't nosy as hell. Once they had an address, Supreme didn't hesitate to make his move. He hadn't been home five days yet and was already putting in work.

"Man, I-I don't know!" Peedie stuttered, his anxiety tipping into a rage. *Fuck this jail-bred, monkey-ass nigga.*

He knew he could've given Supreme a run for his money had he not been paralyzed. But paralyzed, he knew he didn't stand a chance. He was ashamed that he thought he was safe. Getting shot in the back because of Nina's flex should have been enough. But it wasn't.

"Oh, you know, nigga!" Supreme accused and kicked Peedie in the face with his steel toed Timbs. Blood and teeth flew out of Peedie's mouth.

Supreme proceeded to stomp Peedie out until he lay there unconscious. Then he woke him up with a vicious array of slaps.

"Where she at, nigga?"

"Man, the fuck." Peedie fought to clear the fog. "I swear I don't know! She-she was in Georgia, and then she moved to

Florida. After that, she cut off her phone, and I ain't heard from her since!" Peedie snitched. Sister or no sister, he had already lost his legs behind Nina's bullshit. He wasn't about to lose his life too. The bullet that had taken his legs and nearly everything else had been meant for Nina. Stealing and moving the drugs had been her play. Now, she was living her best life, and her homegirl was dead, while he couldn't walk across the room.

Supreme knew Peedie was telling the truth about Florida because Lala had traced her that far before the signal went out, first on Nina's phone, then a few days later, on Jatana's phone. But he still felt like Peedie was holding back.

Supreme grabbed Peedie by the collar, lifted his limp body up, and put him back in his wheelchair.

"Peedie...I always liked you. You was always a good nigga. Too bad your sister is on some straight bullshit," Supreme spat as he pulled out an orange box cutter. "Too bad I gotta use your funeral as bait to bring the bitch outta the cut."

Peedie's eyes got big when he saw the razor's sharp gleam coming toward him.

"Please, 'Preme, don't kill me! I told you all I know!"

"Too bad it wasn't enough," Supreme gritted.

He gripped Peedie by the forehead and pulled his head back while simultaneously slitting his throat ear to ear with the box cutter.

Blood spurted from Peedie's throat as he gargled like he was drowning. A part of him wanted to die. He was no longer the man he used to be. It was better to die than to live how he'd been living. As the last bit of life drained from his body, he smiled, realizing that Supreme had really done him a favor.

"What about *her*, cuz?" Lala asked.

Supreme eyed Natalie.

"Please, please, I didn't see nothin'! I'll do whatever you say!" Natalie begged.

Supreme looked at her scrawny ass and then replied to Lala, "No witnesses."

"Nooooo!" Natalie bellowed. Then all her worries were gone, and her world went black as her brains spewed all over the plastic she had wrapped around her cheap-ass couch. Her body slumped and twitched at Lala's feet.

"Now, burn the place down," Supreme instructed.

"Grab his phone. Nina may try to call," Lala predicted.

Supreme grabbed Peedie's phone. Then they kicked over the kerosene heater and set the house ablaze. As they drove away, the fire engulfed the small wooden frame of the house, the flames licking at the cool night sky.

~

IT DIDN'T TAKE LONG for Mo to break. Being inside that barn was like being inside a living hell. The barn was full of dog cages, but there were no dogs in them. Just people. Men and women that Wicked said, "have stolen from me. Me bring dem 'ere just to watch dem die slow," he cackled. "Me wan' watch dem starve and suffer, breath in dem pain, 'ear dem scream!"

And scream they did. A man can't go too many days wounded without water before their organs begin to shut down. It was a painful way to die, especially inside a barn infested with rats, rats that fed off their injuries like Wicked fed off their pain. Once you were too weak to fight them off, the rats would begin to eat you alive, and all you could do was lie there, begging for death.

Mo watched a rat eat his way into a dude's stomach, saw the rat move around inside as the man screamed and yelled, while Wicked just laughed in his face. It seemed to Mo that Wicked had trained the rats to inflict pain. Once the rats started eating into his wounded shoulder from the shoot-out, he broke down like a shotgun.

"Okay, okay! Cream's in Florida; he's in Florida! He-he got shot, but he lived. He was tryin' to rob a nigga for fifty million dollars. But somethin' went wrong, and somebody stole the money from him!" Mo rasped frantically. His eyes pleaded for the torment to end, already too weak and numb to bat the rat away.

Wicked stuck his staff inside the cage and bashed the rat's head in. The other rats scattered.

"Fifty?" Wicked echoed.

The number sounded far-fetched, but he knew once a man reached the point where he was too weak to fight, he was also too weak to lie.

"Wha' fifty million dem say 'e stole? Speak!"

"Man, I swear! He-he down there tryin'-tryin' to get it back. Please let me have some water!" Cream had told Mo about the lick that got him shot.

Wicked nodded, and one of the Dreads gave Mo some water. He gobbled it down like it was a steak. Wicked looked at Mo, thinking long and hard. If what Mo was saying were true, not only would he have his revenge, but he'd also have a helluva lick as well.

He squatted down at eye level with Mo and watched one of the rats inching forward slowly, whiskers twitching. He observed Mo's fear-filled eyes home in on the rat moving toward him.

"You wan' live, my yout?"

Mo nodded his head vigorously, eyes glued to the roaming rat. Wicked watched the rat start to climb Mo's arm, going for the open wound.

"You take me to dat money, and you will live like a king, eh? But...you try to cross, I..." Wicked warned just as the rat began to nibble on Mo's wounded flesh.

"Please!" Mo cried out.

Wicked chuckled, then crushed the rat's head. Its body

dropped next to the other dead rat. Then Wicked used the staff to stand up.

"Bring 'im inside...for now," Wicked told his dread-headed henchmen.

As two of Wicked's men helped Mo out of the barn, Mo saw a swarm of rats descend on the bodies of the two dead rats. It was a lesson he wouldn't forget.

Rats don't care who they eat. They even eat each other.

$\sim$

Florida

"Mmmm, now, let me show you how much I missed you," Diamond cooed as she wrapped her lips around Cream's dick, then proceeded to try to deep throat all eight inches of his long, hard shaft.

Cream lay back in the hospital bed, loving every minute of it.

"Uhhh," Rhodes coughed to announce his presence as he came through the door. "Excuse me."

Diamond popped Cream's dick out of her mouth with a slurp and stood up, embarrassed. Cream smiled like a Cheshire cat and pulled the cover over his dick. It tented the covers. Diamond went into the bathroom as Rhodes approached the bed.

"Down, boy," Rhodes joked.

Cream chuckled. "My bad, yo," he said, holding his dick down.

He looked at his FBI handler and once again noticed his severe, but weathered, appearance.

"Well, I'm glad to see the shot in your head didn't affect your *other* head," Rhodes snickered.

"You and me both," Cream replied. "The bullet went in my head and came out. That's how I got lucky."

"Not many people get a second chance, Akil. Maybe now, you'll think long and hard about the straight and narrow," Rhodes warned him.

"Man, after this, I'ma be a Boy Scout," Cream swore, playfully holding up two fingers Boy Scout style.

Sure, you are, Rhodes thought pessimistically.

Diamond came out of the bathroom and sat at Cream's side.

"So, what can you tell me about the shooting?" Rhodes asked.

Cream shrugged. "Not much, man. Like I told the cops, me and my friend Shawn were down here on vacation when we got pulled over by a cop. A cop with dreads."

Rhodes scowled. "A cop with dreads? Not many of those around. Go ahead."

"I mean, really, that's it. That's all I remember. The cop was in an unmarked car. He pulled us over. The last thing I remember is reaching over for the registration," Cream explained.

"What about the fifty million dollars?"

"Huh?"

Rhodes smiled. "Come on, Akil. You think I don't know? You're not the only CI we have on this case. I know all about Rinaldo's stash. And I also know you and Shawn came down to rob him. Now, you need to come clean, or our deal is done," Rhodes threatened.

Cream looked at Diamond. She looked at him, her eyes pleading, *Tell him, baby.* She didn't want him to go to prison. Then she would never get her hands on the cash. Cream took a deep breath, then answered. "Yeah, man...Everything you said is true. We...we got the money, but evidently, this cop with dreads—" His voice broke off because suddenly, he was back in the moment. His hands trembled as he thought about the muzzle flash that almost ended him. He had to collect himself as the thoughts flashed through his mind. For a moment, he was lying there dying again. It seemed to stretch forever, but just like that, it was gone.

"What?" Rhodes asked.

"I don't know," Cream answered, shaking his head.

"Baby, are you okay? You want me to get a nurse?" Diamond questioned.

"Naw, it ain't that...anyway...Bottom line is the money is gone," Cream stated glumly.

"Okay. You heal up. But as soon as you're released, I want to see your ass back in Georgia, got me?"

"No doubt, yo."

"Don't try to shit me, Akil. If I find out you're on some bullshit, with all the crap I have on you, I'm going to put you under the jail. Are we clear?" Rhodes said.

"I said no doubt, okay?" Cream retorted irately.

Rhodes looked at Diamond. "You can go ahead and finish what you started now," he smirked, then walked out.

~

NINA WAS HAVING a ball with Rick's credit card. Their new identities meant that she didn't have to look over her shoulder. He had given the card to her to get some more clothes for her, him, and the kids. She was ready to ball out.

A bitch done really came up, she thought to herself, her thoughts full of the fifty million dollars. She couldn't wait until Rick said they could spend the money. But why did she have to wait? Why did Rick have the last word? Wasn't it *their* money? What would be wrong with spending just a little? He wouldn't miss it, and even if he did, it was *theirs*! The max on the credit card was only ten grand. Hell, for five people, that wasn't shit. Nina left the mall with the intention of going over to the storage center and taking out about thirty grand. *Yeah, that would do it.*

"Mommy, that lady looks like you," Daysha remarked as they passed the police station.

"What lady, baby?" Nina asked, looking around.

"Right there," Daysha pointed.

Nina looked, but all she saw was the woman's build and profile. The woman had dreads, and from the little she saw, she could kind of see a resemblance. However, what really bothered her was the funny feeling she got, almost like déjà vu but not exactly. She couldn't quite put her finger on it, but she knew she didn't want to feel it again. She had come to Arizona to recover and focus on healing, not to cause herself more trauma.

KYRA SAW the little girl in the freshly detailed SUV pointing at her as she started to climb into Nurse Wright's car. Her heart leaped. The girl had features so familiar she could have been her child. *Does that little girl know me?* The SUV with the staring child kept going, so Kyra sighed dejectedly, watching the familiar-looking little stranger ride away. *I'm tripping once again.*

Nurse Wright started the car and pulled off. She glanced proudly at Kyra. "Well, Miss Lady, whoever you were, you must really be something," Nurse Wright giggled. "I've been a personal care nurse for a long time, and I've helped many people. Before leaving for Arizona, I had the nursing agency in California send over any information they could find on you so I could answer any questions and help jog your memory. You were a student at UCLA, working on your master's. I'm proud of you for wanting to regain your memory, to rebuild. Most people just seem to sink into themselves after going through what you did. But here you are, fighting to get your life back. You should be proud too."

Kyra mustered a smile. "Yeah, but to be so smart, I feel really dumb. Nurse Wright, can I ask you something?"

"Anything, baby."

"Do you believe everything happens for a reason?"

"I sure do. The Lord places us in certain situations to teach us a lesson that we need. We just have to learn to trust His will."

"Then maybe I lost my memory for a reason. What if... What if the life I had was meant to be forgotten? Even left behind. I mean, why was I lost in the system as a newborn infant, like nobody wanted me? If I'm such a good mother, why can't I even remember my own daughter or what she looks like?" Kyra started to sob, remembering the face of the little girl from a few minutes earlier.

Nurse Wright reached over and patted Kyra's shoulder. "I know it's scary not knowing who you are, but it'll come in time. You now have all you need. All the names and addresses to find your family and get your life back."

Kyra wiped her eyes and nodded. "I want to thank you, Nurse Wright, for everything."

The nurse smiled. "Don't worry none, child. As long as the sun continues to shine on this old body, I'll be there for you whenever you need me."

2

Rick felt good to be home. Rejuvenated. California, to him, was like a trifling old lover. He knew the bitch was no good, but goddamn, the pussy was the bomb! He felt it deep in his gut that he shouldn't have returned. Too many memories, too many painful memories. But like a moth to the flame, he was drawn to California's heat. Besides, California wasn't only his past because if everything went right, it could be his future too.

He drove along Highway 101 in L.A. until he reached North Hollywood. He knew the area like the back of his hand. Even saw some of the same faces. Some things never changed. He pulled the rental over in front of a hole-in-the-wall topless bar named The Wet Nipple. At first glance, it looked run-down. Even the neon sign was only half working and blinked sporadically. But looks could be deceiving. The Wet Nipple was one of the front establishments for some of the most powerful Armenians on the West Coast. His pedigree was strong and, like Kim Kardashian's family, could be traced back to the early Armenian crime wave.

The Armenians controlled the identity theft market, which

was a billion-dollar industry of its own. Not to mention the white slavery rings that ran from Eastern Europe to L.A., worth another billion a year. But best of all, because of the war in Afghanistan, heroin had to be rerouted through Central Europe, primarily via the Caucasus Mountains, which the Armenians also controlled. So, he needed to distance himself from the robbery and make the money harder to trace. If Rinaldo were tracking the money somehow, it would be best for it not to lead straight back to him and Nina. It was for this reason that Rick had come to North Hollywood.

Rick walked into the dimly lit bar. A few lazy strippers worked the slow lunchtime crowd. When he came through the door, all eyes turned to him. He was the only Black man in the place. A large, bald, white man right off the Mr. Clean bottle stood up in front of Rick and folded his arms menacingly. He had to be at least seven feet tall and a solid 320 pounds. Rick looked up at him unconcerned.

The giant leered. "We no serve your kind here," he said in a thick Armenian accent.

"That's good because I'm not the kind of nigga you want on the menu, no how," Rick shot back.

"I have eaten Black pussy before. Taste like chicken."

The two men scowled at each other and then broke into raucous laughter.

"Rick!" the giant exclaimed and enveloped Rick in a huge bear hug, easily lifting him.

"Goddamn, Zev, put me the fuck down!" Rick gasped with a chuckle.

Zev put him down but held him by the shoulders. "It's good to see you, my friend," he smiled.

"Same here. You still ugly as a motherfucka, though!" Rick joked.

Both men laughed.

"Where's Vladimir?" Rick questioned, seeking out the Armenian Mafia's equivalent of a commissioner.

"In his office. Come," Zev replied.

They headed for the back, cut the corner, then went up a creaky flight of stairs. Outside the door of the office at the top of the stairs, a man carrying an AR-15 stood guard. He patted Rick down and took his pistol.

"You can have it back when you come out," the guard promised.

"I'd rather have yours," Rick cracked, admiring the sliding butt stock that made the civilian AR an automatic weapon.

Zev knocked, then waited.

"Come," said the voice behind the door.

Zev and Rick entered. Behind the desk sat Vladimir, the Armenian Don.

He was young for his position, just barely forty, but he made up in ruthlessness what he lacked in age. He was the James Bond type, though darker in both skin tone and spirit. The Russians seemed to revile Armenians, which is why Vladimir hated Russians and made it known whenever he could.

He sat behind the desk with a phone glued to his ear, and every few moments, he would grunt. Rick thought it was because of the phone conversation, but as he approached the desk, he saw a bushy redhead bobbing up and down, giving Vladimir head as he talked. When he looked up and saw Rick, a big smile spread across his face. He ended the call and hung up.

"My old friend! I would stand up, but ahhh..." Vladimir apologized, gesturing to the naked redheaded woman giving him head.

Rick chuckled. "Same ol' Vlad, huh?"

Vladimir shrugged, frowned, and then said, "Wait...hol— fuck," Vladimir grunted, as he came in the woman's mouth.

The bushy redhead swallowed, got up from her knees, and wiped her mouth with the back of her hand.

"Hey, Rick, would you like a shot?" Vladimir offered, gesturing to the woman.

Rick smiled. "Maybe next time."

Vladimir smacked her glistening, white, flat ass and said, "Okay, get back to work."

"I *am* working," the woman winked with a hint of cum in the corner of her mouth, then walked out.

"Where have you been, my friend, eh? I heard you were dead! That was the word on the street," Vladimir remarked.

"Believe half of what you see and none of what you hear," Rick schooled him, adding, "As you see, I'm alive and very well."

Vladimir nodded. "You were always a survivor. That's why I'm not surprised to see you. So, tell me, what brings us the pleasure of seeing you again?"

"Ten million large," Rick answered, getting straight to the point. Vladimir looked at Zev, then back at Rick.

"Those are my kind of numbers. Tell me more."

"I was hoping you could tell me. I'm looking to make a larger-than-life investment in the heroin business, and I need a good partner," Rick announced.

Vladimir leaned forward and put his elbows on the table. "If you have ten mil to invest, that means there is more. Why get your hands dirty, risk it all? It's never enough, eh?"

"Don't concern yourself with my why. I just need a good partner."

"For that kind of money, a good partner shouldn't be hard to find."

"Well, then, I came to the right place," Rick smiled.

"How quickly are you trying to move?"

"I have a few ends to tie up, but you should be hearing from me real soon; that is...if we have a deal."

Vladimir looked Rick in the eyes and replied, "Rick...my friend...We have always been friends but never partners. I definitely would not want to lose a friend simply because I lost a partner."

Rick knew Vladimir was giving him a subtle warning. The Armenians weren't the ones to play with. The scene at the end of *Training Day*, when Denzel got shot up, flashed through his mind. What the movie *didn't* tell you is they were Armenians, *not* Russians.

"Vlad, I would never bring you bullshit. I'm dead serious, and I'm not looking to come up. I'm looking to stay up," Rick assured him.

Vladimir nodded and extended his hand. "Then I'll be awaiting your call."

Rick shook his hand, then got up and left. As soon as he left, Vladimir turned to Zev and said in Armenian, "Make some calls. See what our old friend has been up to. No one comes up with ten million unless someone else somewhere loses it."

Zev nodded and left the room.

∾

"Has anyone ever told you that you look like Don Johnson from *Miami Vice*?"

"Don Johnson? You know how old that would make me? Has anyone ever told you that you look like my future ex-wife?"

"Several guys, although I'm already married."

"That's even better. Somebody else's ex-wife," Houser chuckled.

Rochelle smiled. "In fact, you know my husband."

"You got that right. I *know* your husband is one lucky son of a bitch," Houser remarked, eyeing Rochelle lustfully. *Rinaldo had to be out of his mind for not keeping this one close*, he thought.

She crossed her long, chocolate legs and pushed her hair out of her face. "That he is, and you know his name."

Houser sipped his drink and waited for her to continue.

"Rinaldo Haywood."

Houser smiled and looked around the crowded bar to see if anyone was watching them, feeling like this was his lucky day. What did Rinaldo want with him? Of course, he knew Rinaldo had wanted to get some charges on him that would stick forever but so far had failed.

"And to what do I owe the honor of enjoying the company of the very sexy Mrs. Haywood?"

Rochelle blushed. "Thank you. The honor is mutual...and so is the topic I want to discuss."

Houser downed his drink. "Not here."

"Then where?"

"Follow me."

He got up and began to walk away. Rochelle sashayed behind him. They left the bar, and Houser jumped into his ten-year-old Buick LeSabre. Rochelle climbed into her brand-new pink Bentley and followed him. He drove to the outskirts of Atlanta to a small, dirty, flat-level motel. Houser kept a room there just for the type of conversation he knew Rochelle wanted to have.

They parked and got out.

"You're quite the forward one, aren't you, Agent Houser?" Rochelle signified with a smirk.

"Shut up and don't repeat my name until I say so," he shot back gruffly as he opened the door. He held it open and beckoned Rochelle inside. Then he entered and closed and chained the door. Then he turned to her.

"Okay, strip."

"Excuse me?" she replied, taken aback.

"You want to talk to me? Then I wanna know who I'm talking to. You could be wearing a wire."

"I promise you I'm not."

"Don't promise; assure me. Strip or get the fuck out," Houser told her, then unchained and opened the door to emphasize his point.

Rochelle eyed him for a moment, then said, "Could you close the door? I don't want to catch a draft."

Houser smirked and locked the door again.

Rochelle reached back, lifted one long, delicious leg, took off one of her Louboutin heels, then took off the other. She then reached behind her and unzipped her dress. When she let it drop, she stood before Houser butt-ass naked. Her pert titties stood out firm and juicy, and her nipples hardened because of the room temperature.

"You don't wear underwear?" Houser smirked.

"Not with Versace," she shot back. "Satisfied?"

"Turn around."

She did as he said. His eyes settled on her pretty phat ass. When she turned back around, she asked, "Can I get dressed now?"

"Sure."

Rochelle picked up her dress and put it on again. Then she turned to him.

"Do you mind?"

Houser zipped her up. She sat on the bed and put her shoes back on.

"Now, what does Rinaldo want with me?"

"He lost a lot of money and wants you to help him get it back," she answered.

"Lost?"

"Robbed."

"I see. Am I supposed to find who took it?"

"No. Just get him out so he can find them himself," she answered.

Houser chuckled. "And how am I supposed to do that? Bust him out of a federal detention center?"

Rochelle smiled. "No. He wants you to preempt them… Convince the Georgia DA to indict him on the very same charges, then botch the federal evidence," she explained.

Houser thought for a moment. "How much did he lose?"

"Twenty million," she lied.

"And what's in it for me?"

"Two million. One now, one when he gets out."

"One million now…" Houser contemplated the offer. He was on his way to retirement, and he would definitely need the money. He had never been a dirty cop, but what Rinaldo did, he didn't really see as a big deal. So, he took a few rich people for a fast ride. Nobody twisted their arm. They played the odds and lost. No big deal. But that isn't what finally convinced him. The biggest reward was screwing his brother-in-law, Agent Rhodes. He could just see the look on that smug son of a bitch's face when he saw all his hard work go down the drain and Rinaldo walk free. That alone was worth the two million. On another note, two million wasn't anything to sneeze at.

"Make it three million-plus, and we've got a deal," he said, his greed being the winner.

"Three million plus what?" Rochelle asked.

Houser approached her and pulled her body to his. "Plus… a little taste of chocolate."

Rochelle smiled seductively. "You really think you'll be satisfied with a 'little' taste?"

Houser backed her up against the wall and slid his hand up her dress. Rochelle spread her legs, wrapping one around him while he finger fucked her. She devoured his tongue while unbuttoning his pants. She panted and moaned, cumming in his hand, turning him on even more.

"Stop teasing me," Rochelle cooed in his ear. She pushed him away. "Do we have a deal or what?"

"Tell him I'm all in. Where's the first mil?"

"In the trunk of my car."

She hiked up her dress, threw her arms around his neck, and both legs around his waist. Houser allowed his pants to free fall around his ankles as he slid his short, fat, white dick inside her hot, black pussy. Rochelle began to grind and bounce on him, wishing he had more to give.

"Bang me harder! Harder!" she squealed.

Houser gripped her ass and gave her all he had until she dug her nails into his back and coated his dick.

"Aw, fuck, baby, just...like...that...ahhh," she moaned, thrashing her head from side to side, surprised that he could last past two minutes.

Houser couldn't take it anymore and unloaded his shot. She pushed him away, feeling disgusted.

"I think maybe you're right," he huffed out of breath.

"About what?"

"I don't think I'll be satisfied with just a little taste."

Rochelle knew he wouldn't be.

~

EAST TRENTON WAS one of the Dreads' spots. Wicked controlled the area with an iron fist. Driving through Yard Ave., Reese saw Dreads hanging out, heard the sounds of reggae, and smelled curry goat. It was like they had turned the place into Kingston. Had the Dreads known that Reese was driving the cab, they would have opened fire without hesitation.

But the Rasta tam and fake dreads disguised him enough to give him a pass.

"Everything's good on my end," Reese said into his Bluetooth.

"Then let's make it happen," was Canada's emphatic reply.

That was one thing that he loved about Canada. She was so fucking gangsta!

The homeless woman pushed the cart along Academy Street, talking to herself and laughing. The cart was filled to the rim with bulky green trash bags. She pushed the cart until she approached a group of Dreads on the corner.

"Ay! You! Wha' ya wan', huh? Go way from 'ere. Donu 'ave nothin' for you!" one Dread spat.

The homeless lady cackled.

"But I have somethin' for youuuu," she sang. Then in one smooth motion, reached into the cart and pulled out a fully automatic AK-47, already locked, loaded, and ready to spit rounds.

Brrrrrrrrrapp! Brrrrrrrrrapp!

She let the muzzle spit flame, mowing down Dread after Dread before they could react and fire back. A few Dreads from across the street tried to come to their rescue, but Reese skidded up in the middle of the street, hopped out, and began laying Dreads down with another automatic weapon.

"Surprise, my nigga!" Reese barked.

The trunk of the cab flew open, and another King jumped up and let a riot shotgun rip, lifting Dreads off their feet and leaving a trail of blood, matted hair, and body parts on the sidewalk. The Kings had planned their attack perfectly. They were letting Wicked know who *really* ran Trenton.

"Yo, ma, let's go!" Reese called out to Canada.

She stood over one of the Dreads as he bled at her feet. He was hit up badly but still breathing.

"Why you wan'...kill me?" he asked.

Canada showed no mercy. She put the rifle to his face and blew it off.

"Well," she shrugged, "at least he died hopin'."

With that, she jogged over to the cab so they could make their getaway.

∽

B-Murder sat on the couch in his apartment, smoking a blunt and watching music videos. His chick of the moment brought him over a sandwich and set it on the coffee table in front of him.

"You good, baby?" she asked.

"No doubt," he replied nonchalantly, and the chick walked away.

He sat back, inhaling the exotic and enjoying his power. He was the most powerful King in Trenton, and he was greedy to expand his power. More power meant more money, and more money was really the only thing that truly mattered. No doubt he repped his set. He was King to the bone, but he was no one's fool either. He knew what life was all about, living to its fullest.

He stood up, looked at his reflection in the mirror, and smirked. "Damn, I'm gettin' old!" he joked about the premature gray he had in his hair which was something that ran in the family. His sister, Canada, had it, too. But at twenty-seven, it made him look distinguished and mature, causing strangers to deem him upright, though he was nothing of the sort.

The doorbell rang. He already knew who it was. He turned back to the couch, sat down, and took a bite of his sandwich.

"Ay, yo lazy bitch...Get the door!" he yelled.

Several seconds later, the chick reappeared and did as she was told.

"Who is it?"

"It's Reese."

"Open it," B-Murder told her.

She did. Reese and Canada came in. Canada kissed B-Murder on the cheek, and Reese gave him the signature handshake.

"What up, homie?" B-Murder asked.

"You already know, homie. K's up!" Reese responded.

B-Murder smiled. Reese was definitely a strong captain in B-Murder's army because he got money, and he wasn't afraid to put in work. The mission he had sent him on had proved that.

"It's all good then?"

"No doubt," Reese responded cockily. He sat down in the armchair catty-corner to B-Murder.

B-Murder looked at Canada and her raggedy clothes. "I guess they fell for the homeless trick, huh?"

"Bag Ladddyyy," Canada sang with a snicker, trying her best to sound like Erykah Badu.

B-Murder chuckled. "Sis, you crazy as a muh'fucka."

"Yeah, homie. They never saw it comin'," Reese remarked.

"Now, that fuckin' Wicked knows we ain't playin' wit' his goat-eatin' ass!" B-Murder growled. "But now that we brought the move to 'em, I need you two to lie low. We can't take any chances."

"What's good, homie?" Reese questioned.

"Yeah, what you mean 'lie low'?" Canada added.

"Just what the fuck I said, yo," B-Murder shot back, glaring at her.

She may be gangsta, but she damn sure wasn't about to test B-Murder. She knew her brother all too well.

"I just don't want y'all on Front Street. So, Reese, I want you to reestablish ties with your connects down in ATL. We 'bout to expand the set, and I want you to lay the groundwork down there wit' the homies, you feel me?" B-Murder instructed.

Reese smirked proudly. "*That's* what's up, homie. That will be a good look."

"You earned it."

"Yeah, and on top of that, we can finally track that bitch Nina because I know that's where she ran to," Canada spat, then gave Reese a look that said, *Nigga, you ain't slick.*

B-Murder nodded. "Indeed. The red light is still on that bitch, so see what you can come up wit' on that tip as well."

Reese stood up and gave B-Murder a pound. "Say no mo', homie. I'm on it."

"That's what it is then. K's up."

"K's up," Reese said, repeating the phrase. It was part gang-land bravado, part affirming the success of the Kings.

Reese and Canada walked out. He smirked to himself because he knew when he found Nina, the only thing he'd be killing was that pussy.

～

MO WAS SLOWLY GETTING some of his strength back. Wicked had him locked in a windowless room in the farmhouse. He was close enough to the barn that he could hear the death moans and suffering screams at night. Suddenly, the door opened, and Wicked walked in with two Dreads with automatic weapons.

"The time has come for you to put in work," one of the Dreads announced without a thick accent.

"I'm-I'm ready," Mo replied.

"We'll see."

"What you want me to do?" Mo turned to Wicked.

"Me wan' you to take me to Cream to get the money and the gal seen," Wicked explained.

Mo nodded vigorously as if Cream were some stranger instead of his main man.

"I got you."

"Take me peoples down to Georgia, make 'im tink every-thin' good. Nuting changed. You do that, and you will live. Fuck up, and you die...slow," Wicked sneered.

"I'll-I'll take you to him."

Wicked nodded. Another Dread came into the room and said something to Wicked in Patois.

"Wha'? A 'Omeless 'oman?!" Wicked spat angrily. Then he

turned to Mo. "Don't disappoint me!" he warned, then rushed from the room.

～

RINALDO WALKED to the water fountain to get some hot water for his cup of instant coffee. He held the eight-ounce Styrofoam cup under the faucet, then watched the steam rise as the water turned brown.

"Look at this bullshit," he mumbled to himself.

He loved coffee, but the little packs of instant coffee were starting to get on his nerves because they tasted like dirt. He glanced at the TV, then returned to his cell, not realizing he was being watched. Rinaldo approached his cell and saw a Snickers bar on his bed. He frowned, wondering how it got there, but it didn't take long to find out.

A big cock, diesel, jet-black dude with cornrows followed Rinaldo into his cell and leered at him. At six foot four and 250 pounds solid, he towered over Rinaldo. Rinaldo, however, didn't look worried.

"You get my gift?" the dude growled, flexing his muscles like Debo.

"No, can't say that I have," Rinaldo replied, sipping his coffee.

"The candy bar. Sweets for my sweetness," the dude snickered wickedly.

"Oh, that was from you? Thanks, my man. Now, get the hell outta my cell," Rinaldo answered with a flip of his head.

"Not until I get what I came for," the dude gritted, pulling out a long, prison-made shank that looked like an ice pick.

"And what's that?"

"Either shit on this knife or shit on my dick," he retorted, meaning either Rinaldo was getting stabbed or raped.

The dude took one step toward Rinaldo, and Rinaldo threw

the scalding hot coffee in his face. But he'd been anticipating that. He threw up his massive arm and shielded his face. Rinaldo used that moment to grab the dude's wrist holding the knife and simultaneously deliver a jaw-breaking right hook. The blow staggered the giant, but it only made him madder.

"Now, I'ma kill you!" he roared, then flung Rinaldo across the cell.

He came at Rinaldo, knife raised like Leatherface, and swung down, giving Rinaldo more than enough time to weave away and punch the intruder dead in the Adam's apple. He gasped for air, and Rinaldo struck again, this time with a devastating kick to the nuts, causing the dude's eyes to roll in the back of his head as he fell to his knees in agony. From there, it was all Rinaldo.

"You stinkin' son of a bitch!" Rinaldo screamed, bashing dude's head into the concrete over and over. His face was a bloody mess, and he was out cold.

Rinaldo snatched the dude's pants down around his ankles and dragged him out into the dayroom. Everyone stopped what they were doing and looked on.

"Fuckin' booty bandit! You wanna fuck me? How's about *I* fuck *you*?" Rinaldo spat, then snatched the ice pick out of the dude's grip and repeatedly stabbed him in the asshole.

"Arrgghh!" he cried out, the pain waking him out of his stupor.

Rinaldo didn't stop until his ass was as bloody as his face. Then he stood up, ice pick gripped firmly in his hand, and asked, "Anybody else wanna fuck the white boy? Anybody else wanna fuck me, goddamn it?"

He looked around the dayroom. Some looked away, some smirked approvingly, but no one spoke up. Rinaldo turned, went back in his cell, sat on the bed, and ate the Snickers bar.

~

"NINETY-NINE...ONE HUNDRED," Supreme grunted as he finished his last set of push-ups.

He was determined to stay faithful to his workout regimen to keep his physique in tip-top shape. His motivation, what he used for fuel, was the rage he felt for Nina. In his mind, she had betrayed him. She'd left him for dead, and she would have to pay for that. On top of that, she'd taken his daughter to God knows where and was letting the next nigga play daddy. That was something he couldn't allow! But underneath it all, his heart was broken. He loved Nina, and he couldn't understand why she couldn't see that. Regardless, he'd concluded that if he couldn't have her, no one would. *That* he was sure of.

"Aye, cuz, check this out," Lala called him.

Supreme grabbed his towel and wiped himself off as he went into the living room. He technically should have still been behind bars, but several police officers and lab technicians were found guilty of tampering with evidence, and Supreme's conviction was one of hundreds that had been overturned. Lala sat on the couch Indian-style with the laptop in her lap. He stood behind the couch and peered over her shoulder.

"What's good?"

"I used Nina's Social Security Number to get her credit card bills, right? And I—"

"You can do that?" he asked, surprised.

"If you know what you're doin'," she winked. "Believe me, there's nothing you can't find once you go on the secret internet."

"Secret internet?" he echoed.

Lala nodded. "Most people don't know that. But if you have anonymizing software called TOR, you can access Obama's fuckin' info," she schooled him.

"Damn, cuz, you a beast," he laughed.

Lala smiled. "So, I'm checkin' her shit, and the last time she used her credit cards was in Texas at a convenience store."

"Texas? Fuck she doin' in Texas?" Supreme questioned.

"She used it to buy gas and shit," Lala informed him.

"For her, the kids, and that nigga," Supreme concluded.

"That's what it looks like. And they were near Route 10, so most likely, they were heading further west."

"How you know?"

"Because of the even numbers. Even-numbered highways run east to west, and all odd-numbered highways run north to south," she said.

Supreme paced the floor.

"Where the fuck is the bitch goin'? First, Florida, then Texas headin' west...Cali maybe?"

Lala shrugged. "Your guess is as good as mine. I'll just keep an eye on her info. See what pops up."

She got up from the couch and headed for the kitchen. As she passed Supreme, he made a rat tail out of his towel and popped her on the ass.

"Ow!"

Supreme laughed, eyeing her petite little ass clad in the cheek-hugging gym shorts she was wearing. "I see you got a li'l jiggle back there, La," he remarked, then popped her again.

She jumped and swung back at him, trying to grab the towel. "Quit playin'!" she yelled but with a smile on her face. "Gimme this fuckin' towel."

Supreme grabbed both her arms, wrapped them around her, and held her where she couldn't move. Then he pressed himself against her from behind.

"Supreme, what the hell are you doing?"

"What?" he asked, breathing on her neck. He let go of her arms, then reached up and grabbed her titties.

Lala tried to squirm away, but his massive arms were like vise grips. "Nigga, get your hands off me! We ain't kids no more, playin' house and shit."

She protested, but Supreme was in a zone. Cousin or no

cousin, he was mesmerized by her butter-toned skin and petite but curvy figure. Yeah, they used to play house when they were kids. But now, they were two grown-ass, consenting adults. And those sexy-ass green eyes were mesmerizing. Supreme snatched her boy shorts down and bent her over the couch.

"Supreme, stop! Boy, what are you doing?" Lala cried, but her pussy was screaming something different.

He slid two fingers into her pussy and found it wet. He smiled to himself. "Bitch, shut up. You know you want this dick."

"Nooooo, Supreme, we're cousins!" she weakly protested. But when that thick, nine-inch dick slowly began to fill her pussy, all her protests melted into passion. His grandma being her auntie didn't matter as much anymore.

"Ohhhh, fuck, nooo. This is sooo wrong," she groaned, arching her back.

"But, Lala, this pussy feels so right," Supreme grunted, pushing his dick deeper, admiring his dick sliding in and out from the back. This was the first pussy he had had since he got out.

Lala threw one leg up over the back of the couch and started fucking Supreme back.

Hard.

"Fuck, yeah! Get this pussy! Get it!"

Supreme squeezed and played with her clit while he pounded her pussy relentlessly. He had wanted to fuck her since he had come home. Lala was a sexy chick. Just the thought of knowing his fantasy was coming true made him bust, and she wasn't far behind.

They both lay spent. The mask of passion retracted, and now the moment was just awkward.

"What...did we just do?" Lala asked after regaining her composure.

Before Supreme could answer, Lala's phone rang. She

leaned over the couch, feeling Supreme's long, limp dick slide out of her, and grabbed her phone. She checked the caller ID.

It was B-Murder.

～

NINA WAS HEATED. *Beyond* heated. She felt almost betrayed. She stood in the doorway of the storage space that she and Rick had agreed they would use to stash the money, but it was totally empty. *Nothing.* She imagined a scenario where Rick had said he was going to California, only to take the money and run. The thought made her feel like a fool. She quickly dialed his number. It couldn't ring fast enough for her, so she paced in a futile attempt to speed things up.

"What's up, ba—?"

"Don't baby me!" she barked. "Where is it?"

"Where's what?" he replied but knowing exactly what she was talking about.

Rick pinched the bridge of his nose. He knew this would happen if she found out he hadn't used the stash spot they agreed on. But how would she find out unless she didn't trust him and decided to check behind him? And if she didn't trust him, how could he really trust her? Maybe *she* had decided to take the money and run. The fifty million was playing tricks with both their minds.

"You know what, Rick! The fifty fuckin—"

"Nina, goddamn it! We on the phone!"

"Come home, Rick! Now!" she demanded.

Rick sighed, exasperated. "Look, I'll be there when I get there, okay? I told you I had somethin' to handle."

"Oh, now, it's 'I'll be there when I get there'? You know what, Rick? It's whatever!" she yelled into the phone ending the call. He tried to call back, but it went straight to voicemail.

Fifty million says she ain't who you think she is, Rick remembered his connect saying. Rick hoped this wasn't the Nina she was becoming.

~

NINA COULDN'T EVEN MAKE it all the way home without breaking down in tears.

"Mommy, what's wrong?" Jatana asked soothingly.

"Mommy's okay, baby."

"Then why are you crying?"

Why was she crying? *This nigga got me having mood swings and shit.* She was so confused. She knew Rick was a good man, and he probably had a very good reason for moving the stash. She knew she had trust issues, but how *couldn't* she, after all she had been through? So many men had used and abused her, lied to her, and betrayed her. But was all of that blinding her to the good man standing right in front of her? She was so deep in thought she didn't notice the car pull out in front of her until it was too late.

"Shit!" Nina spat, then turned around to check on the kids. "Are y'all okay?"

"Yes," they replied in broken unison.

She then took a deep breath and stepped out of the car. She looked at the smashed-up taillight on the car she had just hit. It didn't look that bad, but the futility of the moment reminded her of the confusion her life was currently being smothered with. She began to cry in the middle of the street.

"Hush, chile. It's not that bad."

She looked up and saw an older woman with a warm brown face and a comforting smile.

"Ain't nothin' so bad that the Lord can't fix."

"No, no, it's not that," Nina sniffled. "I just...I don't know..."

Like a grandmother, the woman stepped forward and wrapped her arms around Nina and pulled her into her bosom. Nina was surprised at first, but it felt so good to be enveloped by a motherly figure. She embraced the woman back.

"I...I'm so sorry. I'm going to pay for it," Nina promised.

"We'll deal with that. Just tell me what's wrong."

Nina stepped back, wiping her eyes. "It's-it's nothing. Really. I'm just...being silly. I'll be okay."

The woman smiled knowingly. "Just give it to the Lord."

"I will. Ummm, here's the insurance card. It's a rental."

The woman looked at the card, then back into Nina's face. The first thing that had drawn her had been the resemblance. She looked so much like Kyra that it caught her attention.

"Nina...That's a pretty name."

"Thank you," Nina smiled through the tears.

"Just call me Miss Betty."

Nina nodded. "O-okay."

"Now, I get the feeling that you're new in town. So how about me, you, and the kids go get some coffee and work things out," Miss Betty offered.

"I'd like that."

"Okay, Ky-I mean Nina. So would I."

∽

"Where are you?"

"Still in L.A."

"Give me a couple of days, and I'll be out there."

"By then, I'll be back in Phoenix," Rick told his connect.

The connect laughed. "Let me find out you're trying to duck me."

Rick chuckled. "Never that. But the sooner I'm out, the better."

"Mmmm, well, maybe I can give you a reason to stay," the connect flirted.

"Let's keep this professional. Too much is at stake," Rick reminded her.

"It didn't start off as business. It wasn't business when you had your face in my pussy," she cooed. Rick could hear her breathing getting heavy.

"Things have changed. I told you that before."

"Because of her?"

"Because of a lot of things."

"Yeah, like I thought. It's her. Believe me, when you find out that bitch ain't shit, this pussy'll be waiting for you."

Click!

Rick hung up, shaking his head at the antics of women.

He jumped in his ML550 and headed for his destination: Trae and Tasha's house. Ever since he saw Tasha in New York, he had felt drawn back in. He didn't know who the dude with Tasha was, but then again, there was a lot he didn't know. A lot he *needed* to know.

He headed over to his old neighborhood and parked in front of his old house, his new ex-wife's house: a few upgrades but not much. A new Expedition with the temporary tags was parked in the driveway. But other than that, it felt right. His attention turned to Trae's house, across the street and a few houses down. When he looked, he saw a figure sitting with her head down on the porch. He started the engine and slowly drove toward the figure. Every nerve in his body screamed to him for an unknown reason, and as he got closer, he knew why.

It couldn't be. He parked and got out of the car.

His legs felt like jelly, but he willed himself forward. The figure turned out to be a woman. A small, petite woman. A beautiful woman. His woman.

It couldn't be.

It was.

Kyra.

She looked at him as if he were a stranger.

"Excuse me? Do you live here?" she innocently questioned.

He couldn't speak with words, but his tears spoke volumes.

CREAM HAD FINALLY RECOVERED ENOUGH to be released from the hospital in Florida and was back in Atlanta. He walked inside his bedroom and lay back on the bed.

"It's good to be home," he remarked, putting his hands behind his head. It was just another Atlanta colonial, with big windows to let in the sun and a yard made for parties. The interior was tastefully decorated with Ethan Allen furniture, giving it a comfortable yet modern feel. The hardwood floors, with plush carpet in the bedrooms, were so different from the hospital, where everything was hard and sterile.

"Just relax, baby. I got you," Diamond assured him.

"Well, what if I don't want to relax?" he teased, pulling her onto the bed with him.

"Well, in that case, you got me," she purred.

Cream couldn't wait to get up in that pussy. He pulled up her skirt and pushed her panties to the side as she straddled him. He gripped her hips, forcing her to take all ten inches in one deep stroke.

"Oooooh," Diamond sang, sucking in her breath as he impaled her. "I missed you, baby!"

"He missed you too," Cream growled, grunting, then bouncing her onto his hardness.

Diamond placed her hands on his chest and put her legs in a squatting position. Each stroke made her scream out Cream's name, and she loved every minute of it.

"Right *there*, daddy! Oh fuck, Cream! Right there!" she squealed, smacking her own ass and urging herself to ride harder.

Cream watched his dick going in and out of her tight, wet

pussy until she came so hard, she shook like an earthquake. He watched as her juices coated his dick in a milky substance. He then allowed himself to fill her with his load.

"Damn!" she gasped.

Cream chuckled. "Daddy's home."

Diamond smothered his face with kisses. "And mommy damn sure missed you."

Cream's phone rang. He looked at the caller ID. It was his man, Mo.

"What's good, fam?"

"You already know, my nigga. I'm glad to see you doin' better," Mo answered.

"Yeah, yo. I'm back. Now, it's time to get back on the job. And I know just where to start," Cream said.

"No doubt, yo. Say no more. I'm on my way down there. Soon as I get there, you can let me know what's good," Mo said. "So, rest your ass up!"

"That's what it is. I'll see you when you get here, fam."

"Yep."

Mo hung up and looked over at the Dread, who was driving. "It's time to go. He back in Atlanta."

The Dread nodded and headed for 95 South.

3

Peedie's funeral was packed. Trenton had turned out to show Peedie mad love. It was held at the Lighthouse Temple Ministries on Bellevue Ave., the same church his mother attended. Not only were Peedie's friends there, but also a few of Nina's enemies. Many Kings showed up just in case Nina showed her face. They had come with Reese and Canada. Reese hoped deep down that Nina didn't come because he would have no choice but to have her killed. Especially with the way Canada was watching him like a hawk. He knew she knew he had been fucking Nina, but she never told B-Murder. She loved him too much. But face-to-face, there was no way she'd let Nina live to talk about it, so Reese prayed silently that she wouldn't show.

Supreme and Charley sat in the back pew, taking it all in. Supreme kept the .45 he was packing concealed but within reach because if Nina showed up, he wouldn't hesitate. He planned to snatch her up and punish her until she told him where Jatana was. After that, what he decided to do to her was up to how hard she begged. Supreme imagined her groveling at his feet, begging for forgiveness and declaring her undying love. Anything less, and she wouldn't live to see the next sunrise.

"Oh, my baby, my baby, my baby!" Nina's mother wailed, holding onto Peedie's large urn that held his ashes. A friend of Nina's mother tried to pull her back.

He had been burnt beyond recognition, so an open casket was out of the question. Only his lifelike picture sat on the urn.

"My Peedie is gone! Oh my God, what am I gonna do? My baby is dead and-and-and it's all because of that...devil child, Nina!" she exclaimed.

"You don't mean that," her best friend said, trying to calm her down.

"Yes, I do! I mean *every* word! First, she got Derrick killed, and now Peedie!" she cried out. "And I know she killed Deacon Rutherford! I *know* it! She's the devil! My daughter is the devil!"

That last statement made Agent Houser's ears perk up too. He had come to the funeral betting that Nina would show up. He wanted to question her about the attempted murder on Cream. Since he was her ex, Houser wanted to know what she knew. Besides, Cream had told him she was messing with a dude with dreads, so Houser wanted to follow up on that lead. His gut was telling him it was the right one.

After the funeral, Houser approached Nina's mother at the cemetery.

"Excuse me, Miss Coles, I'm Agent Houser," he identified himself, then flashed his badge. "I'm sorry about your loss, but I wonder if I could speak to you? Just for a few moments."

"What about?" she sniffled.

"Your daughter, Nina Coles..."

She visibly stiffened. "I don't have anything to say about that-that-murderer! She's *not* my child!"

"I understand, but what makes you think she's a murderer?"

"I don't think—I *know*! She murdered the good Deacon Rutherford...She thought he was messin' with her daughter, but that daughter of hers is a liar just like her mama because the good deacon just wouldn't do that! He was—"

Agent Houser smoothly cut her off because he wasn't interested in the deacon's eulogy.

"But murder is a serious charge, Ms. Coles. Did you actually *see* her murder the dea—"

"Yes and no."

"Yes and no? Which one is it?"

"You don't have to see what you know in your heart, Officer. Nina did it just as sho' as there's a Gawd in the sky, you hear me? Her and that dread-headed boy. Talkin' 'bout he a po-lice. Humph! He wasn't a bit mo' police than the man on the moon!" she huffed.

Once again, my gut paid off, Houser thought to himself.

"This dread-headed man, as you say, did you by any chance get his name?"

"I sho' did and won't never forget it. I tol' the police when I tol' 'em 'bout Nina. I told them, but they—"

Houser was running out of patience. "The name, Miss Coles. I just need the name."

"Rick. Rick Brown," she answered.

Houser nodded. In his mind, it had all been confirmed. Rick Brown. Former Federal Agent Rick Brown. This was why Rick quit the agency. And why Cream was shot by a dread-headed cop who may have also been behind the deacon's murder. Not to mention, Rick must've also had the fifty million dollars.

"Thank you, Miss Coles. You've been a great help." He smiled.

"What are you going to do about the good deacon's murder?" she asked.

"We'll take care of it," he lied, then turned and walked away.

He pulled out his cell phone and hit speed dial.

"Korn? This is me, Rhodes. It's all been confirmed. Rick is behind all of this."

"Are you sure?"

"Sure enough. Put out an APB for him. We need to see him face-to-face," Rhodes said.

"Done. Anything else?" she asked.

He thought for a moment. "Yeah. Is Charley Adams still on ice?" Rhodes asked, wondering if their CI was still ready and in position to meet their needs.

"Of course. He's turning on Rinaldo Haywood, so he's already in witness protection. How much more ice do you need?" she answered.

"Go see him. Pick his brain. If Rick *is* behind all of this, then he damn sure ain't alone."

"Got you, boss. I'm on it," she assured him, then hung up.

~

CHARLEY ADAMS PACED the floor of the small apartment the Feds had him stashed away in. Two Feds with their coat jackets off and their holsters on sat at a small table playing cards. Charley lit up a cigar and peeped out the window at the Atlanta skyline. At fifty-nine, he was fit with a hefty, beefy build except for the protruding potbelly. He had been a big shot in Vegas with strong ties to the mob. Now, he was just a caged bird waiting to sing.

"Hey, Charley, do you mind? You're making me nervous," one of the Fed agents remarked.

"Don't worry. I'm not gonna make a break for it. I just think better on my feet."

"Yeah, well, what do you do better on your ass?"

Charley chuckled. "Smart guy, eh? Do you think at all?"

Someone knocked on the door. One of the agents got up as if they were expecting company. He opened it, and in walked

Agent Korn. Charley smiled. He always liked Agent Korn because she reminded him of childhood crush he had; a girl with a sweet face that hid all her deceptive intentions.

"Agent Korn as I live and breathe. How are ya?" Charley greeted her cheerfully.

"I'm good, Charley. Thanks for asking."

"I can tell you're not here to shoot the breeze, eh?"

Korn sat down in the armchair across from the couch. "Never."

Charley shrugged as he took a seat on the couch. "Whatever excuse I can get to see your pretty face is good enough," he flirted playfully.

She smiled but didn't comment. "Tell me about Rick Brown."

"Who?"

"Come on, Charley. Remember our deal? You come clean on *everything,* or the deal's off."

"Agent Korn, believe me, this is difficult enough as it is, okay? So, understand, I'm not holding nothin' back. I don't know any Rick Brown," he explained.

"Maybe this will jar your memory," she said, handing him a photo of Rick.

"I remember his face because I never forget a face. Especially one of a cop. He's one of the cops I've seen during a raid. What about him?" Charley asked as he handed the picture back to her.

"We have reason to believe he may have been the man that robbed the guys who robbed you for the fifty million," Korn told him.

Charley laughed heartily. "That's a good one, Agent Korn. You mean we got hit by a crooked cop? Talk about fuckin' irony! What kind of ship are the Feds running?"

"I'm glad you find it amusing, Mr. Adams."

"Actually, I'm laughin' to keep from cryin'. Nothin's funny

about losin' that kind of money, but it's good to know God still has a sense of humor."

Korn crossed her legs authoritatively. "Or maybe you didn't lose the money at all," she smirked.

"Come again?"

"Maybe you and this crooked agent are in cahoots with each other. I mean, it would be genius to pretend you got robbed, especially if it's you doing the robbing. Then you testify on Rinaldo, send him away for a long time with nobody to retaliate—and presto! The money's yours!" Korn analyzed.

Charley nodded. "Actually, that's not a bad idea. I wish I had thought of it. But no, I ain't in cahoots with nobody, let alone a crooked cop. If I wanted to take the fuckin' money, I would've did it in his face! Rinaldo's a fuckin' ant to me. *I'm* Charley the Adams Ace! The only reason I agreed to testify is because I owe a lot of people. Losin' that money put my ass in a sling. So, believe me, if I had that money, I wouldn't be here talkin' to you!" Charley fumed.

He hated the fact that he had to turn rat, but the robbery left him little choice. He owed the mob over ten million, but he couldn't pay without the money.

Seemingly satisfied, Korn nodded.

"Okay, Charley the Ace, I'm going to take your word for it... for now. But if I find out any different, all bets are off," Korn warned him.

"Hey, I'd take those odds any day," Charley replied. "And don't be a stranger."

Korn got up and headed for the door.

"Wow. I really hate to see ya go, but I love watching you leave," Charley remarked, puffing his cigar and watching Korn's ass.

She smiled over her shoulder, shaking her head. "Bye, Charley."

One of the agents closed the door behind her as Charley got up from the couch.

"Where are you going?" the agent asked.

"The shitter. Do you mind, or do you wanna hold it for me? Geez!" Charley exclaimed. He went into the bathroom and shut the door. Then he pulled out his cell and made a call. "Hey, Brandon. We might have a problem," Charley told him.

Brandon sat in the big boss's chair at WMM. No Charley, no Rinaldo. He was the top dog in charge now, and they needed him. He listened to every word and then hung up. He hit the intercom on his desk. "Deanna, will you come in here, please?"

Several moments later, Deanna walked in. Brandon eyed her disapprovingly. She wasn't a pretty woman. Her mother was white and her father Black, giving her a light complexion. She was oddly shaped and Amazon-ish. But she was loyal to him, and she also knew where all the bodies were buried—literally.

"Deanna...Have a seat."

She looked nervously at Brandon. Since taking over for Rinaldo, he had never asked her to take a seat. She wondered if she had done anything wrong. Brandon read her mind.

"Relax, you're doing an excellent job. Matter of fact, I don't know what I'd do without you," he complimented her.

Deanna couldn't hold back a sigh of relief. "Thank you, Brandon."

"But you see...I have a problem."

"Oh?"

"And I was wondering if you could help me with it."

"I'll try, sir."

He looked at her for a moment as if assessing her. "Charley and Rinaldo may never see the light of day, so I have to do what's best for the company," Brandon said, echoing Rinaldo's coaching. "How well did you know Rinaldo?"

"Well, I knew him very well professionally, but personally, I only knew what he told me."

"Like?"

"Very little."

"I'm sure you know by now about the millions he had."

Deanna nodded. Secretly, she had fantasized about having that much money.

"Yes, sir."

"Do you think Rinaldo took it?"

"I'm not sure I follow you. I thought the money was taken *from* him," she probed.

Brandon smiled and sat back in his chair. "Maybe he just wanted it to *seem* that way. Did he seem...shifty before the robbery? Well, *overly* shifty?"

"No, not that I saw."

"Would you tell me if he did?" he inquired.

Deanna nodded vigorously. "Oh, yes, sir, Mr. Ingram."

He looked in her eyes, then replied, "I believe you. And it's important that I believe you because I think I can count on you. Can I count on you, Deanna?"

"Yes, sir," she answered promptly.

"Deanna...What would you do with a million dollars?"

Her eyes widened, and her heart began to palpitate. "A lot!"

Brandon laughed. "I'm sure. I'm going to give you a chance to make a million dollars, but I have to be able to *trust you totally*."

"I assure you, sir, you can."

"And you must do *exactly* what I tell you."

Deanna nodded. "To the letter, sir."

Brandon crossed his legs then casually instructed her to stand up.

She did.

"Now...take off your clothes."

She looked at him in amazement, unsure if she heard what she *thought* she heard. He smiled and added, "Now."

Deanna began to unbutton her flowery dress with trembling hands.

The dress looked like something a Mormon might wear. Once she unbuttoned it, she let it fall to the ground. Underneath, she had on a white bra and white "Madea" bloomers that covered her navel and panty hose. She undid her bra, and her heavy, sagging breasts fell out. Then she removed her panty hose and panties at one time.

She then stood before Brandon butt naked.

He nodded. "Deanna, you know you're not very attractive, don't you?"

"Yes, sir," she mumbled, dropping her head.

"So, you know you'll never get an opportunity like this again, right?" he questioned as he stood up and rounded the desk.

"I-I know."

He stopped behind her and looked at her flat, pasty, pancake ass and wide, flaring hips. He felt his pale skin flush with desire. "Grip the desk and bend over."

Deanna did as she was told. Brandon began to unbuckle his pants.

"Then I trust you will do what I say and *only* what I say, correct?"

Deanna couldn't speak as she quivered with anticipation. Her usually bone-dry pussy was all but dripping with intensity. Brandon rubbed the head of his angry red dick along the crack of her ass, and she tensed up when he ran it over her asshole. Then he positioned his dick at the very entrance of her pussy.

"When was the last time you've been fucked, Deanna?"

"A-A...long time," she answered in a voice choked with lust.

"Good," he replied, then drilled her with every inch of his long, slim dick.

"Oh my...God!" she gasped, clawing at the desk, trying to inch away, but Brandon held her firm as he began beating the pussy hard. He slid two fingers, then a third, into her ass and finger fucked her vigorously.

Deanna cried out, "Yes! Yeeessss, sirrrrr!"

"You will do what I say?"

"Yesss!"

"Who do you belong to?"

"Youuuu!"

"Who?"

"HOMIE-homie-you!" She trembled as her first real orgasm in almost a year erupted inside of her and made her weak in the knees. She collapsed on the desk, but Brandon didn't stop. He continued to pound her pussy until she begged him to stop, and he came all over her ass and back.

Deanna's pale skin was flushed with excitement. She was in heaven. She had never been fucked like that in her life. On top of that, she had a chance to make a million dollars. At that point, she was ready to kill the president if Brandon told her to.

∼

Lala and Supreme stepped inside B-Murder's apartment to find Reese and Canada there as well.

"Yo, ma, I ain't know you was bringing company," B-Murder remarked, sizing up Supreme.

Lala waved him off. "Boy, this my cousin, Teflon," she said, lying about Supreme's alias. She didn't want to tip anybody off about their plans by letting his name drop.

"Teflon?" he echoed. "Where you from, yo?"

"Here," Supreme answered. "I just came home from New Jersey."

"Yeah? You know the homie Kaos?" B-Murder asked.

"Na, can't say that I do," Supreme replied, keeping his words short to let him know he wasn't pressed for conversation.

Lala looked at her watch. "Are we gonna talk business or what, B?"

"Yeah," B-Murder replied, still looking at Supreme, trying to place him.

Supreme already knew why. Supreme knew that B-Murder was the son of the woman Nina's brother had killed. He knew of Supreme. But Supreme was grateful he hadn't made the connection and wanted to get out of there before he did.

Lala pulled out her camera and looked at Canada and Reese.

"Y'all the ones needing the IDs, right?"

"And passports too," Reese added.

"B, you ain't say nothin' about passports," Lala said.

"Ay, yo, Reese, chill. I told you we'd take care of that," B-Murder assured him.

Reese? Supreme's mind echoed. Could this be the same Reese that took Nina to Georgia? It couldn't be. Because then, why was he here with B-Murder? He wasn't sure until after Lala took their pictures and asked, "You said you wanted Georgia IDs?"

Reese nodded.

Supreme flexed his jaw muscles but kept quiet. It was too much of a coincidence for them to want Georgia IDs. It *had* to be the same Reese, he thought.

"That's it?" Reese asked.

"Yeah," Lala replied. "I'll hit you in about an hour when they're ready."

When Lala and Supreme left, B-Murder turned to Reese. Remembering that Teflon claimed he had just come home, he said to Reese, "Get somebody on the phone at the prison and find out who the fuck Teflon is. Something don't feel right about the nigga."

"I got you."

~

FOR SALE.

Kyra stared at the sign planted like a flag on the front lawn of the house. Her information said this was where she lived with her husband and daughter. She tried with all her might, but she couldn't remember anything about the house. After the red-eye back to Cali, she was beat. Kyra wanted to crawl into bed, but she at least had to try, and she had to know. She got on her tippy toes and peered in a few windows, but the place was totally empty. Not even a stitch of furniture.

Where did they go? she asked herself.

She checked the paper again to make sure she had the correct address. It was the right address, but she still felt lost.

"Excuse me, lady. Do you want me to take you somewhere else?" the cabdriver asked.

Kyra wrote down the real estate number on the sign, then responded, "Yes. Give me a minute."

She walked around to the backyard, hoping for something to click, but nothing did.

"Are you ready?" the cabby asked impatiently when she returned from the back.

"I'm ready."

She got in the cab, then told him the address for her contact in case of an emergency, Tasha Macklin.

"Tasha...Tasha...Tasha Macklin," Kyra repeated like a mantra trying to remember a face attached to the name.

"Excuse me?" the cabby asked.

"Nothing. I was just...nothing."

They drove in silence. The farther they went, the more the butterflies in her stomach fluttered. She hoped whoever Tasha was that she hadn't moved too.

When they got to the house, she saw toys on the freshly

manicured lawn, and to her relief, no for sale sign. She paid her fare.

"Thank you."

"Do you want me to wait?"

"No. I think I'll be all right here."

"Well, just in case, here's my card if you need me to come back."

Kyra took the card, gathered up her stuff, and got out. She walked up to the porch and rang the doorbell, but no one answered. She rang again.

Still no answer.

"Maybe I should've asked him to wait," she mumbled, sitting down on the porch and cupping her head in her hands.

She was just about to pull out her cell phone when a Benz ML550 pulled up. The man that got out had long dreads and swagger to match.

When Kyra saw him approaching, she began to get nervous.

Who was he? Did he know Tasha? Did he live here?

But when he approached, the look on his face made her a little nervous. Why was he looking at her like that? Like...he *knew* her.

"Excuse me. Do you live here?"

He opened his mouth to speak, but nothing came out. Kyra felt a funny vibe that made her stand up. That's when the tears began to roll down his face.

"Do...you live here?" she asked again.

"Kyra...is that...you?" Rick questioned intently. "You don't remember me?"

"You know me?" she asked breathlessly, hoping he could help her know herself.

They stared at each other without a word. Rick couldn't believe it was her. But there she was, right in front of him, and he couldn't stop the tears from falling. His intuition hadn't betrayed him. She reached out and wiped his tears with her thumb. He took her hand and kissed her palm gently. The kiss was like a spark that made her tremble, and she whispered, "Rick? Rick?"

She hugged herself, backing away from him.

"Rick. Your name is Rick. I...I remem—" she recalled. Then her eyelids fluttered, and she fainted.

"Kyra!" Rick called out, catching her in her swoon.

He picked her up, carried her to the car, then laid her on the backseat. Then he went back and retrieved her luggage and placed it in the trunk. He didn't know why, but he wanted this moment all to himself. No Trae. No Tasha. This was *his* moment. Just as he was getting into the car, his cell phone rang.

He looked and saw it was Nina. "Shit," he spat.

Rick felt like he had been caught cheating red-handed. His guilt made him answer.

"Nina, baby, I'm in the middle of something. Can I call you back? Is everybody okay?"

Nina didn't say anything for a minute and then asked, "Is everything okay with you?"

He heard the skepticism in her voice, or was it the guilt playing tricks on his mind? "Everything's fine. Let me call you later," he replied, then hung up before she could protest.

He started the car, then checked on Kyra once more before pulling off.

She was beautiful, and his heart cried, *she's alive!* He turned around and pulled off.

Kyra lay in the backseat, eyelids fluttering as scenes flashed before her eyes. Scenes that seemed so vivid, but none of them made sense. Her head started pounding.

"My head," she groaned.

Rick instantly stopped the car, jumped out, and opened the back door. Kyra sat up with a frown.

"Relax. It's me, Rick."

"I...I know who you are, but is it *really* you?"

"Yeah, it's me," he replied, hugging her gently. "I'ma get you to a hospital real—"

"No! Please, no more hospitals!" she exclaimed, grabbing his arm tightly for emphasis. "Do you have any idea how long I've been in the hospital? I was in a coma for months and then in rehab for more months. I couldn't, and still can't, remember who I was or how I got there. So, please, no more hospitals."

Rick listened to her explanation and wanted to ask questions, but he held his tongue. "Okay, okay. Relax. Do you realize that you fainted back there?"

She nodded. "I just need something for my head. It's pounding."

Rick drove straight to the store and got her some Tylenol for migraines. "You can't take these on an empty stomach."

He fed her two graham crackers and some milk, then gave her two Tylenols. The care he took made her heart smile as she lay back down.

Rick.

She thought of the name and thought of his face. The doctor had told her that if she saw something or someone she remembered, it could trigger a chain reaction. *My baby!* her mind screamed, and her eyes popped open. *Aisha Aaliyah.* She could see her face, hear her voice, but where was she?

Her mind saw her creeping around with Rick while she was still married to Marvin! Marvin. That was her husband's name! But where was he? *Then she felt the cold steel of a gun pressed to her temple, and she gasped.*

"...if you want your wife, I suggest you give me my motherfuckin' dough right now," Mook said.

"Mook, get that fuckin' burner away from my wife," Marvin warned him.

"I'm tellin' you, Blue, he's going to split her wig. Just give me my dough. You owe me, remember?" Junie spat.

So many voices. So many faces. She could smell the alcohol on his breath.

"Stop hagglin', Marvin. Just give the nigga the money," she heard herself blurt out and slid Marvin his burner.

Pow! Marvin shot Junie in the stomach.

"See? That's how you do that. I didn't even have to get out," Marvin bragged.

Then Fish shot Mook. Boom! "That's what happens when you send a boy to do a man's job," he turned and said.

Boom!

The light flashed in front of her face. She could hear but couldn't move. The last thing she remembered was her daughter yelling, "Daddy, we can't leave Mommy!"

Kyra's stomach knotted up, and the anguish overwhelmed her. Had Marvin just left her for dead? "He left me!" she screamed out.

"Kyra!" Rick yelled, confused and concerned. He was so happy to see her again that he was terrified of losing her. He wouldn't survive a second loss like that. Heart pounding, he scanned for a good place to pull over. Stopping the car with a screech, he asked, "Are you okay?"

"He—" she started to say, but she passed out again.

4

Rochelle pulled up in her driveway and got out of the custom pink Bentley. Everything was going according to plan. She had to admit, her husband was a genius. Who would've thought of robbing themselves of the fifty million? She remembered when he had come to her and asked, "What do you think about the guy Shawn that works for me?"

"What do you mean, what do I think?"

Rinaldo smiled. "I mean, would you fuck him?"

She knew her husband was into some kinky shit. They had participated in swingers' parties which were nothing but glorified orgies, but he knew Rochelle wasn't really into it. So, when he mentioned Shawn, she just blew him off. "No, Rinaldo, I'm not interested."

"I don't mean for pleasure. I mean for business," he told her. Then he broke down the perfect plan.

Once she knew it was about fifty million dollars, she was willing to fuck any and everybody. She knew Rinaldo was getting money, but she didn't realize he had stacked over twenty million.

"Throw the dumb mutha'fucka a little pussy and a couple of

stacks for his lame-ass magazine," Rinaldo chuckled. "Then tell him about the stash down in Florida. Once he goes down there, Charley and Brandon will think we've been robbed."

"Then what about Shawn?" Rochelle quizzed.

Rinaldo smirked. "What you *think* happens to Shawn?"

It had been a perfectly executed plan—until somebody killed Shawn and his friend, Cream. The thought froze Rochelle in her tracks.

What if that someone had been Rinaldo? Maybe Rinaldo had someone take Shawn out so he could jump ship and leave *her* high and dry. The thought made her see the whole situation differently.

"Yeah, Rinaldo, you may be a slick-ass white boy, but I'ma badass bitch!" she said to herself as she put the key in the door and went inside their house.

As she turned to go for the lights, she felt a hand cover her mouth and another arm wrap around her throat.

"Thought you got away, huh, bitch?"

Rochelle tried to scream, but he muffled the sounds. Her body tensed to fight, but before she knew it, he was choking all the fight out of her, lifting her off her feet as he applied more pressure. She kicked frantically, sending one of her shoes flying.

"Yeah, bitch, now you see what dyin' is like!"

She could barely hear his taunts. Her kicks got less frantic, her determination less intense. She was just on the verge of giving up when he released her and allowed her body to slump to the floor.

Rochelle breathed in gulps of air like a man dying of thirst would guzzle water. She was dizzy, and her head hurt, but she was happy to be still alive as she gagged and gagged some more.

He cut on the lights, and she looked up into his face. Instantly, her eyes bulged like she was seeing a ghost, especially with the white gauze bandaging one side of his head.

"I...thought—"

"I was dead?" Cream spat, finishing her sentence. "Naw, bitch, but you might be if you don't tell me where that fuckin' money is!"

He pulled out a .45 automatic and kissed the barrel to her forehead.

"I swear, Cream, I don't know!"

Cream laughed and snatched her to her feet. She stood on wobbly knees.

"Bitch, you think I'm stupid? Who the fuck else knew besides you, me, and Shawn? Shawn's dead, I'm not, and that only leaves *you!*" Cream deduced.

"And Rinaldo!" she reminded him.

"Rinaldo? We were *robbin'* his ass. How the fuck did he know?"

Rochelle smiled despite her fear. "Because *he* set up the whole thing."

Cream looked at her, amazed. "What?"

"It was Rinaldo all along, *not* Shawn! He-he wanted me to come on to Shawn to seduce him and convince him to take the money!"

"Why the fuck would Rinaldo rob himself?"

"Because only a third of the money is his. Charley Adams and Brandon also have a cut. Rinaldo knew he couldn't just rob Charley because he had long arms. He'd never get away with it. But if Charley thought they had *all* been robbed, then Rinaldo would be in the clear," she explained.

Cream lowered the gun as he thought about what she had just said.

"Damn!" he remarked, "The muh'fucka was settin' us up the whole time we thought we were settin' *him* up. Ain't that some shit!"

"Exactly."

"So, what was supposed to happen to us after we took the money?"

She just looked at him, afraid to answer. Cream grabbed her by the throat and slammed her against the wall, throwing the gun in her face.

"You bitch! You were gonna kill us!"

"It wasn't my idea. Shawn brought you in!" Rochelle replied, talking as fast as her tongue would carry her, trying to stay a breath ahead of the trigger.

Cream thought about it. She was right. Shawn had brought him into the scheme once Cream told him he could get the Feds off his back. It was a mutual deal, both hands washing the face-type agreement.

"So, if everything went according to plan, then where's the money?"

"As I said, I don't know. Rinaldo set me up too," Rochelle admitted.

"Explain."

She took a deep breath and then replied, "Whoever killed Shawn and...tried to...kill you, Rinaldo's acting like he doesn't know about that. He says somebody else robbed him!" She shook her head at the complexity of the deception. "I think he's trying to set me up. Tell Charley Adams I seduced Shawn to make it seem like *I* really robbed him! Then Charley will kill me, and-and..." She broke down in tears.

Cream paced the floor. He didn't know who to believe. First, she said she and Rinaldo had set them up; now, she said Rinaldo had set her up to take the fall. Somebody had the fifty million and, win or lose, Rochelle was smack-dab in the middle of it.

"But...I have a plan," Rochelle said, wiping her eyes. "Fuck all the bullshit. I wasn't born yesterday."

"Bitch, I've had it up to here with your fuckin' plans," Cream huffed.

"No, please...Hear me out. Whatever happens, it won't happen until Rinaldo gets out."

"In fifty years!" Cream laughed. "That cracka's goin' under the jail!"

"Not if there are no witnesses," Rochelle smirked. "Rinaldo has an agent from the Georgia Bureau of Investigation on the payroll. He's agreed to make it so Rinaldo walks. Once he walks, he's goin' for the money, wherever it is."

"How do you know?"

"Because I know my husband."

"Shit, you ain't know he was settin' *you* up," Cream countered.

"That's...That's because I thought he loved me...loved his family. Now, I see it's all a game. But if it is, then I'm damn sure ready to play," Rochelle assured him.

Looking at her, Cream could tell she was telling the truth. "So, what's the plan?"

"Continue to go along with Rinaldo. Help him get out. Once he's out, he'll lead us straight to the money," Rochelle replied.

"Help him? So both of y'all can cross me? I don't think so."

"Look, Cream, I'm just as blind as you are in this, okay? *Nothing* is as it seems, but that's how it is when you play for big stakes. If you can't keep up, then I suggest you walk away," she told him.

"Oh, I can keep up. The question is, how do I know *you're* not settin' me up?"

"You don't," she smirked. "So, you either have to trust me... or be smarter than Rinaldo by staying five steps ahead."

Cream walked up to her and put the gun to her cheek. Her breath caught in her throat.

"I'm smarter than that fuckin' white boy, and if I ain't..." he responded, tracing the barrel of the gun down her neck and between her breasts, "then I'm definitely smarter than you...

because if I even *think* you bullshittin'...*Bang!*" he hissed, pressing the barrel into her stomach for emphasis.

"We want the same thing, Cream," Rochelle whispered. "Revenge."

He smiled and ran his free hand down to her ass. He squeezed it, and his dick got hard just feeling how soft it was.

"Well, since Rinaldo tried to fuck me, I'll get some revenge by fuckin' his wife."

"Not if I fuck you first." Rochelle eased to her knees and unzipped Cream's jeans.

She reached in and pulled out his semihard dick. Her pussy moistened as she marveled at his size, eager to feel him deep inside of her. She took him into her mouth and ran her hand along the shaft at the same time. Slowly, she devoured every inch of his dick, taking him deep in her throat, working her throat muscles, and making him groan with pleasure.

"Shawn said you had a crazy head game, but goddamn..." Cream grunted.

She worked her throat muscles like a pro, making Cream grab her by her hair and fuck her face. He felt himself about to cum, so he pulled back.

"Come 'ere and sit on this dick," he demanded.

He sat on the couch, and Rochelle straddled him facing away, reverse cowgirl style. She gripped the base of his dick and slid it inside of her.

"Oh...fuck!" she yelled out as his huge dick maxed out her pussy.

He grabbed her by the waist and began to bounce her on his shaft. "Grab your ankles," he ordered gruffly.

"I-I can't," she gasped; his backbreaking thrusts paralyzed her with pleasure.

"Grab your fuckin' ankles," he repeated, pushing her forward.

"Okay!" She did it, and it made her feel every inch. "I-I-I feel it in my stomach!" she cried.

Her sexy moans only made Cream go harder. He pounded her until she came twice, back-to-back, screaming his name and beggin' him to cum. He couldn't help but oblige her.

Finally, Rochelle leaned back against his chest and cocked one leg up on the couch. "So, I take it you've chosen to trust me," she teased.

"Naw, ma, not you. I trust your greed."

~

TWO OF RINALDO'S LAWYERS, Mack and David Abramoff, sat in the hot tub on the third floor of their office. It was a place to unwind with no cell phones and entertain very important clients, particularly wealthy divorcees who wanted to thank them personally for making them richer.

The two brothers drank bubbly and toasted another victory when Brandon walked in.

"Brandon, how did you—" Mack started to ask, surprised by his presence.

"I came to join the party. That is, if I'm not too late," Brandon replied smoothly. "So...What are we celebrating?"

David scowled at him. He noticed Brandon was wearing leather racing gloves.

"What're the gloves for?"

"So I won't leave prints," he gritted before aiming his gun.

Both brothers dropped their glasses and put up their hands at the same time.

"Brandon! What the hell is going on?" Mack quizzed frantically.

Brandon walked up to the edge of the hot tub and rested his gun hand on the edge while still keeping it aimed at them. "Come on, fellas. Let's not play dumb, okay? I know Rinaldo wouldn't make a move without dotting his i's and crossing his t's, and you two are his pencils. So...I'm only going to ask once. Where did Rinaldo move the money to?"

David and Mack looked at each other, too scared to answer.

"Brandon...if...if I tell you everything, will you let us live?" David, the younger of the two siblings, pled.

"Of course, you two are only pawns. In a very dangerous game, I might add, but pawns, nonetheless. Now...answer."

Mack gulped. "Rinaldo set it all up himself. He planned to use his wife to seduce the guy, Shawn, that worked for him. Then once the money was in his hands, he would make you and Charley believe she took the money."

Brandon chuckled. "Interesting. Where's the money now?"

"Somebody robbed him," Mack blurted out.

"Nothing beats the cross but a double cross, huh?" Brandon remarked.

"That's all we know," Mack assured him.

"How do you know Rinaldo didn't rob himself again, just to cut you two out?"

The two brothers looked at each other. Of course, they hadn't thought of that.

"Looks like Rinaldo was planning on robbing us all," Brandon concluded.

"Son of a bitch," David barked, slapping the water.

Brandon shrugged. "Well...I guess Rinaldo no longer needs you, so...." he remarked. Without lifting the gun, he pulled the trigger and shot David in the throat.

"*Gggrrkkk!*" David grunted, grabbing his throat as he slowly sank underwater.

"Brandon! You said you'd let us live!" Mack reminded him frantically.

"Never trust a man with a gun."

Brandon shot Mack twice in the head, blowing his brains to the wall and leaving him sprawled half in and half out of the hot tub. With the brothers dead, two fewer people knew about the whole fifty million. The fewer people looking for a piece, the better. They knew too much anyway, making them loose ends, and Brandon didn't like loose ends. It was the only way he could ensure they didn't run to Charley The Ace Adams.

He turned to leave, and as he walked away, he pulled out his cell phone. "Deanna."

"Yes, sir."

"I want you to go see Rinaldo."

"Yes, sir."

"And this is what I want you to say..."

∿

AGENT KORN SAT in the corner of Starbucks, nursing a latte she had spiked with vodka. Her mind was a thousand miles away, so when Houser appeared unexpectedly, he startled her.

"I'm sorry, Melissa. I hope I didn't disturb you."

"No, no, I was...thinking," she replied.

"Mind if I sit down?" he asked.

"No, be my guest."

"Thanks."

Korn watched Houser sit down and gave him a friendly smile. She had always liked him whenever they worked on a case together. He was a cop's cop, unlike his brother-in-law, Rhodes. She and Rhodes had history that Korn had tried to forget.

"So, Agent Houser, what—"

"Call me Daniel...Melissa." Houser smiled charmingly.

Korn blushed. "Okay...Daniel. What brings you to my side of town?" The posh, Midtown Atlanta neighborhood not being somewhere she would peg as his usual haunt.

He shrugged. "I like Starbucks," he chuckled. Then added, "Actually, I came to see you."

"Me?"

Houser nodded, eyeing her reaction. "To be honest with you, I'm thinking about going to the DA with everything I have on Rinaldo Haywood. I think State should prosecute this case, not the Feds," he explained. He was tired of the Feds getting all the glory, especially after the GBI did all the actual police work. There's nothing like cops as crooked as any criminal getting to be the heroes and building careers off it.

"Or would you prefer you get the collar instead of your brother-in-law?" she replied with a playful smirk.

Houser leaned in, resting his elbows on the table. "To be honest with you...yes. Yes, I want the collar. You and I both know Rhodes is a son of a bitch just trying to make a path to Washington on the backs of everybody else's hard work."

"Can't argue with you there," she admitted.

Houser nodded and looked out the window. He knew he had to be careful, so he chose his next words carefully.

"Tell me, Melissa. How does *your* path to Washington look?"

She sipped her latte. "It's...doable." She smiled because she grasped his agenda instantly. "Of course, I'd need a few more *good* collars," she replied.

"Well, the head position of GBI is going to be open soon. I'm next in line, but I'm retiring. I'd rather die in a fishing boat than behind a desk, you know? But my recommendation would carry a lot of weight," he explained.

"So...Daniel, what do you want from me?"

He eyed her flirtatiously, then replied, "I'll plead the Fifth on what I *want*." Every man he knew on the force wanted a taste of Agent Korn, and he was no different. "What I'm offering is head of Georgia Bureau of Investigation in return for your complete cooperation in the Haywood case."

She nodded. "Rhodes would piss a bitch if we stole this case right from under him."

"All the more reason," he smiled.

Korn giggled. "You're too much, Daniel."

"And to think I'm just getting started." He winked as he stood up. "I'll be in touch."

"I'm sure you will," she replied.

He smiled and walked away. Korn turned to watch him go with a smile on her face that said his offer was right on time.

~

NINA SAT ON THE BED, rubbing cocoa butter lotion all over her barely protruding pregnant stomach. "All this drama while I'm pregnant. *It'll be a miracle if you make it.*" Nina felt the life stir inside her.

"I know, boo. I want your daddy too," she said to her unborn, but her mind was on Rick. At twenty weeks pregnant, there were many things on her mind. The hormones were sending her from one extreme to another: arousal, trepidation, frustration, *Rick.*

Why was he taking so long, and what was he doing back in California? What could be so important? *Who* could be so important? She tried to stop her mind from wandering, but it was hard when she didn't know what was going on. She needed someone to talk to, someone she could share her thoughts with. Her mind instantly thought of Peedie. He had always been there for her as a big bro, even after he got shot helping her steal the bricks that had built the foundation of her dreams. She felt guilty not being there for him, especially since all his bad luck centered around her bullshit. She thought about calling him, but she remembered Rick's warning not to contact *anyone* from the past until everything was situated.

But who is Rick? she huffed. *He ain't even here.*

That thought alone made Nina want to defy him. She decided to call Peedie but blocked the number as a precaution.

The phone rang several times, and she was just about to hang up when the call was answered, and she heard, "Hello?"

It was a woman's voice, one Nina thought she recognized but couldn't place.

"Umm, I'm sorry. I must have the wrong number. I was trying to call my brother, Peedie's phone."

"This him-I mean," the woman giggled lightly. "This is his phone. I'm his girlfriend. Is this Nina?"

"Yes, can I—"

"Peedie just stepped out, but he's been waitin' for your call. Where are you?" the woman asked a little too anxiously.

Nina's street sense went off. "Ummm, just tell him I called."

"Is there a number where you could be reached?" the woman asked. That's when recognition hit Nina.

"Lala?" she blurted out.

There was a short silence. Then, "Lala, I know this you! Where's Peedie?"

The line went dead in Nina's ear.

"Hello? Lala! You bitch!"

Now she was positive something was wrong. She called Peedie's phone again, but it went straight to voicemail this time. Nina's heartbeat was speeding a mile a minute. Her thoughts were racing uncontrollably. She called her mother's phone after blocking her number again as she paced the floor. Her energy surged, and she was beginning to feel light-headed.

The phone rang. It rang again. Her mother answered, yelling, "Oh God! Oh God!"

"Mama!"

The voice she heard next made her grab her stomach and damn near drop the phone.

～

LALA HUNG UP. She was busted. Nina had recognized her voice.

"Yeah, what up?" he answered on the second ring.

"Nina just called."

"You get a number?"

"It was blocked," she told him.

He hung up because now Miss Coles's phone was ringing.

Supreme had been vexed because Nina hadn't fallen for the bait and come to the funeral. He was obsessed with getting his hands on her, so he decided to make an example of her mother. He had waited patiently for her outside of her house. When she finally came home, he ambushed her and dragged her old ass inside.

"Oh God, Lord!" she yelled as Supreme flung her on the living room floor. He put the gun to her forehead.

"Where the fuck is your triflin'-ass daughter?"

"Oh, Lord Jesus! Jesus, help me!"

Supreme smacked the dentures out of her mouth. "Bitch, you 'bout to meet Him personally if you don't tell me where that daughter of yours is!"

"I-I don't know! I swear!"

Supreme punched her in the face and broke her nose. She passed out. Then he slapped her awake. Just then, her phone rang. He snatched it. When he saw it was a blocked number, he knew it was Nina. Supreme put the phone in Miss Coles's face.

"Answer it!"

She did.

"Oh God!" Miss Coles exclaimed.

"Mama!" Nina cried.

Supreme put the phone to his ear. "Naw, bitch, scream Daddy 'cause that's who home!"

"Supreme, what the hell—"

"Where are you, Nina? Where's my goddamn daughter?"

"Nigga, fuck you!" Nina spat, wishing she had a gun, and it was pointed right at his head.

"Oh, you think I'm playin', huh?" Supreme laughed evilly. "Listen to this!"

He put the phone to Miss Coles's mouth and began choking her with the other hand. Nina could hear her mother retching and gasp for air.

"Talk fast. Your mom's turnin' blue!" Supreme warned before loosening his grip. But Nina's mother spoke first.

"You demon-spawned bitch!" her mother rasped. "My boys! My boys are gone, and it's your damn fault! First, Derrick died behind your larceny, and now because of you, Peedie is dead! His legs and dreams weren't enough!" She sobbed, fear and pain coalescing into hatred. "All I know is death because your greed brought the devil into our lives, you filthy, faithless, murdering harlot! You infidel disbeliever—whore of Babylon! I hate you...Good Lord, forgive me, but I...HATE YOU! I wish I had flushed you down a toilet! You're a curse—" The sounds of choking sounds resumed.

Nina listened to her mother's words, and she couldn't help but break down and cry. Half of her wanted to save her mother, but the other half didn't care what happened to the bitch. Nina hadn't forgotten that her mother had knowingly left her daughter in the hands of a monster. She thought of her daughter's pain, the loss of her innocence, and the darkness her child would have to live with forever. She knew she couldn't tell Supreme where she was. But her mother was right about one thing: Peedie's blood was on her hands, which left her feeling heartbroken.

"What's it gonna be, Nina?" Supreme questioned.

Before Nina could answer, her mother stopped fighting, and her body went limp. "You a cold bitch, Nina, lettin' your mama die like that. But trust me, I *will* find you!" Supreme vowed.

"You damn sure will, you fuck-ass nigga! First, you lookin' for me, but now, I'm damn sure lookin' for you!" she spat as she hung up the phone.

Feeling light-headed, she staggered to the bed as the torment hit. As much as she wanted that old bitch dead, even when she was ready to do it herself, Nina still hadn't been prepared. Rick had been right. Killing her in a righteous fury and to hear her strangled by that monster were two different things. It was too much for Nina. Her heart raced wildly, darkness beat at the edge of her vision, and she passed out, collapsing on the floor.

5

Wicked paced the floor of his condo in Philly. He knew the war with the Kings was getting out of hand. He had lost too many soldiers, too quickly. He wasn't the type to surrender, but he knew he needed to fall back and regroup. Besides, this was having a serious impact on his business. If something didn't change soon, his paper would be too short to war with the Kings.

His thoughts turned to Mo. He was glad he had spared him. He could be the answer to all his problems. With a fifty-million-dollar war chest, he could annihilate the Kings. Mo had become the key to this victory, so he definitely would take the blame if he fell.

Wicked turned to his chief Dread.

"We gon' take a trip, star."

"Where to?"

"Atlanta." Wicked smiled, and the Dread knew precisely why.

∾

MEANWHILE, Mo was already in Atlanta, playing his hand with Cream.

The Dreads stripped him of all his money, so it wouldn't be easy if he decided to try to ditch them. But Mo was just as interested in the fifty million as anyone else. Cream may've been his man, but he knew where the fifty million was, and Mo intended on being right there. Cream lived life like every day was a music video, and he was the star. They were lucky to be extras on his set. Fly cars, fast women, and enough jewelry to stock a mall kiosk were normal for him. Likely why they called him "Cream." Mo wanted all that—and more. And if that meant selling him out to the Dreads, at least he hadn't sold for cheap.

"My nigga!" Cream said, surprised when he opened the door. They had known each other back in Jersey, ran the streets at the same time, and moved in the same circle. It had always been love, but in a fake "see-you-at-funerals" kinda way.

He gave Mo a big brotherly hug. Diamond stood on the other side of Cream, so he gave her a hug and kiss, then patted her pregnant stomach.

"So, what up back home?" Cream asked him as they sat on the couch, and Diamond disappeared in the back.

Mo shrugged. "Same ol', yo, except that shit turnin' into King central."

"Yeah, I figured that."

"But what's good wit' you, fam? You lookin' good for a muh'-fucka that ain't 'posed to be breathin'," Mo remarked. "Yo' head is the only thing fucked up," he joked.

"No doubt. Maybe it is a God up there after all. All I know is a nigga was given a second chance." He patted the gauze on his head.

"No doubt. But what up? You ain't heard nothin' on the dough?" Mo questioned.

Cream thought about telling Mo about Rochelle but decided against it. He may have been his man, but Cream had no intention of bringing him in. He didn't mind throwing him something, but he definitely wasn't looking for a partner.

"Naw, but I can tell you this. I know somebody that might know, and if we can find them, we good."

"Who?" Mo asked.

Cream smiled.

"Nina?" Mo hit it dead on.

"Yo, remember I told you that day when I thought a mutha'-fucka had stolen my truck while I was in the bank?"

"Yeah. I remember that bullshit. That was fucked up."

"Naw, fam, the bitch got my shit repo'd! But check it. I had all them tapes in the trunk, and the white boy was on them bitches talkin' about the stash. So that's why I think Nina knows what's up too," Cream explained.

Mo thought about it. "Yeah, that makes sense."

"Plus, as soon as I got shot, the bitch got ghost. You can't tell me shit is a coincidence."

"Well, where she at?"

"Nigga, you think if I knew I'd be sittin' here talkin' to yo' ugly ass? I'd be on my yacht!"

"*Our* yacht, yo. You know we always break bread," Mo reminded him.

"No doubt," Cream replied, shooting Mo the bullshit.

They grinned at each other like they were both hiding knives behind their backs, each ready to stab the other.

"So that might explain what happened to Peedie and her moms," Mo remarked.

"What happened?"

"You ain't heard? Somebody killed Peedie, burned down his crib, wheelchair, and all. And Miss Coles, her throat got sliced."

"Yo, that's foul." Cream shook his head. "Nina is a scandalous-ass bitch. Her shit finally startin' to catch up wit' her. Real talk, though, that shit just prove my point. *Somebody* want

92

this bitch, and I bet it's for that gwop." Cream was confident about that.

Mo was getting more excited by the minute. If Nina had the money, he certainly didn't need Cream. "Bottom line is, fam, we gots to find that bitch first!" Mo exclaimed.

∼

NINA WOKE up in a hospital room, groggy. It took her a minute to focus, but when she did, she saw the faces of her children and Nurse Wright standing around her.

"Why...am I in a...hospital?" she asked. Then her hands shot to her stomach. "The baby!"

Nurse Wright patted her hands and gave her a reassuring smile. "The baby's fine. But you passed out. Thank the Lord, your daughter, Daysha, knew to get your phone and pull up my number." Her time with the Deacon had made Daysha sharp and forced her to grow up sooner than she should have had to.

"Thank you, Daysha," Nina said, sat up, and leaned over to kiss Daysha on the forehead.

"I remember you said Nurse Wright was our contact if anything happens, so I just called," Daysha explained.

Nurse Wright had really become a godsend for Nina being in a new city, considering Rick hadn't been home for weeks now. She turned to Nurse Wright. "You're an angel. Do you know that?" Nina smiled.

Nurse Wright returned the smile. "No, I'm just one of the Lord's workers. That baby of yours is the angel. She said she heard you hit the floor. Do you remember what happened?"

Nina remembered precisely what happened, but she wasn't ready to share that information with Nurse Wright. She knew if she told her about hearing her mother being killed and her brother's death, it would open the door for a whole litany of questions, so she simply responded, "I-I just got a little overly excited. I'm fine now."

Nina started to get up, but Nurse Wright put her hand on her shoulder to gently restrain her. "The doctor wants you to stay a day or two. It was a pretty nasty fall. He just wants to monitor you."

"Is everything okay?" Nina asked, worry apparent in her voice.

"That's what he wants to make sure of."

Nina started to say something, but the door opened, and the man walking in caught her attention. He looked studious in his round-rimmed glasses and blue button-down. The sparkle of his eyes was brightly making an effort to shine from behind his lenses. He smiled at her as he approached the bed.

"I hope you're feeling better, Miss Coles."

"I am, and you can call me Nina," she replied, extending her hand. "And you're Doctor who?"

He shook her hand with a chuckle.

"He's not a doctor, baby. This is my nephew, Dion," Nurse Wright told her. "I asked him to come with me when your daughter called because I figured we'd have to carry you."

Nina looked at Dion's muscular build and broad shoulders and imagined him carrying her. The thought gave her a slight sensation, even if he didn't look a day over twenty-one.

"Well, umm, thank you, Dion. I hope I wasn't too heavy," Nina remarked, suddenly feeling self-conscious.

"You were as light as a feather." He winked.

His wink let her know he was checking for her, making Nina feel a little guilty. "I-umm-I need to make a call."

Daysha went and got Nina's phone and gave it to her.

"Well, baby, we'll go, but I'll be back tomorrow to check on you," Nurse Wright told her. "And don't worry about the kids. They can stay with me."

"I will too," Dion added with a sexy smile.

Nurse Wright playfully hit her nephew. "Boy, come on here."

The kids all kissed Nina as they got ready to leave.

As Dion walked out, his and Nina's eyes lingered on each other. She dialed Rick's number as soon as the door shut. It went straight to voicemail. She frowned. She dialed it again. Voicemail. Frustrated, she sent him a text.

Call me ASAP. In hospital.

The moment she sent it, she regretted it. Why did she put the fact she was in the hospital in the text? Was she trying to make him respond, or did she feel she had to compete to be a priority? Compete with whom? Her thoughts turned to his ex. *Was that what was so urgent?* She shook off the thought, then called him again. Voicemail once more. Nina put the phone down to watch TV but ended up dozing off.

～

Nina was standing in front of a full-length mirror, looking at herself.

She didn't recognize the room, and in a mind-boggling way, she didn't recognize herself. Her mind simply said, "This is you." But there was something different.

Suddenly, she saw Rick behind her in the mirror. She turned around to look behind her, but he wasn't there. She turned back to the mirror, and there he was! He was only in the mirror. She watched him walk up to her reflection and wrap his arms around her waist.

Her reflection turned to kiss him.

"No!" Nina cried out.

She reached for Rick, but her reflection's hand reached out and grabbed hers.

"No!" her reflection barked. "He's mine!"

"Yours? But you're me," Nina emphasized.

Her reflection laughed. "You're nothing more than my reflection!"

The reflection then grabbed Nina around the neck, and Nina grabbed it by the neck. They wrestled and threw each other around wildly, both seeking the upper hand, while Rick stood on the side looking dumbfounded, repeating, "I'm sorry...I'm sorry...I'm sorry."

~

"NINA! NINA, WAKE UP!" Dion repeated, trying to restrain her flailing arms.

He had walked in and found her thrashing on the bed. He thought she was having a seizure and was about to call the nurse. But then he saw she was just dreaming.

When she finally came to and looked at him, the first word she mumbled was, "Rick?"

"Even better," he smiled. "It's Dion."

She sat up in the bed, looked around, and pushed her hair aside. "I...I was dreaming."

"Are you okay?"

Nina looked at him as if she were still getting her bearings together, then nodded. "Yeah...I guess."

"I came in and saw you thrashing around and mumbling. I hope whoever it was, you beat the hell out of them. And by the way, the kids are fine. I told Auntie I would circle back and check on you."

She smiled. Dion reached down to the end of the bed where he'd laid the white roses and handed them to her. "I got you these."

Her face lit up. "Thank you. They're beautiful," she gushed, smelling them.

"Here, I'll put them in some water for you."

After he did that, Dion sat on the edge of the bed. "So...did you?"

"Did I what?"

"Beat the hell out of whoever you was fighting," he smirked.

Nina knew it was his way of asking what she was dreaming about. "To be honest, I don't know."

"I take it Rick is your child's father."

She nodded. "Something like that."

Genuine concern showed in his voice as he said, "I hope it wasn't him you were fighting."

"No, no, definitely not. It was nothing like that," Nina answered.

Dion looked into her face just to gaze upon her beauty. He remembered seeing her passed out on the floor, helpless. The moment he took her into his arms, he knew he'd never want to let her go.

"Has anyone ever told you that you look like—"

"Janet Jackson. Yeah, they have," she answered but mentally subtracted points for the cliché. "You can't do better than that?"

"Actually, I was going to say Josephine Baker. That's who Janet based her early look on," he corrected her.

Nina couldn't help but be impressed. Everybody had always said she looked like Janet, but ever since she was a little girl and saw Josephine Baker in an old *Ebony* magazine, she thought she favored her. Now, here was a man who finally saw her as she saw herself. He got his points back, plus one.

"Thank you."

"Don't thank me. Thank your moms," he cracked.

Mentioning her mother made Nina withdraw, and despite herself, her eyes welled up.

"I'm sorry, Nina. Did I say something wrong?"

"She...She was recently killed," she sniffled.

"Oh my God, I'm sorry. What happened?"

"It...It was because of me," she admitted feeling comfortable enough with his presence and needing to unbottle some of her emotions.

Dion pulled her to him and gave her a warm hug. Being in his arms gave Nina a sense of purity that soothed her spirit.

And for a moment—a short but powerful moment—she forgot about Rick.

~

RICK HAD FORGOTTEN to charge his phone and hadn't noticed that it was dead. He hadn't noticed much but Kyra. He had taken her to the hospital and never left her side. He had lost her once, but he was determined not to lose her again. Rick watched her resting peacefully. The doctor walked in, and Rick stood up to greet him, shaking his hand.

"How are you, Doc? What can you tell me?" Rick questioned him.

"Are you her husband?"

Part of him screamed, *Yes!* But he answered firmly, "I'm all she's got."

The doctor nodded. "I understand. Well...Miss Blackshear has had a lot of trauma. You mentioned that she didn't recognize you at first?"

"Yeah, and once she did, she passed out shortly afterward," Rick informed him.

"The MRI results says it's highly possible she may have neurological problems. It looks like she's been shot or suffered through an explosion. Either way, she's probably going to have problems recognizing others, and quite possibly herself as well, but let's hope for the best," the doctor explained.

"Herself? What do you mean?"

"She may have periods of what's called 'conscious blackouts,' where she'll be consciously engaged but won't recall any of it later on."

"Like...a split personality?"

"Not quite. Split personality is usually caused by psychological repression. Conscious blackouts are the brain wiring an... alternative self."

Rick didn't fully understand, and the doctor could tell that by the look on his face. "Just try to keep her from becoming stressed. Once she recovers, we'll know more," the doctor concluded.

"Thanks, Doc," Rick said, and then the doctor left.

Alternative self, he thought as he gazed down into Kyra's sleeping face. He prayed that whatever it meant, it didn't mean that Kyra would have to be put away.

While Kyra lay there, her brain practically rebooted itself. All her memories began to play back on her closed eyelids. Faces, places, names, emotions, she remembered it all. The last memory she had was of her walking into Rick's mother's house and seeing his childhood bedroom.

"Can I have a kiss?" he had asked her.

"You are tall, dangerously and forbiddingly sexy," she had told him.

The attraction had been undeniable. Inescapable. Despite her marriage and love for Marvin, Rick did something to her that no other man had done, and she couldn't resist him.

Kyra's body played back the moment he'd entered her for the first time. Her nipples hardened, and her pussy got wet. They say Sleeping Beauty awoke to a kiss, but this Sleeping Beauty awoke to the rhythm of the dick.

Her body remembered every stroke and how he spread her legs, then put one in the crook of his arm. His grind was absolutely toe curling, and once he found her spot, she melted.

"Oh, Rick!"

"Turn over."

Despite being only a memory, it was so vivid as if it were just happening. The last thing she remembered him saying was, *"I'ma make you mine, Kyra."*

Her eyes popped open, and Rick was right there. The first thing she said was, "I love you, Rick."

Without hesitation, he replied, "I love you too." The words

came out on their own, only to be followed by a tinge of guilt. *Nina.* She seemed like another lifetime, one he was just living in, even if only temporarily until he got his real life back.

Kyra squeezed his hand and looked into his eyes intently. "Rick, I remember everything. Even...even Marvin. But I know where I want to be. I want to be with you."

Rick was speechless. Since he had first laid eyes on Kyra, those were the words that he wanted to hear come out of her mouth. But his circumstances had changed, and though he truly loved her, he also loved Nina.

"Rick, say something. Tell me you want to be with me too," Kyra urged him. Her female intuition told her his silence had a deeper meaning.

"I-I do, Kyra. I do want to be with you, but—"

She pulled him to her, wrapped her arms around his neck, and held him tightly.

"Then that's all that matters. I still love you, Rick."

Rick had to pry himself from her hold. When he did, he took her by the shoulders and looked into her eyes. "Kyra, please...We have to talk."

"About?"

"All this. It's...It's crazy! You have to understand, I thought you were...dead."

"But I'm not. I'm here."

"I know." Rick shook his head. "But...things are...different now."

"What do you mean...different?"

He didn't respond.

"Rick...what's her name?"

He looked her in the eyes. "Nina," he replied.

At the same time, Nina lay in a hospital bed peering into Dion's eyes, but her mind was elsewhere, thinking of Rick and wondering if he was thinking of her.

RINALDO COULDN'T BELIEVE his ears. He stared through the Plexiglas window at Deanna.

"Dead?"

She nodded. "They were found shot to death in their office," she told him.

Mack and David dead? Rinaldo wasn't concerned that they had been killed. His only concern was *what* they might have said before they died. And *who* did they say it to?

The last question was answered when Deanna said, "You know Brandon's running the company, umm, right? He said you guys left it to him."

"He told me. I mean, hell, he's the only one of us left standing. He should be," Rinaldo responded.

"He...He...umm...came on to me," Deanna revealed timidly.

Rinaldo's ears perked up. "He did?"

She nodded. "He...wanted to know if you had been acting...shady."

Rinaldo smiled. He knew now that it had been Brandon that had killed Mack and David. Brandon obviously thought he was on to Rinaldo, that he'd figured it all out. "And what did you tell him?"

"I told him you always act shady."

She was deadpan serious, and Rinaldo couldn't help but burst into laughter.

"Rinaldo, he tried to turn me against you. He wanted to know if I knew about the money. He thinks you set up the whole robbery yourself. He even asked me to come see you today," Deanna informed him over the prison phone.

Rinaldo chuckled. It made sense for Brandon to try to turn Deanna. After all, she was his secretary. But what Brandon didn't know was that she was Rinaldo's personal guard dog. She idolized him. She would never turn on him, and her coming clean about the whole thing proved it.

"Good girl! Listen, believe me, if I had that bag, I'd be somewhere on an island speaking Spanish. So, Brandon can snoop all he wants. I ain't got nothin' to hide. But between you and me, Deanna, I can't say the same for Rochelle. I want you to keep an eye on her because I think she knows something."

"How can I keep an eye on her? She doesn't even like me."

"She will if she thinks *you* know something about the bag, you follow me?"

Rinaldo grinned mischievously. "She knows I trust you, so make her think you know something only I could tell you. Then if she does know something, she'll know you're lying, and *that's* how we'll catch her!"

"Wow, Rinaldo, you're a genius."

"Chess, baby; this is chess." He winked.

Their visit was over. Deanna stood to leave.

"And, Deanna," Rinaldo said right before she put the phone down.

"Yes, Rinaldo?"

"I do trust you...You know that, right?"

She smiled. "I know."

"Okay. Go handle daddy's business."

∽

"Yes, daddy! Yes! Yes!" Deanna squealed as she bounded up and down on Brandon's dick, reverse cowgirl style. She loved the fact that she had some dick twice now in the same month.

Brandon lay back on her bed and watched her broad, flat ass going buck wild on his semihard pipe. It was easy to fuck Deanna for hours because she didn't turn him on. The only thing that kept him hard was the thought of the fifty million dollars.

"Oh, daddy, I'm about to cum! Oh fuck, here it comes," she gasped, then her whole body spasmed like she was being hit with a thousand volts of electricity.

She looked back over her shoulder, panting, "Did-did you cum?"

My God, she's ugly, Brandon thought with disgust. But he answered, "Of course I did."

She smiled, delighted she'd finally gotten a man off. She collapsed beside him and began planting kisses from his chest to his stomach. Brandon rolled his eyes and said, "Deanna. Deanna. Deanna!"

She looked up at him with a mouthful of dick. "Humph?"

He gently but firmly pulled her off his dick. "What did Rinaldo say? How did it go?"

"Just like you said it would," she smirked. "I could tell he swallowed it. He thought just because I told him everything, I was on his team. You're a genius, daddy."

"Yes," Brandon smirked. "I know."

He had anticipated Rinaldo's reaction. Brandon knew if he sent Deanna to Rinaldo to get information, he would've seen her coming a mile away. But by having her reveal what Brandon was doing, Rinaldo would think Deanna was double-crossing Brandon, only to triple-cross himself.

"And you were right about Rochelle. He wants to blame it on her. He told me to watch her," Deanna added.

"Then she's the key. The bottom line is we must get Rinaldo the fuck out of prison. He'll lead us straight to the money," Brandon concluded.

"What do you want me to tell Charley Adams?" she inquired.

"Who?" Brandon smirked.

"Oh, daddy, you're so bad!" she squealed. "We're going to cross Charley too?"

Brandon shrugged. "Why not? If he thinks Rinaldo took the

money, let him think that. When it's all said and done, Charley may have his revenge but not the money." Brandon plotted. He had it all figured out.

His mind turned to the one word Deanna used that irked him. *We.* In Brandon's mind, there would be no *we.* As he watched her gobble up his dick like a starving immigrant, he decided once the smoke cleared, Deanna would have to die too.

～

"Nina? You think *Nina* has the money?" Rochelle questioned Cream. They were standing in her living room. She had called him over as soon as she heard about the killing of the two lawyers, fearing that she was next.

"Naw, yo, I don't *think.* I know!" he emphasized. The more he had thought about it, the more he was convinced.

"And how do you know?"

He couldn't tell her about the tapes from the bug he planted because then, she would know he was also working with the Feds.

"Look, I just *know.* Plus, I remember who shot me now! The cop with the dreads? That was the same dude I saw goin' over to Nina's house a few times. So, they must've found out about the stash somehow and fuckin' tried to kill me," Cream explained.

Rochelle paced the floor. "Dude with dreads...dude with dreads...Why does that sound familiar?" she mumbled until it hit her. "The dude with the dreads!" She snapped her fingers. "She met him in the club one night. It has to be him because she was crazy about him!"

"Now you see? The bitch got the money! I can feel it in my gut!" Cream spat, punching his fist for emphasis. "We *gotta* find her."

"But what are you going to do about the murders?" Rochelle

asked anxiously. "I mean, if they killed the lawyers, whoever it was won't hesitate to kill me."

Cream took her in his arms to comfort her. He really didn't give a fuck about her, but she was still vital to his plan. "Get your things. We'll go pick up your son from school, and I'll put you up somewhere, okay?"

"Okay." She mustered a weak smile.

He tipped her chin up with his finger. "Don't worry...I got you."

He leaned in and kissed her with an urgency that said he wanted more.

Rochelle responded by tonguing him down while at the same time putting her hand inside his jeans. She felt him growing hard in her hand and couldn't wait to feel him inside of her again. They tore off each other's clothes until they were both naked. Cream got ready to lay her on the couch, but she put her hand on his chest.

"Wait. I want to taste you," she whispered.

Rochelle dropped to her knees and took his big dick in both hands. She ran the head around her lips, teasing it with her tongue before sliding him into her mouth. With every bob of her neck, she swallowed more as she played with his balls.

Cream threw his head back with a grunt. Fucking her mouth was like fucking a wet pussy. She began licking up and down his shaft, taking his nuts into her mouth one at a time. Finally, unable to take anymore, he pulled her to her feet and laid her on the couch. She cocked one of her long chocolate legs over the back of the sofa and the other in the crook of his arm. Cream watched his dick slide deep inside her hot, juicy pussy.

"Ooh, this dick is sooo good," Rochelle cooed, throwing her pussy up at him.

"I'ma make this pussy mine," he grunted.

"It's already yours," she moaned.

The sweet sound of making love was suddenly shattered by the stuttering terror of automatic gunfire.

Rochelle screamed.

"What the fuck?" Cream barked.

The windows shattered as a barrage of gunfire tore through everything in its path. Cream and Rochelle fell to the floor as bullets tore into the couch, sending stuffing flying everywhere.

"Shut the fuck up and come on!" he urged her, crawling on all fours.

They scrambled out of the living room and headed for the back room. Several seconds later, the gunfire ended. Cream's heart was beating a mile a minute as he looked over at Rochelle, stunned.

"We *definitely* gotta get you outta here *now!*"

They were both shook up, which was Brandon's intention. He had sent the gunman not to kill them but to make them react. He knew the first rule of rats is to make them move. *Make 'em scatter, and sooner or later, they'd lead you to the cheese.*

~

HOUSER PULLED up to the small house in Dunwoody. It was a federal safe house, and it was being used to house Armand, Rinaldo's ex-bodyguard-turned-federal-witness. He wouldn't have known where he was if it weren't for Korn. She was turning over all evidence so Houser could take over the case. She just didn't know what he planned on doing with it yet.

Houser walked up to the door and knocked.

"Yeah? Who is it?" a woman asked from the other side of the door.

"Agent Houser. I'm with the Georgia Bureau of Investigations."

"Who?"

"Could you just open the door?"

She did but stood in the doorway, blocking his path. He flashed his badge. She still didn't move. "What's this about? No one informed us you were coming," the female agent protested.

"Life's full of surprises," Houser stated sarcastically. "I need to speak to the witness. Here are my clearance documents."

She eyed him for a moment, assessing the situation, then stepped aside.

"Thank you kindly," he smiled, tipping an imaginary hat as he entered.

Inside was another young, Black agent. He and Armand were watching TV. The female agent closed the door and stepped to Houser's side.

"What's this about?" she asked again.

"This won't take long. I just have a few questions for the witness," Houser answered.

"Who are you?" Armand asked suspiciously.

"Georgia Bureau of Investigations."

"I only talk to Feds," Armand remarked arrogantly. "GBI? You guys are a joke. Not real police."

Houser smiled. "You sound like a whore that claims she don't do chinks. This is what you signed up for, Armand."

Armand eyed Houser. He had a strong sixth sense. Something was wrong. "Rinaldo sent you...didn't he?"

Houser smirked. "Smart guy."

Before either agent could react, Houser pulled out a revolver from the small of his back and shot Armand twice in the chest, center mark, exploding his heart and killing him instantly. Then he turned the gun on the Black agent and blew his brains all over the wall behind him.

The female agent went for her gun, but Houser back-handed her so hard, blood flew from her mouth before she slammed into the floor. Her weapon slipped from her grasp as she lay there dazed. She looked up at him.

"You...You're no cop."

He shrugged. "Only when I need to be."

Houser aimed the gun, then pumped two into her brain. As he walked out, he texted Rochelle: *Problem number one solved.*

~

THE FOLLOWING DAY, Rhodes was furious. The front page of the *Atlanta Constitution* read:

FEDERAL WITNESS GUNNED DOWN IN CUSTODY

The proverbial egg was all over his face. Washington was all over his back, and Houser had his nuts in a sling. On his desk was the paperwork Houser had sent informing him GBI was taking over the case.

He jumped on the phone and called Houser.

"Good morning, brother-in-law. Lovely day, huh?" Houser gloated.

"You rotten son of a bitch! This is *my* case, and I'll be goddamn—"

"Correction...It *was* your case. There was a murder on Georgia soil, which now makes it *my* case!"

"Bullshit! Federal law dictated that the FBI has jurisdiction!"

"Over the dead *agents*, yes. But over a *citizen* of Georgia, no. Besides, you guys couldn't even protect the poor son of a bitch," Houser chuckled.

Rhodes was seething. He had worked too hard to let some country bumpkin steal his shine. "Houser, I will fight you every step of the way!"

"On what grounds? Face it, *Agent* in charge...you blew it. Now...if you'll excuse me, I have to get to work on *my new case*," Houser snickered, then hung up.

Rhodes wanted to throw the phone through the window. He didn't like the way this felt. Rinaldo had the balls to blatantly have a federal witness killed, and he couldn't do anything? He vowed to get to the bottom of it all—jurisdiction or no jurisdiction.

A moment later, a young Asian agent stuck his head in the door.

"Don't you know how to knock?" Rhodes growled.

"Sorry, Chief, but we just got a tip that ex-Agent Rick Brown is in L.A."

Every cloud has a silver lining. Most assumed Brown quitting the FBI had to do with his lawsuit against the bureau, but something about that just didn't feel right, Rhodes thought as he hurriedly grabbed his suit jacket and headed out the door.

6

Reese may have been Brooklyn to his heart, but he couldn't stunt. He loved the ATL. The pace may have been slower, but the flow was laid-back in a way he appreciated.

He felt good being back in the "A" as the man in charge of overseeing the Kings' expansion. Being in B-Murder's shadow was beginning to suffocate Reese. He was tired of being the man next to the man. ATL would give him the chance to be exactly who he wanted to be.

One of the first things he did was ride through his set's hoods and check the traps. He scooped up his lieutenant, a young, lanky dude named T.J. He had malevolent-looking eyes and a Snoop Dogg-like demeanor, but his hammer game was nothing to play with.

"What up, big homie?" T.J. greeted as he jumped into the car, giving him the King handshake.

"You already know, King. How you?" Reese returned, adding, "B-Murder told me a lot about you. He said you get it in."

T.J. took the compliment in stride with a nonchalant shrug.

"I'm just a soldier, big homie, but King to the heart."

"That's what's up."

"But check it, big homie, I already hollered at the connect. So, we should be able to get them AR-15s modified and have 'em up top in no more than a week," T.J. informed him.

Reese nodded. The King's main moneymaker was copping guns and selling them up top in places like Jersey, New York, and Connecticut, then bringing coke down to the ATL and flipping that profit in firearms. With each flip, more money was added to the cycle.

"That's cool but, yo, I need to know about this company, WMM. B-Murder is lookin' for somebody that works there."

"That ain't no problem, yo. It's mad smokers work over there. Whoever it is, they won't be hard to find. Let me know who it is, and I'll get it handled," T.J. offered.

"Naw, I'ma take care of it personally," Reese replied, not divulging any more details than necessary.

T.J. snickered. "You can chill, big homie. You ain't gotta put in work no more. You made."

"Yeah, but I don't want to get rusty."

"I heard that."

Reese dropped T.J. off and headed to his new apartment. He purposely drove by Nina's old condo in the Cherry Ridge subdivision in Decatur. *Memories.* He thought about all the times he would come through, sexing her like crazy, knowing he had been the person assigned to kill her.

～

"A FUCKIN' crackhead, man, a fuckin' crackhead killed my moms," B-Murder cried as he paced the floor.

Reese held a sobbing Canada in his arms. They were both crushed by the death of their mother and wanted revenge.

"Word to King, they whole family gonna pay, King," B-Murder seethed, looking at Reese.

"I got you, big homie," Reese had vowed.

"Word is the nigga got a brother named Peedie and a sister named Nina. Find 'em and kill 'em, ya heard?" B-Murder ordered.

"Say no mo'," Reese had said, thinking about Nina. *I know it can't be the same Nina that I just met!*

～

But it was, and he found out for sure when Nina had told him to meet her at the pizza shop. She told him everything. He was supposed to kill her on the spot by law, but he was feeling her too much. So instead, Reese ended up giving her a gun and helping her move ten bricks. Now, he was determined to find her once again. Like he told T.J., it was truly personal.

When he got to the apartment, he found Canada unpacking and getting the place in order. He stood back and admired her in her belly shirt and gym shorts, her pretty, bare feet padding around the polished hardwood floors. He was definitely loving his baby mother. Canada was everything a hood nigga needed. She was the lady every thug wanted. But Nina was the one that got away, which made her that much more desirable.

Canada bent over to pick up a box. She knew he was watching her ass. She looked over her shoulder and said, "Instead of gawkin' like a stalker, you need to be grabbin' a box."

"I'ma grab somethin' all right, but it won't be a box," he returned, grabbing her ass with both hands.

She jumped up, and he wrapped his arms around her waist. "Boy!"

"Where the baby?"

"Asleep."

"Then you know what it is," he remarked, kissing her neck.

"Nigga, you see how much stuff I gotta do?" Canada giggled and pulled away.

He snatched her back. "You know you want it," he whispered in her ear, slipping his hand up her shirt. She turned around and wrapped her arms around his neck.

"Want *what*?" she asked huskily, tonguing him teasingly, then pulling back. "What you gonna give me?"

Reese responded by tonguing her greedily as he laid her on the floor. Then she began kissing him all over his face while she pulled off her own shorts.

"I told you, you wanted it."

"Shut up and give me this dick," she replied, her tone full of lust.

Reese filled her with his hard, thick dick, cocking her legs back to her shoulders so he could drill her pussy.

"Yeah, baby...fuck me just like that!" Canada groaned, gripping his dick with her pussy muscles.

"Whose pussy is this?"

"Yours, baby, yours!" she squealed.

He turned her over and beat that pussy from the back until they both came. Then Canada lay on the floor, and Reese lay on top of her, both out of breath.

"Nigga, uh-uh. Get your heavy ass up," she giggled. Reese chuckled and rolled over beside her.

"So, how you like the 'A' so far?" he asked. ATL moved at a snail's pace compared to New York or even Jersey. Most niggas from up top couldn't stand it, but to Reese, it was an opportunity to make moves. The change of pace excited rather than frustrated him. Think, plan, then do. It was nice.

"Hot!" she replied. "How you like it...big homie?" she teased, knowing that he was feeling being the top dog.

"Go 'head wit' that," Reese smirked, playing it off.

"You deserve the position, but you gotta earn the rank," she remarked. He watched her face suddenly take on a cold, sober expression.

He knew what she was referring to. "Don't worry, yo. I'ma find her," he replied.

"I'm sure you will. But will you find her for us...or for yourself?" she probed, looking him dead in the eye.

Reese had to look away because he couldn't meet her gaze.

"Oh, you ain't know I knew? I been known you was fuckin' the bitch, but I ain't say nothin' then because I love you more than she could. Silly me, huh?" Canada explained, punctuating her conclusion with a cold smirk.

"Yo, Canada, listen—"

"No, *you* listen. I see she bigger than just a fuck to you, so I'ma make sure you handle this shit 'cause if you don't, the green light gonna be on *you*...big homie," Canada declared, then got up, grabbed her clothes, and walked off, ass jiggling.

∼

Mo stood at Cream's door, ringing the bell nervously. The two Dreads were off to the sides of the door where they couldn't be seen. Mo hadn't planned on setting Cream up so soon, but Wicked's presence in Atlanta had sped up everything. Mo couldn't tell if Wicked was more obsessed with the money or with Nina. Either way, Wicked had told him it was time to go see Cream. In the back of his mind, Mo hoped he would kill Cream. That would be one less nigga with his hand in the pie.

Mo's mind refocused on the present when he heard footsteps approach the door.

"Who is it?" Diamond called out.

Mo smiled to himself. He was glad she answered the door. Then the plan would go a whole lot smoother.

"Mo," he answered.

She unlocked the door and greeted him with a smile—a smile that quickly went sour when the two Dreads simultaneously appeared with guns drawn and put both muzzles to her head.

"What the—" Diamond started to scream, but Mo put his hand over her mouth and a finger to his own lips.

"Shhh. You scream, you're dead, Diamond. I'm sorry, but your man fucked up. Now, it's time to pay the piper," Mo explained as if he weren't facing the same consequences. He didn't lead his own crew, but he was the inner circle with a reputation as a standup hitter.

They all stepped inside, then several seconds later, Wicked and his chief enforcer, Soon Come, followed them in, closing the door behind them. Wicked looked at Diamond with his jet-black glass eye reflecting her own terrified image back at her.

"Where is he?" he hissed.

"In-in the back, asleep," Diamond muttered.

Wicked nodded, and the two Dreads headed for the back. Wicked looked at Mo. "Ya did good, my yout. Maybe you live."

Mo nodded his acceptance. He felt like a part of the team more and more each day.

There was the sound of a slight skirmish, then the thud of a body hitting the floor. A few moments later, the two Dreads came out, dragging Cream. When Cream saw Wicked, his whole soul shook. Wicked recognized the expression on his face and welcomed the fear.

"So, we meet again, eh, Cream?" Wicked chuckled. "You look like you nah expect to see I and I."

"Nah, Wicked, man, listen...I'ma get your money, man, I swear," Cream pleaded.

Wicked stepped over to Mo and put his arm around him. "If it nah fi me friend 'ere, me neva woulda catch you."

Cream shot Mo a murderous glare. "You bitch-ass nigga!"

"Nigga, they was gonna kill me for *your* bullshit!" Mo shot back.

Wicked laughed. "Me guess there really is no honor among thieves, eh?"

Cream turned his attention back to Wicked. "Wicked, word on everything, I got a major move goin' on. I'ma have your money, plus interest!"

"How much interest?"

"Double!"

"Eh, mill...'ow 'bout *fifty* million?" Wicked asked. "Yea, Mo told mi about that too. So, you want to live, eh? Well, mi want it all...and de gal."

Cream felt dizzy. It was one thing for Mo to have crossed him for Wicked, but to tell him about the fifty million was the straw that broke the camel's back. "You stupid muh'fucka!" Cream barked as he lunged at Mo and caught him with a vicious left hook.

The blow caught Mo totally by surprise and knocked him on his ass. Before he knew it, Cream was on him, pinning his shoulders to the ground with his knees and drilling him with a barrage of punches. The two Dreads moved to pull Cream off him, but Wicked stopped them.

"Him deserve it."

"You! Bitch! Ass! Nigga!" Cream spat, punctuating every blow with a curse.

He beat Mo bloody and unconscious, then began to choke the life out of him. Mo's eyes popped open momentarily, but he was too weak to fight back. Slowly but surely, the air seeped out of his lungs, and after a few moments, his dead body lay limp. Wicked stepped over and nudged Mo's lifeless body with his foot.

"Him dead. Now, do we 'ave a deal?"

Cream stood up, breathing hard, blood covering his shirt and hands. He looked at Wicked. "I guess I ain't got a choice."

"You always 'ave a choice, see? You *could* die." Wicked shrugged.

Wicked looked at Diamond, who was standing in shock, looking at Mo's dead body. She snapped out of it when Wicked rubbed her pregnant stomach. She started to step away, but Wicked quickly grabbed her arm.

"Don't be afraid, little gal. Me nah 'urt you...as long as your man plays fair," Wicked leered, then looked at Cream. "You *will* play fair, eh, star?"

Cream seethed, watching Wicked caress Diamond's stomach. It wasn't because of her. It was his seed *in* her that had him pissed at Wicked's threat.

"Yeah, yo...I'ma play fair."

"Me 'ope so. Now, go find me fifty million!" Wicked bellowed.

The sounds of screeching car tires filled the room. One of the Dreads ran to the window just in time to see Rochelle speeding off in the Bentley with her son. But there was no time to chase her. Instead, they had to clean up their mess and dump Mo's body.

Rochelle had been in Cream's guest room when she heard the sounds coming from Cream's bedroom. She immediately jumped up, grabbed her son, and hid under the bed. One of the Dreads opened the door and peeked inside, but they were out of sight. Once he returned up front, Rochelle picked up her son and headed for the window. She looked out, but the jump was too high from the second floor of the building. Then she remembered Cream's bedroom had a fire escape window. Slowly and carefully, she ventured out into the hallway with her terrified three-year-old son, Raymond, in her arms.

"Mommy, wh—"

"Shhh, baby!"

Rochelle heard Cream punching someone repeatedly and hoped he'd overcome the intruders, but she wasn't about to stick around and find out. Instead, she entered Cream's room and headed straight out the window. As soon as she was on the ground, Rochelle hightailed it to her Bentley. She started the car but tried to back out too fast, causing the tires to squeal. She glanced up at the window as she put the car in drive and saw one of the Dreads peek out.

"Are you okay, baby?" she asked her son.

"Yes, Mommy," he answered.

Rochelle breathed a sigh of relief, then dialed Houser's number.

"Yeah?"

"I'm coming to see you."

"Now's not a good time."

"Make it a good time!" she shot back.

Click!

Houser looked at the phone, then put it down with a grunt.

"Is everything okay?" Korn inquired.

He looked down and admired her naked body. He traced his finger around the nipple of her breast, making her moan with pleasure.

"Never better," he smirked.

He leaned in to lick her nipple. She closed her eyes and hugged his head to her, and then she subtly shook her head.

"Dan-Daniel."

"Hmmm?" he replied, still sucking.

"Daniel, we really need to finish the conversation. I didn't know you would kill Armand," she said, reminding him of Rinaldo's former fixer.

He sighed and sat up. "You're in the big leagues now, Melissa. Some pawns are expendable. Plus, CIs come, and CIs go. The road to the director's office is lined with 'em," Houser schooled her. *Plus, loose ends don't make clean cases*, he thought to himself.

"But we're the *law*, right? So, we can't just *kill* the criminals."

He smiled at her naivety. "Look, Melissa, you want to be chief or not?"

"Yeah, but—"

He shook her off. "No buts, no ands, no ifs. Armand had to go. Now, I need that confidential list of cooperating witnesses."

"There's only two more. Charley The Ace Adams and Jill Stevens. But security has been doubled on Adams, and Stevens is an addict. She's refusing protection, almost like a hostile CI," she explained.

"She's irrelevant," he mumbled to himself.

"And what about Adams?" Korn probed.

"Charley's a lucky son of a bitch...for now," Houser chuckled.

He had no plans to kill Charley. He needed him. If Rinaldo tried to play him, his plan was to go to Charley and spill the beans. With his connects, Rinaldo wouldn't be able to hide anywhere in the world.

Korn started to get up.

"Where you goin'?" he asked.

"I have to go."

"What about round three?"

She smiled as she slid on her panties. "I'll have to take a rain check. I'm supposed to be on my way to Cali."

"Why?" he probed.

"Agent Brown, or I should say *ex*-Agent Brown. We got a tip he's back in L.A."

Houser lay back down. "Have fun."

"Maybe I will," she winked, pulling on her slacks and shirt.

"And, Melissa, don't worry. I've got everything under control."

"Let's hope so."

~

"YOU REALLY THINK YOU SHOULD GO?" Dion asked.

He and Nina were standing beside her van. The three kids,

Jatana, Daysha, and Jermichael, were waiting inside, ready to go.

Nina sighed as if resigned to the decision.

"I'm sure, Dion."

"How 'bout you just forget him and stay here with me?" Dion smirked, flashing his dimples.

Nina smiled. He had been a good friend, almost like a shelter in her life's storm. He had dutifully checked on her, popping by regularly to make sure she was good and the kids had everything they needed. And while Nina had enjoyed the time to reconnect with her kids, she missed Rick, and Dion helped fill that void.

"I really do appreciate you for all you've done, Dion. Really. And if things had been different...who knows? But Rick's my fiancé, and I love him."

He nodded. "I understand. He's a lucky guy."

"Yes, he is," Nina giggled, then kissed him on the cheek. "See you soon."

"I'll be waiting for you," he replied solemnly.

Nina climbed into the van and pulled off.

≈

"Kyra, we've both been through a lot since the last time we saw each other. This isn't easy for me either," Rick expressed as he drove.

Kyra just gazed out the window at the passing landscapes.

"I...I feel like I just found you, Rick, and now I'm losing you again?"

"You're not going to lose me. I'm always going to be here for you, but I can't forget about Nina," he replied.

"You know in your heart she's not me, Rick! So, why are you going through the motions?"

He had told Kyra how much Nina looked like her and how he so wanted Nina to be her. "I can't just walk away, Kyra."

"Oh, but you *can* just walk away from me?"

"Look, let's just put our focus on you right now, okay? You're about to see Aisha."

Hearing her daughter's name gave her butterflies. She gripped Rick's hand tightly as she played various scenarios out in her mind.

"Oh, Rick, I'm so nervous. What if she doesn't love me anymore?" Kyra asked, tears welling in her eyes. "What if she doesn't even know me?"

"Don't be silly. Aisha loves you."

They turned onto Trae and Tasha's street and pulled up to the house. "Okay, we're here," Rick remarked as he pulled into the driveway.

"Oh no, we're here already?"

"Kyra, you're going to be fine," Rick assured her.

He had already reached out to Trae while Kyra was in the hospital, so everyone expected their arrival. Aisha had been peeping out the window every five minutes, so she dashed out the door when she saw the car pull up.

"Mommy!" Aisha yelled as she jumped off the porch.

"Aisha!" Kyra cried as she jumped out of the car, just as excited.

"She called me Mommy, Rick! She called me Mommy!"

They ran into each other and exploded in an embrace, falling to the lawn and covering each other with kisses.

"Look at you! You are beautiful!" Kyra gushed as she pulled her up off the ground, giving her a once-over.

"I'm sorry I left you, Mommy!" Aisha blurted out.

"You didn't leave me, baby. Don't think like that."

"Yes, I did. I left you, Mommy. I'm sorry," Aisha cried.

She had been plagued with nightmares for so long as guilt filled her young mind.

"Aisha, Mommy is fine. I love you. We won't be separated ever again, okay?"

"What about Daddy?"

Kyra bit back her words. Marvin was nothing but a regrettable memory. "I don't know about your father. I haven't heard from him. But for now, you gotta give Mommy some more love!"

Rick watched with a smile on his face. He was happy to see Kyra back with her daughter. Tasha came running out of the house, followed by Trae, Marva, and all the kids. He turned to Trae and gave him a gangsta hug.

"It's good to see you," Trae said.

"Same here," Rick returned.

"Yo, we got a lot of catching up to do," Trae remarked.

Rick smiled and said, "Nigga, you just don't know the half of it."

Knowing Rick, Trae questioned, "Nigga, what you done got up your sleeve? Or better yet, what you done got into? I smell something big and risky."

"You still got the man cave in the basement, or did Tasha take it over?"

"Oh, you still got jokes."

Trae and Rick went into the house, leaving Kyra on the lawn, delirious with happiness. They went down in the basement. "Fuck a blunt! You look like you need a drink," Trae said and went to pour Rick a shot of Grey Goose.

"Fuck a shot! Bring the whole damn bottle!" Rick chuckled.

Trae laughed, grabbed the bottle by the neck, and brought it to Rick.

"So, talk to me, fam, what's good?" Trae asked. "And where the fuck you been?"

"Around, nigga! You still fuck with that Chinese chick?"

"Man, you know that's on a need-to-be basis; why?"

"Well, we about to flip the script on them mutha'fuckas. We

about to be their supplier. I'm putting a deal together with the Armenians worth ten million," Rick explained.

Trae nodded, impressed but skeptical. "Ten mill? Shit, nigga. Ten mill comes with ten mill in risk. Tell me more, just in case I want to be down," Trae chuckled.

"Shit, my li'l nigga, you already factored into the equation. You saved my life that night."

"What? That shit was two years ago."

"Whatever, nigga. I will never forget that. You may have, but not me," Rick replied, giving him dap. "Just identify your team for now. A real solid team. And I'll be getting back."

∼

SUPREME SAT in the parking lot of WMM, patiently waiting to make his move. He scanned the faces of people coming out of the building as they got off work. He was looking for the perfect personality to get what he needed.

"House nigga," he chuckled when he saw Milt. Milt looked like he was leaving the pulpit instead of a telemarketing job.

"Big Amazon bitch. Bet she don't know shit," he remarked when he saw Deanna.

"White bitch..." he said, contemplatively thinking about approaching Vera, but the next person that emerged seemed to be a better choice.

As soon as he laid eyes on her, he knew she was a functional addict.

Her gear was up to par, but her erratic movements gave away the inner workings of her cracked-out mind.

Supreme got out of the car and crossed the parking lot just as she reached her car. "Excuse me," Supreme said as he approached her.

She jumped and turned around like somebody had taken a shot at her.

"My bad, ma. I ain't mean to scare you or nothing," Supreme apologized, giving her a charming smile.

He knew his effect on women. And crackhead or not, she was still a woman.

She looked at him and liked what she saw, so she decided to hear him out.

"You didn't. I just...had somethin' on my mind," she told him.

Yeah, a blast. "My name is Harv, and I'm lookin' for a friend that works here. Her name is Nina Coles."

"Nina Coles? She don't work here no more," she replied.

"Damn," Supreme spat as if he didn't already know that. "I'm sayin' do you know her, though? It's kinda important that I get in contact with her."

Supreme pulled out a wad of money and peeled off five twenty-dollar bills. Her eyes bled with greed as he handed them to her.

"I know who you talkin' about. Kinda short and favor Janet Jackson?"

"That's her."

"Yeah, I know her. She one of the ones who got indicted."

"Indicted?" Supreme echoed. *Fuck! I need to get to her before they do.*

She nodded. "This place was under investigation, and Nina was one of the major players along with my ex-fiancé, Pete. May God rest his soul. She's probably in jail," she stated.

Supreme had known nothing about the indictment, so he was all ears.

"What was she indicted for?" Curiosity got the best of him.

"Fraud, I think, and money launderin.' Some shit like that."

"You think she in jail?"

"I don't know for sure, but she could be. But I know somebody that *might* know," she admitted.

Supreme understood her tone, peeled off a fifty, and gave it to her.

"Her boyfriend, Cream. I know him through a mutual friend named Petra. We all...party together, you know what I mean," she explained, giving him the flirty eyes. "Do you...party?"

Supreme knew what she meant by party. *Get high and freak off.* "From time to time," he lied with a flirty smirk of his own.

She held out her hand. "I'm Jill."

He shook her hand. "Well, when is the next time you and Cream gonna party? I wanna join you."

"I don't really party with him. I party with Petra. But if you give me your number, I'll call you and let you know," she offered.

They exchanged numbers then parted ways. Supreme drove straight to the small apartment he and Lala had rented. "Ay, yo, how the fuck you miss the fact that Nina had been fuckin' indicted?" Supreme barked as he came through the door.

"Indicted? For what?" she questioned.

Supreme paced the floor like a raging bull. "My fuckin' daughter coulda been in foster care this whole time!"

Lala grabbed her laptop and went to work. Twenty minutes later, she said, "*That's* why I missed it."

"Why?" Supreme probed as he glared at the screen.

"Because she was indicted under an alias, Alexis Greenspan. But see right here, a.k.a. Kelly Short, a.k.a. Melissa, a.k.a. Nina Coles. That's why it didn't come up."

"Is she locked up?"

"No...In fact," Lala replied, then hit a few more keys, "it looks like the charges were dropped. She was the only one who walked away," she explained.

"Think she snitched?"

Lala shrugged her shoulders. "I don't know. Maybe. It's not saying. I need some more time."

"Fuck!" Supreme growled, punching his hand. "Where the fuck is this bitch? Yo, Lala, look up that Alexis whatever and see if she's using that."

"I'm on it."

"Stay on it! Find her goddamn ass!" Supreme instructed, then pulled out his phone.

He felt they were getting closer because they'd uncovered some new information.

Cream. She was fuckin' with that lame?

Supreme hit Jill's number. She picked up on the third ring.

"Ay, yo, let's party tonight. It's on me, a'ight? But don't invite Cream. Just the other chick."

"Oh, it's like that, huh?" Jill flirted greedily.

"Just like that," he responded.

"Well, if the party's on you, I ain't complainin', baby," she giggled.

"Then I'll see you tonight," Supreme concluded the call, thinking how he couldn't wait to see Cream.

RINALDO LISTENED INTENTLY through the thick glass on the prison phone as his wife, Rochelle, showed all the cracks in her composure. Under the harsh lights of the dingy visiting room, she looked tired, washed out, and scared. She practically slumped into the faded fabric of the visitor's chair and picked up the phone as though the effort exhausted her.

"I need you to listen to me. Somebody shot up our house." Rinaldo could hear the fear in her voice. He could tell by her tone there was more. "Cream is compromised. He..." Rochelle sighed, "There were some guys with dreads. I didn't stick around long enough to find out what happened. My gut is saying he sold us out."

"Did you fuck him?" Rinaldo asked with a familiar gleam in

his eyes. She told him about the ease of her seduction, relaying the ins and outs of her dealings with Cream.

He took it all in as Rochelle continued to talk. Rinaldo computed it and decided it had to be Charley or Brandon, or Charley *and* Brandon. It was time to see who was with whom.

"What did our friend have to say?" Rinaldo questioned, staring at Rochelle through the prison Plexiglas.

Rochelle knew *our friend* meant Houser. "He put us up in a hotel out of the way. He said not to worry; you'll be home in no time."

Rinaldo smirked. He had already read about Armand's assassination in the paper, so he knew Houser was upholding his end of their agreement.

"A'ight. Look....Obviously, whoever it is thinks you and this Cream guy know something, so just lie low. Lastly, I need you to go see Deanna. But be careful when you leave here. Make sure you're not being followed. Matter of fact, stop driving that fucking Bentley around."

"Deanna? Why?"

"Because I said so," he snapped. "You got a problem with that?"

"No, baby, I'm just saying...You trust her?"

Rinaldo laughed. "Bitch, I don't even trust you. But I trust myself, and that's all I need. Besides, Deanna's my lapdog. So even if she can't be trusted, I can still count her. She too goddamn dumb to pull any surprises."

Rochelle didn't like his tone, but she needed to play the good wife just a little while longer. "Okay, baby, I'll call her."

"I didn't say call. I said go *see* her and tell her to tell Brandon we need to talk once I get out."

"Anything else?" she asked sarcastically.

"Yeah," Rinaldo smirked. "Pull up your dress and pop that pussy for daddy."

Rochelle placed down the phone, stood up, hiked up her skirt, and did as she was told.

~

"KYRA, I'M LEAVING TONIGHT," Rick announced as he and Kyra sat on Trae's front porch, chilling and trying to enjoy the moment.

"Why? Why do you have to go back? I need you here with me, Rick," she whined.

As hard as it was, Rick knew he needed to go. He had seen Nina's text about being in the hospital, but ever since then, her end had been silent. She didn't answer when he called or respond to any of his texts. He had no idea what was going on, and he was worried.

"Kyra, you're in good hands here with Tasha and the family. I'm at ease now, knowing that you're safe and pretty much settled in."

"Rick, you know damn well what I mean when I say I want you here with me. I don't want you to go back," she replied, expressing her deepest desires.

"Kyra, you know my situation. What do you want me to do?"

"Stay here with me. It's only a situation if you make it a situation," she said, then climbed over on his lap and straddled him.

"Kyra, don't make this harder than it has to be."

"What am I supposed to do, Rick? You know I'm a fighter. You don't expect me to put up a fight for you? I had you first," she remarked softly, then kissed his lips.

She had stopped trying to convince him with words and decided to persuade him with her love. Feeling him growing hard beneath her, she knew it was working.

"Kyra...baby."

"I like the way you call me baby," she snickered.

"Kyra—"

Kyra huffed, "Rick, if I'm going to lose you, at least let me have this moment. I haven't been kissed or fucked in God knows when. I don't even remember what it feels like to be fucked."

Rick wanted to give in so bad, but his guilt wouldn't let him. And when he tried to stand, Kyra wrapped her arms and legs around him.

"Kyra...baby. We can't do this now."

"Do what?" she asked with faux innocence as Rick set her on the banister.

She reached in his pants and grabbed his dick. By now, he couldn't help but be all in.

"Let's go inside," he growled.

"Nope, you're gonna fuck me right here. Right now." She purred so seductively, Rick had to yank up her dress over her ass. He hoped nobody came out because he was past the point of giving a fuck. He unzipped his jeans and slid up in her tight, wet pussy, her walls gripping him for dear life.

"Rick. Rick. Rick...oh...Rick," she moaned, grinding slowly, wanting to savor every stroke while digging her nails into his back.

"I'm here, baby," he groaned, enjoying her tightness.

"I'm...Rick, baby. Oh, that feels...soooo...soooo good. Fuck me. Keep fucking me like that. Now I remember what it feels like," she moaned, wrapping her legs tighter around his waist.

Rick felt the nut building in his stomach. He gripped her ass and began pumping harder and faster.

"Oh yes, baby, cum in this pussy! I wanna have your baby!"

Just as he was about to cum, he saw a van slow down in front of the house.

He didn't realize who it was until they turned up in the

driveway, but by then, he was too far gone to care as he exploded inside of Kyra, filling her with his seed.

◁∽

THE WHOLE DRIVE FROM PHOENIX, Nina watched Rick blowing up her phone with texts and phone calls.

Baby, R u OK? Call me. I love you.

Ma, where R u?

Part of her wanted to respond, but the other part, the rational part, said she was responding by driving to L.A. She didn't know what she would find. Her rationale told her Rick's old flame was dead, but her intuition was screaming, *He's cheating on you!*

What other reason would a man just totally cut a woman off for? Not to mention the fact he had changed the place they had stashed the money. *Drastic times called for desperate measures!* her mind screamed. Only she wasn't prepared for what she found.

Nina pulled onto the street where Rick used to live. She spotted his Benz parked in the driveway, realizing this wasn't his old house. *"What the fuck?"* She parked next to his car, unsure what to do next. Then she looked around, surveying her surroundings, and saw two figures on the porch. The man had dreads. She looked closer. *Are they?* They were fucking! And it wasn't just any man and woman. It was Rick, fucking another woman!

Nina felt like she might throw up. She could tell by how his body was jerking that he was cumming inside of her. Finally, Rick's eyes met hers. Nina's stomach may have felt queasy, but as she killed the engine and jumped out of the van, the Westside Trenton came out of her.

"Nina, what—" Rick tried to say, standing at the top of the stairs.

He knew he was busted. Kyra scrambled to fix her clothes.

"Don't *what* me!" Nina barked as she stormed up the stairs. "You got me at home worried the hell about you, wondering if you're all right, and you're out fucking your ex-wife on porches."

Rick restrained her. "She's *not* my ex-wife."

"Then who is she, Rick? Who is—?" she started to say, but when she looked at Kyra, she knew exactly who she was.

It can't be!

But it was, and the resemblance was undeniable. Kyra may have been a little more petite, but it was obvious who she was. They eyed each other for a moment. Then Nina snapped out of it by slapping the shit out of Rick.

"You told me that she was dead, you lying piece of shit!"

Rick took the slap, knowing he deserved it. But when she swung to slap him again, he grabbed her. Nina pulled away but fell down.

"You pushed me!" she cried out in disbelief.

"I *didn't* push you," Rick replied, trying to help her up.

Nina scrambled to her feet, yelling, "Get away from me! Rick, you lied to me! How could you lie about something like that? That is so cruel."

"Nina, I—"

"And you—Bitch? Did you know that he had a family? That I'm pregnant? Didn't he tell you that?"

All hell broke loose as Angel, Jaz, Trae, and then Tasha raced out of the house. Trae came out to help Rick because Angel and Jaz were trying to jump Nina after Nina had slapped Rick. They finally got Angel and Jaz back into the house, but Rick still had his hands full with Kyra and Nina. He tried to grab Nina, but she shoved him off.

"Get off me, Rick! I'm leaving, and by the time I get home, you *better* have your ass there!" she warned.

Kyra ducked under Rick's arm and punched Nina in the

face. "You bitch!" The one thing she didn't forget was how to beat a bitch's ass.

Nina rolled with the blow and countered with a jab of her own. Rick quickly separated them. Tasha grabbed Kyra, who kept yelling, "Yeah, bitch, I'm back! So, you might as well step the fuck off. It's over!"

"Bitch, in your dead-ass dreams!" Nina spat back while trying to loosen Rick's grasp on her. "Get off me, Rick!"

"Then calm down, a'ight?" Rick snatched open the car door and forced Nina inside.

"Mommy, Mommy! Are you okay?" Daysha, Jatana, and Jermichael all rushed to her side. Daysha was crying.

"I'm fine, baby. Stop crying. Mommy's fine," Nina assured them as she did her best to mask her tears.

Seeing her children cry just made Nina madder, reminding her that her kids had just seen everything that happened.

"Nina, I swear I didn't know—" Rick started to explain, but she cut him off.

"Didn't know *what*, Rick? That you were fuckin' that ho on the porch? Is *that* the type of bitch you want? *Is* it?"

"Rick, I need to talk to you—now!" Kyra yelled from the second-floor window.

Nina stuck her head and hand out the window. "Bitch, what part of 'he ain't your man' don't you understand? Do you see this rock on my finger? Tell her, Rick! Tell the bitch to comprehend the fact that you are coming home to me."

Rick dropped his head with a frustrated sigh. "Nina, it's...it's not that simple," he admitted.

"Not that simple?" she repeated. Her heart was crushed by the weight of those three little words. She had to fight back the tears.

He looked her in the eyes. "Nina, I love you...I do. But I...I didn't know she was alive," he stressed.

Despite her fighting, the tears erupted from within. "You know what, Rick? You can have her!"

"Nina, don't—"

"No! Don't 'Nina' me! You can have her! But we still have business, Rick. So don't think you can play me out of mine!" she gritted.

Rick ignored her threat. "Baby, just give me a few days. I just...need to think," he reasoned.

She looked in his face, but instead of the usual strength and confidence, all she saw was vulnerability and confusion.

"Pathetic," Nina spat, shaking her head.

She backed up the van, then drove off, leaving Rick knee-deep in his own bullshit.

7

Rick knew he was wrong for spending the night with Kyra after Nina left. Sex on the porch had been spontaneous; therefore, he could charge it to his lust. But the second time was totally on him. He didn't just want to fuck her. He wanted to make love to her. Rick was caught up between the love he always wanted and the love he never had—Kyra and Nina. He needed to get out and clear his head. He drove around L.A. in a mental fog that rivaled the Los Angeles smog.

"I gotta go back," he mumbled to himself. But deep down, he wasn't sure which "back" he meant. Should he go back to Nina or back to the love he felt he'd lost?

When he turned onto Trae's street, he popped out of his stupor instantly. Trae's house was surrounded. There were unmarked federal cars and L.A. Sheriff Department cruisers *everywhere*. Everything seemed to go in slow motion as his eyes met Rhode's. Rhodes was coming out of the house when he spotted Rick sitting at the corner.

"There he is!" Rhodes barked, and everything went from slow motion to fast forward in a split second.

"Fuck!" Rick spat as he threw the Benz in reverse and took off, squealing tires.

He zoomed down the street backward as the Feds and sheriffs raced out after him in hot pursuit. Rick hit the brake and the gas. He threw up the emergency brake and locked up the steering wheel, causing the car to spin 180 degrees. Then he threw the car in drive and dipped off without missing a beat.

Rick glanced in his rearview and saw the convoy of cops way behind him. He knew, given the right circumstances, he could get away from the cops on the ground. It was the ones in the air that worried him. The familiar sound of the helicopter overhead had him glancing up every five seconds. He took corner after corner, dipping in and out of traffic at over 80 miles per hour, but he knew he was running out of time.

His only option was the airport. Helicopters can't fly over airports because of the preponderance of air traffic. Rick knew if he could get to LAX, he had a slight chance of getting lost in the crowd.

"He's going to the airport!" Rhodes barked over the radio. "Alert airport security!"

"I'm on it!" Korn hollered back over the radio. She mashed the gas, picking up speed in hot pursuit.

Rick saw the airport security cars trying to form a line and block his entrance. But he skidded into oncoming traffic, dodging cars like bullets as he went in the exit and bypassed the roadblock. He headed straight for underground parking. His maneuver had helped him pick up precious seconds, but he knew he would have to move fast to fade into the crowd.

However, he didn't move fast enough.

Korn was determined to get Rick first. She mimicked his oncoming traffic move perfectly. By the time he had skidded up inside underground parking, heartbeat racing, she was on him. Rick jumped out of the Benz, staying low between cars and tried to duckwalk up the aisle. Korn spotted his head and skidded to a stop inches from him. She jumped out of the car and yelled, "Freeze!"

Rick froze.

~

SUPREME KNEW NOT to make a sound. Instead, he squeezed the pistol in his hand like a lethal security blanket as he listened to Jill struggle and gag.

Earlier, she had called and told him where to pick her up. She lived in a run-down plantation-style house with a wrap-around porch. It had definitely seen better days. She and her lover, Pete, were going to fix it up and then sell it for a profit, but that was before the fast money of WMM turned their cocaine indulgence into a full-blown crack addiction. So, the house deteriorated just like their miserable lives. And now that Pete was dead, she didn't even bother fixing the steps or cutting the grass, so the front porch looked like it had a scraggly beard and missing teeth. Supreme thought it was abandoned as he stepped up on the squeaky porch and rang the bell. When he didn't hear anyone, he figured it didn't work, so he knocked. Hard. She appeared almost instantly, her crackhead nerves frazzled.

"Damn, why the hell are you knockin' like the police?" she snarled.

"You didn't tell me your bell don't work," he replied with a shrug.

She gave him a look that said, *you're lucky that you getting me high*, then said, "Come in."

He entered the long hallway that ran the length of the house. Beside it was a staircase. She started up the stairs.

"Make yourself comfortable. I'll be ready in a minute."

"Where's your bathroom?"

"Go straight back. It's on your left."

Supreme headed for the back. He hadn't even finished his piss when someone else began banging hard on the door. His ears perked up. He had been in prison too long to believe in coincidences. He pulled out his gun, kicked off the safety, and peeped out the door. He had a clear shot at the front door from where he squatted. Supreme watched Jill come back down the stairs. She yelled, "Who is it?"

"Agent Houser. Georgia Bureau of Investigations" came the grave reply.

Jill looked over her shoulder nervously. She remembered that Supreme was using the bathroom. She opened the door as if she would talk to Houser from the doorway, but he deftly sidestepped her and came in as he flashed his badge.

"Jill Stevens, I presume," Houser smirked, looking her over.

She had once been a pretty girl, but he could see how the drugs leached her beauty.

"I was on my way out."

"This won't take long. Mind if I take a look around?" Houser asked and began walking toward the back.

"Yes, I do," she replied. "Unless you have a warrant."

Houser chuckled. "Actually, I do!"

"Let me see it."

"It's in the car."

"Then go get it."

He turned around and was back in no time, flashing some papers, now with gloved hands.

Houser wanted to make sure no one else was there. Supreme saw him coming straight for the bathroom. He wasn't sure why he was there, but Supreme didn't want to be found. It was too late to go out of the small bathroom window, even if he could fit, and he damn sure wasn't about to shoot a cop unless he absolutely had to. So, he did the only thing he could. He headed for the hall closet.

Seconds later, Houser opened the bathroom door and flipped on the light that didn't turn on.

"Excuse you!" Jill huffed. "What the hell do you want?" she yelled out, trying to get him to focus on her. "My fiancé is dead. No one else is here."

Satisfied they were alone, he turned his attention to why he came.

"You."

"Me?"

He nodded. "I'm here to protect you."

"I told the FBI I don't need no protection. Besides, I don't know shit," Jill stated defiantly.

"Oh, Jill, that's not what I heard," he snickered. "But it doesn't matter. I'm here to let you know we don't need you anymore. So..." he explained, then grabbed her by the throat before she even realized what was happening. The last thing she expected was for the police to attack her. Once her mind realized what was happening, she tried to fight. But Houser had her in a death grip.

He knew just how to squeeze. Even, gentle pressure so the coroner would never find the bruise marks. By compressing her jugular, he caused the blood to back up in her brain as she slumped to the floor. He didn't want her autopsy to reveal she had been strangled to death. No. He wanted it to appear as an overdose. He pulled a syringe filled with uncut heroin, too pure for Jill's fragile system. He found a vein and fed her death in one long squirt. Despite her unconscious state, the drug made her body spasm within a few seconds, and she flopped around like a fish. Her eyes popped open only long enough to roll up in the back of her head as she had a seizure, then cardiac arrest, then, nothing.

She lay still. Stiff. Dead. Houser looked down at her and breathed a sigh of relief.

"Last witness," he said. Then he heard a noise come from the shower.

Supreme had seen it all. He couldn't believe his eyes. Either the man wasn't really a cop, or he had just witnessed an official hit. He eased back to the bathroom, hiding behind the shower curtain. Houser's footsteps were headed his way.

Supreme stayed as quiet as he could, but it wasn't enough. His weight shifting as he squatted behind the curtain caused him to rub up against the curtain, which was more than enough noise to Houser's well-trained ear. Then instinctively, his head snapped up, his hand went to his holster, and he reached for the curtain.

Supreme saw him reaching for his gun and the curtain simultaneously. He could've easily shot Houser, but he knew the consequences of shooting a police officer.

Supreme sprang out of his squat like a cobra uncoiling, ripping down the curtain and landing on top of Houser.

"What the—"

Houser unholstered his gun and got off one shot before Supreme launched a Tyson-sized hook that broke his nose on contact. Blood squirted on Supreme and the wall. Houser was dazed, but not out, so Supreme kept it hot. Two more lefts and a right knocked Houser unconscious.

Adrenaline pumping and breathing hard, Supreme stood and rested his hands on his knees as he assessed the situation. He knew that Jill was dead, and the cop wouldn't be out for long, so he had to move. But he was determined to get what he came for. Therefore, he went into Jill's pocket and pulled out her phone.

He quickly scanned the numbers. She had dialed 911 a few days ago and then a few calls down, he saw a number marked "Cream."

Bingo!

He pocketed the phone, then headed for the door. He

wiped his bloody hands on one of the rungs of the banister before dipping out the door.

A few minutes after Supreme left, Houser came to. He looked around. "Fuck!" he cursed.

He knew he had fucked up. His fingerprints and blood were all over the bathroom and hallway. He did his best to clean up, even finding some bleach and wiping down the bathroom. Then he dug the bullet out of the wall, where it had been embedded above the showerhead. Some of the crumbled tiles fell into the tub. He double-checked his work. He didn't know who the perp was that ambushed him, but he was a dead man for sure if he found him. As he walked out, he felt confident that the crime scene was clean of any traces of his presence that he might have left behind, and he was right. He just didn't know about the smudge Supreme had made.

~

REESE PICKED T.J. up in the trap. He looked calm and collected on the outside, but his mind was in overdrive. He didn't have a clue where Nina was, but Canada thought he did because she thought he was still fucking her. And he knew Canada wouldn't hesitate to make good on her threat.

How long would it be before her patience ran out and she told B-Murder? He couldn't take that chance, so he had a decision to make; her or him?

It took him all of a split second to decide for himself, which led to his next question:

How to get rid of her?

A train of thought is like a thread in a giant tapestry. Once you pull on one, you realize it connects to another one, and before you know it, you've got a pile of yarn at your feet. Reese liked the power of being a big homie and having his own set. His greedy mind reasoned, *Why not have it all, my nigga? If you get rid of her, what about B-Murder? Get him out of the way, and you can be the man for real!*

But Reese knew he couldn't just kill B-Murder. It would be too obvious. He had to set him up. Then, in the power struggle that would ensue, take over his whole East Coast set. He had it all planned out, but he needed one last piece of the puzzle.

T.J.

"Yo, Reese," T.J. called out, impatience coloring his tone.

"Huh?" Reese replied, stopping at the light.

T.J. chuckled. "You a'ight, big homie? I called you like five times."

"My bad. I was just thinkin,' yo."

"What's good then?"

Reese glanced over at T.J. He knew he had to proceed with caution.

"Naw. I just...you know...I was thinkin' like, real talk, I know before I came down here, you was the big homie."

T.J. shrugged it off. "Ain't no biggie, yo. I'm just down for my nation."

"No doubt. But...is your nation down for you?"

"What you mean?" T.J. questioned.

The light turned green, and he made a left. "I mean, keepin' it real, I know a lot of the li'l homies feel like niggas with the rank eatin' big while they eatin' crumbs."

"You know how niggas talk. It ain't about shit, though."

"Naw, homie, I feel 'em. Muh'fuckas is greedy up top, and I ain't feelin' it. I hollered at B-Murder too," Reese told him.

"What he say?"

Reese smiled to himself because he knew he had T.J.'s attention. He had no choice but to chance the fact that T.J. wouldn't rat him out. "Between me and you?"

"No doubt."

"Word on what?"

"Word on King."

That was the first step to a coup. Coconspirators willing to keep secrets.

"He said them country niggas need to be satisfied wit' what they get."

T.J. didn't respond, but Reese could see his jawline flex. A sure sign when a man is vexed. Reese knew no matter what nation, flag, or set, that North/South shit always got under niggas' skin. Nobody from the South liked when northerners came down and tried to make them feel small.

"He said that?" T.J. finally asked.

"Word on King," Reese lied.

T.J. shook his head. "Yo, big homie...No disrespect, but that up top shit is played. Niggas ain't slow in the 'A' by a long shot. Real talk, I'm 'bout tired of hearin' that shit."

"I feel you. My word, if I was callin' the shots, I'd break bread, feel me? If I was callin' the shots, it wouldn't be about no fuckin' North/South shit. Real is real, and real get rank. If I was callin' the shots, I'd handle up top, and you'd handle down here across the board," Reese rambled like he was giving some kind of campaign speech.

T.J. heard him loud and clear. "Sounds like if you were callin' the shots, a lot of shit would change, huh?" he smirked.

Reese looked at him and returned the smirk. The second rule of a coup: The conspiracy must only be implied but never spoken. "Exactly, homie. A lot would change. And with the way shit is right now, if anything happened up top, I got a good shot at callin' the shots," Reese explained.

"Something happen?"

Reese shrugged. "You know like...if somethin' happens to B-Murder."

There it was. It was do or die. If T.J. turned him down, Reese would have to kill him, so he didn't go back to B-Murder. But that would truly weaken Reese's position. He needed T.J. to keep the soldiers in line in the ATL just in case of an internal war.

But he had nothing to worry about because T.J. wanted to be the man in his own hood, just as much as Reese wanted to be that man in every hood.

"I'm sayin', big homie...if somethin' was to happen...I'm rollin' with you."

"That's what it is then."

They gave each other the King handshake. They slapped hands before hooking each other's thumbs and raising their pointers and middle fingers to form the crown.

"Then check it. This is our next move," Reese said, breaking it down because he had it all figured out.

BRANDON AND RINALDO sat on either side of the Plexiglas like two professional chess players sizing up each other. Both men thought that he was the one holding all the cards. Only time would tell who truly did. They picked up the phone simultaneously.

"Hello, Brandon."

"Rinaldo."

"You look well."

"You look better," Brandon returned with an ironic smirk adding, "despite the circumstances. I was sorry to hear about your lawyers. Any idea what could've happened?"

Rinaldo shrugged and snickered. "Lawyers are like women; they can always be replaced. I haven't heard from Matt either, have you?"

"If I did, you'd be the first to know," Brandon replied.

The size up was over, so Rinaldo decided to play his first card. "I fucked up," he admitted.

"How so?"

Rinaldo leaned forward, resting his elbows on the slight lip of the table in front of him. Brandon did the same.

"How long have we known each other?"

"Long enough to know each other," Brandon stated matter-of-factly.

Rinaldo smiled. "So then, you know how I fucked up."

Brandon listened to the words and was unable to hold his poker face.

"You mean—"

Rinaldo nodded. "Love, my friend, can make you do some crazy things. I'm not...blaming her. Charge it to my heart. But what's done is done. Tell me what I can do to fix this," Rinaldo requested.

Brandon hadn't expected a confession. When Deanna told him Rinaldo wanted to meet, he expected the old, arrogant Rinaldo, not the sullen, apologetic one.

"Rinaldo..." He sighed and shook his head. "Despite our friendship, you tried to steal from me. How can we fix that?"

"I'm willing to...compensate you. My share of the money is a little less than twenty. Keep ten and leave me the change," Rinaldo offered, like the spider to the fly.

If this had truly been a chess game, Rinaldo had just offered Brandon his queen, unavenged. Not being cautious but greedy, Brandon took it.

"Ten? That's very generous of you, Rinaldo," Brandon remarked.

"No. The other forty is being generous. You can have it all. Charley doesn't know. He thinks I took the money. Therefore, you find it, just give me ten, and keep the rest. Deal?"

Now, Brandon overstood, or rather understood, what Rinaldo wanted him to understand. Brandon thought Rinaldo needed his help to find the money, so Rinaldo would take the rap with Charley in exchange for finding it and letting him live. And just like that, Brandon's greed blinded him to the catch.

Brandon's smile said, *checkmate.*

"So, that's it? You'll let me have it all?"

"Except my ten."

"Except your ten. In exchange for taking the rap and letting you live?"

Rinaldo nodded. "It's the least I can do. So, therefore, it's the least I can ask."

"Deal. I accept your...apology," Brandon chuckled.

The Plexiglas stopped them from shaking hands, so instead, they bumped their fists against it.

"I'll work Rochelle from this end; you watch her from that end, and together, we can get paid in full," Rinaldo smiled, thinking, *checkmate.*

∼

"I SAID, FREEZE!" Korn yelled again as she jumped out of the car.

But she wasn't aiming her gun. Instead, she was aiming her finger.

"This is no time for fuckin' games, Melissa! Pop the fuckin' trunk!" Rick barked.

"No time for games? Then why are you still in L.A.?" she shot back while simultaneously popping the trunk.

Rick dove in. She closed it. Seconds later, more cop cars skidded into the parking lot. She spun, unholstered her revolver, and fired off two rounds toward the corner of the parking lot. The cops jumped out everywhere.

"He's over there! I almost got him!" Korn barked.

In seconds, the whole parking lot was crawling with cops. Rhodes jumped out of his unmarked car and approached Korn.

"I was right behind him, Chief, and then he just...disappeared!" she exclaimed as if she had witnessed magic, not letting on that she was the magician.

"I want this whole area searched!" Rhodes barked. "Car for fuckin' car if we have to! I want *every* manhole overturned! Whatever it takes! Find Brown!" Rhodes seethed. He couldn't believe Rick could get away in a crowded airport and vanish.

"I've been on duty for nine days," she said, releasing her belt holster. "I can't see straight."

He turned to Korn. "I don't give two shits, Korn. You haul your ass back to headquarters. I want you manning the phones. If we have to get a warrant for any vehicle or private plane, I want the judge on the phone, ready, pen poised. You got me?"

"Yes, sir," Korn nodded, then jumped into her vehicle.

Meanwhile, Rhodes stood by the trunk of her car without the slightest idea that Rick was right behind his back—literally.

Korn pulled off. When she felt she was far enough away, she pulled over near an old, abandoned warehouse. She got out, keeping her eyes peeled, then popped the trunk. She looked down at Rick and smirked.

"I should've left your ass in there."

Rick climbed out. They both stepped out of sight into the shade of the warehouse alley. As soon as they were, Korn wrapped her arms around him and kissed him passionately. Rick palmed her ass and pressed her up against the brick wall. She grinded against him like she was ready to fuck right there in the dark alley. Finally, they came up for air.

"Hello to you, too," Rick smirked.

Korn rolled her eyes but couldn't help but smile.

"Don't be cute. I'm still mad at you. And I want an answer to my question. Why are you still in L.A.?"

"I'm still waiting on word from the Armenians."

"Bullshit. You could've closed the deal on a burner. It's your ex, isn't it? Don't lie, either!" Korn hissed.

Rick shook his head. Here they were on the run from the Feds, her being a federal officer herself, and she was worried if he was still fucking his ex-wife.

Women.

"No, it's not her, okay?"

"Then who is it, Rick? I know you, and I'm tellin' you, I can put up with Nina for now, but I'm not about to put up with anymore," she complained.

Rick took her in his arms and kissed her gently just like he knew she liked to be kissed.

When Nina had brought him the tapes from the bug under Rinaldo's desk, Rick knew two things: One, Cream was working for the Feds. And two, he'd need another Fed to help him set up the robbery. Korn was the obvious choice. He practically had the pick of any of the female agents, but Korn was in the best position to help. So, he laid his mind game, then his dick game, and the final part of his plan would unfold shortly. He and Nina had just found a house. They had a child on the way, and something about impending fatherhood drove him from calculating to ruthless. He didn't *want* to do this. Rick didn't enjoy any of it, but he had to pretend. It was just part of the plan. No different than working a CI. *Part of the job.* He had to muddy the trail, cover his tracks, and protect his family.

"Did you switch the stash spots like I asked?" Korn checked.

"Yes, my sexy connect," Rick smirked.

"I'm telling you, Rick, I don't trust Nina. So, the sooner you're out of the country, the better."

"There's been a slight delay."

"What?"

Rick couldn't tell her that Kyra was back in his life, so he answered. "Nothing major. I just need to wrap up a few more loose ends."

"Then you need to hurry up. We don't have forever."

"You don't have to remind me."

"The quicker we get the money exchanged for international currencies, the harder it'll be to trace," she remarked.

Rick chuckled. "I worked the financials too, baby. So, I know the art of money laundering."

Korn pushed up on him again. "I've missed you, baby. I'm almost tempted to get me some of this dick right now," she purred, gripping his hard-on.

"Shit, why be tempted?" he replied and maneuvered his hand awkwardly into her uniform pants.

"Rick," she gasped. "We can't."

That's all she got out before he had pulled her panties aside and was gently squeezing and pulling her clit.

"Can't *what*?" he teased her as he slid two fingers into her pussy.

"Can't stop," she breathed, angling her hips out so he could play with her wetness.

Rick turned her around to face the wall and worked her pants down to her knees. He dropped his own, then guided his big, hard dick inside her.

"Rick!" she cried out, arching her back to accommodate his every inch.

The alley was narrow enough where Rick could lean back against the opposite wall and use it for leverage for his powerful thrusts.

Korn was damn near lifted off her feet with every back shot. He was long-dicking her relentlessly, his balls slapping against her ass.

"Ohhh, Rick, I missed you!" Korn squealed.

He banged her out until her pussy squirted cum all over his dick. Then he withdrew while Korn pulled up her pants and caught her breath.

"I damn sure needed that," she giggled while out of breath.

"And I need you." Rick lay down his game while pulling her tight.

She kissed him lustfully, then replied, "Remember that."

"How can I forget?"

"Call me," she said, kissing him one more time. Then she put her shades back on and stepped out of the alleyway, resuming her façade.

Rick turned and disappeared down the other end of the alley.

~

NINA WAS DEVASTATED. She felt totally betrayed, and it was tearing her to pieces. But she tried to be strong on the drive back, in front of the kids.

"When is Rick coming home?" Daysha inquired.

"What was happening with that lady?" Jermichael asked.

"Who was that lady anyway?" Jatana questioned. The kids were relentless. Nina wanted to be annoyed, but instead, she found herself sad. *Fucking hormones.* The fact that Rick had done nothing but love her kids and treat them like they were special made him a hero to them. He literally threw away his career and had endangered his life for Nina and her family. *He even killed for me, that deacon who was molesting my baby.* Nina was confused and hurt.

She had seen the look in Rick's eyes when he pleaded for her understanding. Despite herself, Nina wanted to believe him. At the moment, she had been too mad to admit it, but watching them had turned her on. And when she slapped Rick, she had put some extra snap on it just because. Just thinking about it made her want him. *What the fuck is going on with me?* Nina had to suppress a sob laced with a crushing tide of arousal.

Indeed, who was she? When Kyra was supposedly dead, Nina felt like she couldn't compete, so how could she even hope to compete with Kyra alive? She waited until she got home, and as soon as she reached the familiar comfort of her own bed, she broke down until the sobs wracked her body. The pain was torture. She had honestly thought Rick would be different. She had given him her heart. Now, what did she have left?

～

"Mommy! Mr. Dion is on the porch." Jermichael barged into the bathroom while Nina was in the shower.

"Who?" she snapped.

"Mr. Dion," he said and shot out of the bathroom before she could digest what he had just told her. "He on the porch. I didn't let him in." He shut the door before his mom could get a word in.

"Shit! He's here? Now?" *What the hell?* Nina attempted to gather her thoughts. The opposite sex was always attracted to her gangsta. "I gotta see how I can use him." *Shit, girl. I thought you said you wasn't that chick no more? Chill. You got Rick. You got money. You got all three kids. Enjoy the peace. Don't bring any unnecessary drama into your life.* She smiled at that thought as she rushed to get out of the shower.

When she opened the front door, he was standing there waiting. "Oh my God! Dion! What are you doing?" she gasped, a smile spreading across her face.

"Making sunshine," he replied, referring to her smile.

"I-I don't know what to say."

He handed her another bouquet of roses. "Wow, white and red ones. Two bouquets in one day." She took them and smelled them. "They're beautiful. Thank you."

"Can I come in? I came to check on you. To see how your trip went."

And just like that, Nina went from peaceful to wanting to take a head. But she tried to play it off. *Stay calm.*

"You have me feeling like a stalker. Are you going to let me in or what?"

Nina smirked. "You brought these just so you could be nosy, didn't you?"

"I plead the Fifth." He laughed, adding, "But I will say, my mama ain't raise no fool."

"Um-hmm. Follow me to the place where y'all think women belong," she joked. "Let me hook you up with my award-winning coffee."

"Okay. Let me see what you working with." He followed behind her, a smirk plastered to his face.

Nina stuffed the roses into a vase and put it in the middle of the kitchen table, admiring her handiwork.

"So, how did it go?"

Nina shook her head. "Trust me. You *don't* want to know," she said, forgetting all about the coffee she was supposed to be making.

"Try me."

Nina looked at him. She could see the concern in his eyes, and deep down, she needed to be comforted, but even more, she needed to vent. Jatana came into the kitchen and began to raid the refrigerator.

"Let's move to the den." She damn sure didn't want to relive the shit in front of her child.

"I-I drove to California. I needed to know what was going on. I kept calling and calling, but I didn't get an answer. Then, when he finally called me back, I wouldn't answer. I needed to see for myself. When I got there...it was dark. But I could see...I could see..." Her voice faltered and cracked as she broke down in tears.

Dion put his arm around her. "It's okay, Nina, I'm here. Let it out."

"I saw Rick on the porch with *her*! She was supposed to be dead. Why couldn't she stay dead? Why did she come back?"

"Who is she?"

"Kyra! Oh my God, Dion, he loves her! I could see it in his

eyes! They were fuckin' right there on the porch for the whole world to see, like they didn't care!"

She fell into his embrace. He held her close and tight as she sobbed on his shoulder.

"Right there on the porch, Dion...How could he! I love him so much, and he wasn't there when I needed him the most! They killed my mother and brother because of me, and I can't even go and visit their graves. He wasn't here for none of this trauma."

Dion caressed her arms. "Why can't you go back? I'll go with you," he offered.

Nina sat up out of his embrace and shook her head. "I-I can't. They'll kill me and my baby," she cried, rubbing her stomach.

Dion took her by the shoulders and looked into her eyes. "Nobody will kill you as long as I'm here," he vowed firmly.

"You just don't understand, Dion. My life is so crazy right now. I'm in love with a man who's in love with a dead bitch. My baby's father wants me—" she had to catch herself. "The world is looking for me." She felt herself about to open the floodgates of her problems onto his lap.

"Why is the world looking for you?"

She looked him in the eye and said, "The money."

"The money? What money?"

"Yeah, Nina...What money?" a familiar voice said, shattering the fragile sense of peace and joy that had so recently buoyed her spirits. They didn't even hear him approach. Nina and Dion turned in the direction of the third voice, and both their eyes widened in surprise. Nina felt the familiar sinking feeling that came with knowing she'd fucked up. She was mad at Rick, but looking at him now, with that hurt in his eyes, Nina wanted to crawl into a hole. He wouldn't have looked that hurt if he didn't really trust her. Nina felt like she had broken something special, and that hurt her more than she thought it could. Nina had never been afraid of Rick. But that was *before* she had been prepared to betray his trust. Now, looking into Rick's eyes, she felt an icy tendril of fear for the first time.

REESE SNUCK BACK into Jersey under the cover of night. He didn't want anyone to know he was in town, especially the Kings. So, he drove a rented Civic and headed straight for Kelsey Avenue, the hangout for Wicked's crew. Wicked's people were called Dreads, but they didn't really have a name as far as he knew. The last time he had been there, he had come as an enemy. This time, if everything went right, he would leave as an ally.

He parked up the block then debated with himself about taking the pistol with him. He didn't want to give the wrong impression. But then again, he wanted to be able to deal with any wrong impression he made. In the end, he decided to take it.

Reese got out of the car and headed up the block. The spot was heavy with Jamaicans. Several gave him the screw face. But it wasn't until he tried to enter the bar that his path was blocked.

"Where g'wan?" a Dread in a Rasta cap the color of the Jamaican flag asked as he stood in the doorway, hand on his gun.

"I need to speak to Wicked!"

"Who?"

Reese smiled, seeing the Dread wanted to play dumb. "Put it like this. Wicked definitely gonna want to see me once he hear what I have to say, a'ight?" Reese said with confidence.

The Dread looked him up and down. "What' a bloodclot King wan' wit' de bredren, eh?"

"Look, yo, I don't want no problems. This shit can benefit both of us, or I wouldn't be here. I need to speak to Wicked."

The Dread looked at him for a moment like he was chewing it over. Then he said, "Wait 'ere."

The Dread stepped inside the bar and left another Dread to keep watch. He never took his eyes off Reese. About ten minutes later, the Dread came back out.

"Come," he gruffly called Reese over.

When Reese approached, he patted him down and took his pistol. Then he motioned for Reese to follow him. Inside the bar, the sounds of Dance Hall Reggae pulsated through the room. Two Jamaican girls were dancing like only island females could. Reese admired how they moved as he walked through and headed for a back staircase. He paused before descending and looked at the Dread skeptically.

"What's down there?"

The Dread snickered. "'Ho you look fi see?"

Reese looked down the darkened stairs. At the bottom was an open door with a red light bleeding into the darkness. He knew anything could be at the bottom waiting for him. He took one last glance at the Dread and went down.

The Dread was behind him. The music went from clear to just a rumble overhead. When he got to the bottom of the stairs and entered the room, what he saw made him stop at the door. The Dread put his own gun to the back of his head and shoved him inside.

"You said you wan' see Wicked, eh? This is the Wickedness!" the Dread cackled.

Inside the room, a young King was tied to the chair, slumped, and badly beaten. One of his eyes was black, puffed, and swollen shut. His lips and teeth were busted, and the whole front of his shirt was covered in blood. Reese thought he knew him, but he wasn't sure. Standing over him was a big Amazon bitch. She had extensions that were dyed the color of a crazy rainbow. She was at least six foot three, but in her spiked boots, she was damn near six foot eight. She had big lips, big titties, a big ass, big thighs—big everything. She was just a big bitch all around. She looked like she could fuck the shit out of a nigga or beat the shit out of one. From the looks of the King, the chair, and the bloody little bat in her hand, she had already proven the latter.

She stepped to Reese and towered over him.

"Wha' g'wan say, eh? If nah good, you next! Ya fa sure g'wan bow ta Queen Nanny!" she hissed.

"I want to see Wicked. I got a deal for him," Reese answered.

"Wha' deal you speak? Talk!" she demanded.

The tension was quickly building in the room, so Reese knew he had to lay his cards on the table fast.

"I'm about to make a move on B-Murder, but I need Wicked to back me. When it's all said and done, we split Trenton, and Wicked will be my exclusive supplier on my side of town."

She looked at him. "You speak treachery. Wha' make you tink oonu trust you?"

Reese smirked, then held out his hand. "Gimme that bat, and I'll show you."

She frowned, but then once she caught on, she smirked and handed it to him. It was already slick with blood. He gripped it carefully, then raised it and cracked the King over the head. He moaned like a wounded mule, but it didn't last long. Reese beat the misery out of him, hitting him repeatedly until his brain jellied and began to ooze out of his ears. There was no question at that point Reese had beaten him to death.

He handed the bat back to her. "*That's* how you know."

She looked at the other Dread. He shrugged. She turned back to Reese, grabbed a towel off the table, and handed it to him to wipe his hands.

"So...You wan' do business wit' us, star?" she grinned.

"This war shit is played. We can both eat, but the nigga B-

Murder on some bullshit. Once I talk, the war between us ends, and we get back to gettin' gwop...together," Reese offered.

She nodded, then pulled out her phone. "Give me eh number."

He gave her the number to a burner.

"Okay...Me talk to the Bredren. Reason, seen? If him say we talk, seen?"

"No doubt. Tell Wicked don't take too long."

"Me tell him. G'wan. Soon come," she replied.

Reese walked out. As soon as he was back outside, he hit T.J.

"Yo," T.J. answered.

"Everything's a go. The next move is on you," Reese told him.

"Say no more then, big homie. It's done."

They both hung up.

~

CREAM CHECKED his watch for the umpteenth time in five minutes, then let out an aggravated sigh. He had been waiting for Jill for almost twenty minutes. She had told him to meet her in the parking lot of the McDonald's on Snapfinger Road. He would've left if she hadn't been such a good customer.

He texted her again:

Yo! Where the fuck u at?

Supreme texted back:

Sorry, baby. I ain't gonna make it. TTYL

He was sitting in his car across the street watching Cream's every move as he used Jill's phone to bait him.

Cream started up the car and pulled out. As soon as he hit the street, Supreme was right behind him. He knew Cream could lead him straight to Nina, so he had no intention on losing him.

He stayed two cars back, but he kept the tail tight. Cream was oblivious to notice. He was too busy trying to get Rhodes on the phone.

"I'm sorry, but Special Agent Rhodes is out of the office," the woman said.

"Yo, I've been trying to reach him on his cell, but I ain't get no answer. Did he change numbers?"

"Not that I know of, sir, but I will tell him you called."

Cream hung up without saying goodbye. He was vexed. He had been trying to get Rhodes for two days. Cream needed to talk to him because he was desperate to get Wicked off his back. Not only was he trying to take the fifty million, but he also had his unborn seed kidnapped, and Cream didn't know where. He knew what Wicked was doing to Diamond. That didn't matter. As long as his seed was okay, Cream would be okay. He had to get at Rhodes.

Cream was still preoccupied, so he didn't even check his surroundings as he entered his building. He was too busy texting Rhodes. By the time he turned around to close the door, Supreme was on him and had a big boy .357 kissing the tip of his nose.

"Yo!"

"Shut the fuck up, nigga, and let's go to your spot," Supreme gritted.

"Man, I ain't got no—"

Blah, bloom, bloom!

Supreme hit him with a straight right that crumbled Cream to the floor. Then Supreme grabbed him by the collar.

"Get the fuck up, and let's go!"

This time, Cream followed instructions.

When they got inside the apartment, Supreme slammed the door, then backhanded Cream so hard he slid a few inches across the slick hardwood floor. Supreme put the gun to his forehead and barked, "Where's Nina, nigga? And don't lie!"

"Man, I don't know!" he yelled out.

"Wrong answer!"

Supreme slapped Cream with the pistol until he was dizzy. "Where is she?"

"That's my word. If I knew, I'd tell you!" Cream swore.

Supreme cocked the hammer and jammed the gun up against Cream's temple. "You must think this a game! Goodbye, nigga!"

Cream saw death in Supreme's eyes, and he wasn't about to call his bluff. He didn't know who Supreme was, but Cream felt there was only one reason Nina was worth killing him for, so he blurted out, "What-whateva Mo told you is a lie! We don't even know if Nina got the money! I swear!"

Supreme scowled, but his interest was piqued. "Money? What money?"

That's when Cream knew he had fucked up. His fear had made him let the cat out of the bag.

"I-uh-uh—"

Slap!

Supreme rang his bell with the butt of the pistol again. "Nigga, don't stutter! What goddamn money? How much?"

"Fifty," Cream started but then caught himself and said, "thousand! Fifty thousand!"

Supreme thought about it. Fifty grand was a lick but nothing spectacular. His gut instinct told him Cream was holding back. He turned and put the gun to Cream's boot and blew off his big toe.

"Ahhh!" Cream bellowed.

"Talk!"

"Fifty million, nigga. Goddamn! Fifty million! My goddamn toe!"

"Nigga, shut the fuck up. You got nine more!" Supreme huffed.

He stood up and paced the floor while Cream writhed and whimpered.

Fifty million? Pain has a strong tendency to make a nigga tell the truth, so he felt like it had to be true. *But Nina with fifty million?* His greed leaped around inside him like a rabid pit trying to get a nigga's ass from behind a fence. He kneeled down and grabbed Cream by the throat. His breath was hot against Cream's face when he said, "You gonna tell me everything. And if I even *think* you lyin', you'll have more than a big toe to worry about!"

Cream knew it was a wrap. There was no wiggling out of this—no point in begging a man who had no mercy. Wicked had Diamond, and Diamond had his baby. Even if he didn't love her, she deserved better than whatever nightmare Wicked and his killers would unleash. Images of Wicked doing unspeakable things set Cream's hands to shaking violently, and his breath came in ragged, gulping gasps that he hadn't felt since he was a child getting whooped. Supreme waited, managing to radiate menace, like a teacher listening to a student's excuses.

Cream didn't hesitate to spill his guts. "Man, listen...a'ight? Nina helped herself to some of my work. Next thing I knew, her people got popped, and she got ghost. So, imagine my surprise when I see the bitch down in Georgia. I snatched up her ID and shit and reminded her that she owed me. So, I set her up with a little job situation to have her in place on this cracker, Rinaldo. The Feds was closing in on his ass, so I finessed a little sumthin' for a big score."

Cream got into his story, relaying everything he knew, including the robbery. Silently, he apologized to his unborn seed. If he lived, he could make more. Only God, or maybe the devil, knew what Wicked would do now.

~

RICK GAZED at his features in the dingy bathroom mirror. He could hardly recognize himself. He ran his hand over his smooth, bald head. It was lighter than his face because it had been hidden under dreads for so long. But he knew they had to go. Deep in his heart, he hated it because his hair was a part of him. But like a wolf that will gnaw off its own paw if it gets caught in a trap, Rick hadn't hesitated.

He splashed water on his face, then went back into the bedroom. On the bed was the same redheaded hooker that had been giving Vladimir head before. Vladimir had sent her up to help Rick "relax." But relaxation was the last thing on his mind. After escaping the Fed dragnet and making it to Vladimir's place, Rick knew he had to stay on his toes.

He eyed the girl on the bed. She was a natural redhead. Even the silky hairs between her legs were red, with big, firm Irish breasts and bird-skinny legs. Her gaze stayed glassed over, so he knew she was high, and from the looks of it, her drug of choice was likely meth.

"You sure you don't want a go, baby?" she cooed seductively. "I used to be a gymnast," she added, then showed Rick how she could put both legs behind her neck. Her pussy spread, and it seemed to pucker and blow him a kiss when she popped it.

His dick jumped, but he knew he had more important things to handle. Plus, he wasn't fucking no methhead.

"Some other time. Go tell Vlad I need to talk to him."

She shrugged and slithered off the bed. "Suit yourself," she said before walking out.

Rick put on his shirt again. Half an hour later, Vladimir walked in.

"Did she do the trick with her throat?" Vladimir teased.

"I didn't have time to try her out," Rick chuckled. "Anyway, thanks for the cover."

Vladimir nodded his acknowledgment. When Rick

contacted him, Vladimir sent someone to pick him up and bring him to the bar.

"You're on the news again. They're calling you 'Houdini.'"

Rick laughed. "Leave it to the media to find a way to sell it."

"I won't ask you how you did it."

"Don't."

"I'm not talking about your miraculous escape."

Rick looked at him. Vladimir clasped his hands behind his back. "I know who the money belongs to," Vladimir remarked.

"And?"

"And...it presents a problem. Bear with me. You see, the money belongs to Charley Ace, as I'm sure you know. That...is *not* the problem. The problem is Charley owes a madman named Borcelli. Even *that* is not a problem. But you see, Borcelli owes me, and *that*...is the problem. Because if I let you pay me with money somebody else owes me, then I come up short. You see my problem?" Vladimir explained.

Rick eyed Vladimir evenly. He could just as easily be bull-shitting just to put the squeeze on Rick. But Rick knew he was in no position to bargain.

"How much?" Rick questioned.

"Ten million."

"Ten million! Goddamn, Vlad, this is *me*!"

Vladimir smiled. "And this, my friend, is me. You have an avalanche of bad people waiting to fall on you. I am the only thing keeping them back. Now, I could always throw you under the bus and charge Charley the same ten for a finder's fee. But as you put it, this is you. And while I do consider you a friend, ten million is enough to kill my own mother for, so it's more than enough to kill a friendship. Do we understand each other?"

Rick knew he was caught between a rock and a hard place. If he told Vladimir no, he could certainly become an enemy.

But by telling him yes, that put Vladimir at twenty million, almost half his stash.

Rick sighed.

"Doesn't look like I have much of a choice."

"Rick, Rick," Vladimir tsk'ed as he put his arm around his shoulder. "Don't look at it like that. It's just the cost of doing business. You wanna play in the big leagues? Well, these are the rules, eh? Believe me, it is *not* personal."

"Then maybe someday I can return the favor," Rick eyed him, and Vladimir caught the innuendo.

He laughed. "Only if you get up very early in the morning, as they say in this country."

"I'm gonna need a few days to get the money," Rick stated.

"Take all the time you need. No rush. Zev needs a vacation anyway," Vladimir replied.

Rick stopped walking and turned to him.

"What do you mean, 'Zev needs a vacation'?"

"My friend, surely you didn't think you were leaving without insurance, did you? Zev will be with you when you leave," Vladimir told Rick firmly, looking him dead in the eyes.

"Of course, Vlad. No problem," Rick replied with a nonchalant shrug. *Bodyguard...or assassin*, Rick wondered. Deciding he was both, he resolved to stay on his guard.

~

RICK ASKED Vladimir if he could keep the redhead hooker with him. "So she can show me that trick," Rick had told him.

And that's what exactly she did in the murky motel room. Except she wasn't showing Rick, she was showing Zev. His eyes were rolled up in the back of his head as she deep throated him. Then instead of bobbing her head, she used her throat muscles to give him a blow job.

Rick's mind had been too busy establishing a plan to duck

Zev to enjoy a blow job himself. He didn't have a gun, but Zev did. Zev also had over 300 pounds of Russian bear in his blood. That's why Rick wanted to bring the hooker. A man is at his weakest point when he ejaculates. Rick was just waiting for the right moment. So, when he heard the big man grunt, he knew the moment had come, literally.

"Fuuuuuck!" Zev groaned as he grabbed the back of her head and unloaded down her well-worn throat.

Rick knew he could never knock Zev out with one blow, so he did the next best thing. He knocked the hooker out. Rick hit her in the back of the head, which caused her to bite Zev's dick with the weight of the force. She bit down so hard she drew blood.

"Aaaarrrgghh!" Zev roared, grabbing his bleeding crotch, still managing to stand up, right before kicking the redhead with a force that sent her tumbling away.

Rick used that moment to catch the big man with a haymaker hook. He put all he had into the blow; yet he barely staggered the giant behemoth.

Zev looked at him with murder in his eyes. "Now I must break you!" he growled, then hit Rick with a blow so hard it lifted him off his feet and through the plate glass in front of the motel room.

It was nighttime, so only a few people saw Rick come flying through the window. Zev stepped out, crunching glass as he stepped. He snatched up Rick by the collar. Rick was dazed but not so out of it that he couldn't feel the crushing bear hug Zev put on him. The pain was intense. Rick knew the Russian bear would crack his ribs if he didn't do something. That's when he went Mike Tyson on Zev and bit the shit out of his ear.

"Uurrgggh!" Zev yelled out and let Rick go.

Rick spit out the piece of earlobe he bit off, dropped low, and straight jabbed Zev's bleeding dick, which was still hanging out, as Zev doubled over. Next, Rick kneed him in the face, which broke Zev's nose and dropped him to the pavement, half-conscious.

"My bad, homie, but drastic times," Rick huffed as he went through Zev's pockets.

He pulled out the keys to the suburban, then quickly jogged off, jumped in the car, and peeled off. While he drove, he called Vladimir.

"What is it?" Vladimir asked.

"Change of plans," Rick responded. "I didn't feel comfortable takin' Zev where I rest my head."

Vladimir didn't answer. Rick knew he was vexed.

"Don't worry. You'll get the money. You have my word on that, and then hopefully, we can complete our business," Rick said.

"Don't strain my patience, Rick."

"I told you, you'll get your money."

"One week. Not a minute over. Do you understand?"

"Done deal."

Silence.

"Hello?" Rick called out.

"The movie *Training Day*, Rick? Do you remember how it ended?" Vladimir asked, then hung up.

Rick got the message.

He drove through the night, taking the lesser-traveled roads until he got to Phoenix. He didn't know what to expect, but he anticipated there would be drama and tried to prepare himself mentally for what was to come with Nina. When he pulled up, Jermichael was shooting baskets in the driveway.

"Hey, Rick, you cut your hair!" Jermichael exclaimed in amazement.

Rick laughed and ran his hand over his bald head. "I'm cutting yours next!" he teased.

"Uh-uhh!" Jermichael shot back.

"Where's Mommy?"

"In the room."

Rick nodded and went inside. Daysha and Jatana were in the pool, so they didn't see him come in. He took the stairs two at a time. Then he took a deep breath before entering the bedroom.

That's when he heard voices. Nina's and a *man's* voice. His blood pressure whistled in his ear. He opened the door, but they were so caught up in their conversation they didn't even know he was right there in the doorway.

Dion got up too, not knowing what Rick's next move would be. Rick's fist balled up. It was a good thing he didn't have a gun because there was no telling what he would've done. He and Dion stared at each other. Nina kept quiet.

"Nina. Who. The fuck. Is this?" Rick seethed.

The initial surprise was gone, but the anger remained. Especially since he heard them mention the money.

"A friend," she sassed with a roll of her neck.

"Maybe I should-um-should go," Dion remarked, looking at Nina.

"Why?" Nina retorted.

"My man, you got about ten seconds..." Rick said in a tone, leaving no room for debate. He met Dion's eyes with a glare. He would kill this nigga here and now—just because. And his look said it all.

"Just leave." *Leave or get carried out*, Rick thought.

Dion looked at Rick. They were about the same size, and Dion was the type of dude who would knuckle up with anybody. But he knew he was in the wrong in this situation, and this wasn't the right time or place.

"You got it, man. I'm out."

Dion stepped around, keeping him in his peripheral. Rick eyed him until he was out of the house and had closed the door.

"So, this is how you do? We on some tit-for-tat shit?"

"I should be!"

"I better not hear about that nigga in my house again. And let me find out you fuckin' that nigga, Nina."

"I should have. You did it to me!" she accused.

"That was different!" he yelled and regretted it as soon as he did.

"Different?" Nina barked and stepped up to him. "How dare you—"

"Roses, Nina?"

"Don't try to change the subject, Rick! What do you mean by 'different'? You told me she was dead! How low can you go, Rick?"

Rick sighed in frustration. "Look! We've got bigger problems right now, okay? You telling mutha'fuckas about the money! The Feds almost caught me in L.A.! I just barely got away. That's why I cut my hair. We may have to bounce sooner than we planned," he explained.

"And go where?"

"I don't know. Maybe back to L.A." Which would go a long way toward showing Vladimir that Rick's attack on Zev wasn't treachery.

"L.A.? Didn't you just say you got chased *out* of L.A.?" she probed.

"But that's where all my contacts are."

"You mean that's where that bitch is!"

"Nina, goddamn, can you just forget about her?"

"Can *you*?"

They stared at each other until Rick said, "Listen, baby, I know I hurt you. I'm sorry, and we will talk about it, just not now, okay? We gotta be on the same page with our next move. We need clear thinking. You're pissed and seeing red. I'm pissed and seeing red. And the Feds are on my ass."

"Fuck you, Rick. What about the money?"

"What about it?"

"Where is it, Rick? I need to know now more than ever. What if something happens to you? We are still partners in this shit. Did you conveniently forget that? You just going to leave us hanging?"

"I'm glad I did. You telling niggas all about the shit!"

"We're supposed to be partners, mutha'fucka!" she screamed.

Rick knew how a woman scorned could be. He didn't know how mad she really was. But she was right. They *were* partners. But if she was angry enough, would she turn him in? There was no way he could tell her now.

"Why? So you could tell your little boyfriend? What the fuck were you doing talkin' to that nigga about it anyway?" Rick questioned. "And who the fuck is he? And where did you find him? Damn, Nina, what were you thinking? You're from the streets."

Nina didn't want to answer his questions. She was still pissed at him. "I wasn't thinking, okay? I was in the hospital. He's the nurse's nephew. Hell, his aunt had to keep the kids while you were away fucking your bitch. I-I just needed someone to talk to, and-and...I'm sorry. I admit, I fucked up. It was a rookie move. But still, Rick, really, I need to know."

"Damn, Nina. How much did you tell him?"

"Nothing, Rick. He doesn't know anything. I didn't get a chance to tell him anything. You walked in just in time. So, what do we do now? Is someone coming here?"

"I told you it's safe. You do still trust me, don't you?" Rick asked as though he had been reading Nina's mind. The question in the air was left hanging. Neither one of them could answer that one.

8

L ala held Supreme's ankles as she rode him reverse cowgirl style, bouncing and bucking like she couldn't get enough of her cousin's dick.

"Ooh, fuck! Right there, 'Preme, fuck!" she squealed, her pussy cumming for the second time.

Supreme slid his thumb in her ass, making her jump and ride him harder. He gripped her waist and pulled her back until she was lying flat on top of him. He cocked her legs up, slid his dick out of her pussy, then before she protested, he put his dick in her ass and slowly penetrated her.

"Wait, baby, it's...too big!"

"Shhh," he whispered in her ear, playing with her clit as he pumped himself deeper.

"Ooh, daddy, daddy, it burns," she whined, but her body was already beginning to respond. As she got used to it, she began to moan with pleasure. "Mmmm... Fuck my ass, baby," she gushed.

Supreme didn't last long in her tight asshole that got wetter as he stroked it more. He reached around, gripped her by the inside of her thighs for leverage, and began to pound her deep.

"Yes! Yes! Yes!" Lala squealed, her pussy cumming for the third time, and Supreme was right behind her.

Once he had unloaded his nut inside her, Lala turned over and kissed him on the chest.

"We are so wrong," she snickered.

Supreme shrugged. "They do this in West Virginia all the time."

"You stupid," Lala giggled. "But for real, for real, Supreme, we gotta stop."

"Why?"

"Because I'ma fuck around and fall in love wit' my own cousin. You blood Preme" Lala admitted. "And if my moms find out, I'm fucked." She had been thinking about their relationship because she knew she was catching feelings.

Supreme looked at her. "La! We only fuckin'. What the fuck you catchin' feelings for?"

"Nigga, what?"

"Naw, ma, I'm dead ass. You heard me! We only fuckin' like when we used to play house when we were kids."

Lala looked at him sincerely, but before she could say anything, her laptop began to beep. She jumped up and went to it. She had been running a "Hoover Check," which was a tactic hackers used to run a person's information to pinpoint their last location. It was a highly complex algorithm only the criminally inclined could work out.

She clicked a few keys, and several columns of names and numbers filled the screen, but only one was blinking. "Bingo!" she cried out excitedly. "I think I've got her. She checked into a hospital not too long ago."

"For what?"

"It won't say all that, but it does have the hospital's name. It's Banner-University Medical Center in Phoenix, Arizona."

Supreme smiled. He had already told her about what

Cream had told him. Fifty million dollars! If Cream was right, then Supreme just knew he was about to be a very rich man.

"Then I guess we on our way to Phoenix," he remarked.

"No problem. Just give me a day to make the IDs," she told him.

He smacked her on the ass playfully. "Handle your biz quick, ma. We talkin' fifty million! We 'bout to blow!"

～

No AIR SMELLS as fresh as the air of first being free. Rinaldo tilted his nose back and inhaled the freedom. He stood on the steps of the federal jail in downtown Atlanta and smiled as Rochelle approached him with a sultry strut, then wrapped herself around him and gave him a long kiss.

"Welcome home, daddy," she whispered in his ear.

"I never left," he arrogantly stated.

Houser had done his job well. He had elbowed the Feds out of the way, asserted jurisdiction, then dismissed the case precisely because there were no longer any witnesses. Now, Rinaldo was a free man and ready to take over the world.

"Houser said he needs to talk to you as soon as you get settled," Rochelle said.

"Where's my Raymond?"

"With the babysitter."

"Then I'll talk to Houser after I see him. As for you, I need to see that kid, Cream, ASAP," Rinaldo instructed.

Rochelle got nervous. *What does Rinaldo have in mind?* "What if he's afraid to come see you?"

Rinaldo shrugged. "Then don't tell him. Just have him in place, understood?"

"Yes, daddy."

"Now, go handle your business."

~

ROCHELLE DROVE straight to Cream's apartment. Whatever Rinaldo had up his sleeve, she would be on him like a hawk. She was convinced he knew where the money was but knew he wouldn't make a move until all the loose ends were tied up. And Cream was definitely a loose end.

She climbed the stairs to the apartment and knocked on the door. The force of the knock pushed the door open.

"Cream?" she called out timidly as she walked in.

She was hit in the face by an awful smell. It almost made her throw up.

"What the hell? Cream, are you here? Open a window. I can't breathe."

She went to open the window, and that's when she saw him. His body was behind the couch, brains blown out, and guts spilled. The flies were swarming, and maggots were crawling.

"Oh, my—" was all she got out before she threw up her lunch, some of it splashing on Cream's boot.

"Need some tissue?"

She heard the voice behind her and quickly spun around to see who it was. It was Agent Rhodes. He held out his handkerchief to her.

"Who are you?"

"No, the question is, who are *you*? And what are you doing messing up my crime scene?" Rhodes asked, even though he already knew of her from Rinaldo's investigation.

He was vexed that Rinaldo was out and even more annoyed that Houser had dropped the case. He could smell something fishy.

He watched as Rochelle greeted Rinaldo on the jail steps. He had Rochelle followed and was glad he did. He hadn't known Cream was dead. He knew Cream had been trying to call, but he'd been so caught up with trying to catch Rick he'd put Cream on the back burner. Now it looked like everything was finally coming together.

He flashed his badge at Rochelle. "Special Agent Rhodes... Mrs. Haywood."

"If you knew my name, why did you ask who I was?" she sassed him.

"Names don't matter at this point, only motives. And I ask you again, what are you doing here?"

"Motives?" Rochelle echoed with alarm. "I know you don't think—"

"I don't know what to think, Mrs. Haywood. I just walked in and found you puking all over the dead body of my CI," Rhodes shot back.

"Cream was an informant?" Rochelle said, genuinely shocked.

Rhodes smiled. "Cream. So, you knew him pretty well, huh?"

Rochelle mentally scanned all she had told Cream. *If he was an informant, did the Feds know he tried to rob Rinaldo? How much do they know about me?*

"Not well enough."

"What do you mean?"

"I didn't know he was dead." Rochelle gagged, holding the tissue to her nose. The stench was almost unbearable.

Rhodes chuckled. "That was cute. But too bad this isn't a time to be cute. Turn around," Rhodes told her, pulling out his cuffs.

"For what?" she demanded to know.

"I'm arresting you," he replied, turning her around with force. "For tampering with a crime scene, obstruction of justice, and accessory after the fact to murder one."

He slapped the cuffs on her.

"Murder one? You can't be serious! I didn't kill anyone!"

"Serious? Oh, I'm *dead* serious! I may have lost one, Haywood, but I won't lose two!" he threatened.

As he marched Rochelle toward the door, she understood what the arrest was all about from his comment. She stopped short.

"What do you really want, Agent Rhodes?"

"What makes you think you can give it to me?" he replied sarcastically.

"Try me."

He spun her around to face him. "Who killed Cream?"

"That, I can't tell you."

"Can't or won't?"

"I...don't...know," she replied, aggravation in her tone.

"Are you aware that Cream tried to rob your husband?"

"Very."

"Were you involved too?"

She hesitated, then nodded her head.

"Okay, then I want to know, number one, how did your husband get out? Who helped him, and why do you think you can play both sides of the fence?" Rhodes wanted to know.

Rochelle smiled and replied, "The answer to all your questions is money, money, and more money."

Rhodes snatched her by the elbow and started for the door. "You have the right to remain silent, any—"

"Okay, okay! It was Houser, okay? Agent Houser," she snitched.

"How can you prove that?"

"I can get you proof," she offered.

"Don't jerk me around, Mrs. Haywood," he warned.

"I wouldn't jerk your anything," she replied, looking him up and down disdainfully.

"You've got a real slick mouth. But it's all right because today is your lucky day. I'm going to give you a pass. But guess what? *You're* my new CI, and if I even *think* you're holding back, you'll wear this murder. Remember, I have your DNA," Rhodes stated, then removed the cuffs.

"My husband and Houser are supposed to meet soon."

"Will you wear a wire?"

Rochelle smiled mischievously. "If I know my husband, I won't be wearing anything."

∽

"Boy, I know you ain't wet again! I just changed you," Canada huffed good-naturedly.

The goo-goo gaa-gaa baby talk made her chuckle.

"What you laughin' at? What you laughin' at?" she cooed, tickling the baby.

She loved her son to death. But despite enjoying her gangsta life, she yearned to be able to settle down and just live a square life, drama-free. She had been a Kingette since she was twelve, but that was only because of her brother. Her mother had been a hustler, and when she died, she took part of Canada with her, leaving her with a burning taste for vengeance against God and the world.

Canada also loved Reese, but she loved her mother more. So, her ultimatum wasn't because she hated Nina or because he was fucking her. She just wanted to know who he loved more. The irony of it all was that's exactly how he planned on proving it.

T.J. used the same kilo that Reese had used to come home. Now he was using it for a come-up. This was the work he had to put in to get the rank Reese had promised him, and he was down to handle it. He kicked the safety off the gun with his thumb as he tiptoed through the house.

Canada never saw it coming.

T.J. saw her leaning over the bed. As he approached, he raised the gun. She heard him draw close.

"Reese, I—"

That was all she got out before T.J. blasted her full of dum-dums. Hollow points. But he was so close, they didn't just blast through her. They went through her son too, killing him instantly. T.J. emptied the clip. Reese had told him to make it ugly. They wanted it to look like the Jamaicans had done the deed. The front of her face was blown off, and the exit wounds were big enough to fit a fist in.

T.J. stood over her body sprawled on the bed. He wouldn't have known there was collateral damage if he hadn't seen the tiny foot sticking out from under her.

His heart sank to his feet.

"Fuck! I know I ain't—" he began to say, but when he shoved Canada to the side, he saw exactly what had happened.

He had murdered Reese's son in the process.

"Man...goddamn," he cursed as he paced the floor. It seemed like an injustice to call such a thing an "accident." T.J. was never scared to put in work, but killing a baby, accident or not, was something different altogether. To make it worse, what the fuck would he tell Reese?

Reese had told him to bring him his son. He knew he couldn't bring him like that. He had fucked up, and he knew it. The only thing he didn't know was what would Reese do.

∼

TASHA WAS WORRIED ABOUT KYRA. Since Rick had left, all she'd done was mope around in a daze. She had Tasha nervous because she didn't know what to expect next.

"Kyra, did you call Nurse Wright?"

"No," Kyra answered, sitting on the couch in her sweats, eating popcorn, and watching *Meet the Browns*.

Tasha sat down next to her. "You need to."

"Why? So she can tell me how crazy I am? In case you

haven't noticed, something's wrong with me, Tasha, and I'm too fucking scared to find out what it is."

Tasha could feel her friend's pain as she put her arm around her. "Girl, we will be with you and don't worry, 'cause you've always been crazy," Tasha teased.

Kyra mustered a smile. "I know. Thank you, but I just...I don't know what to do. I haven't heard from Rick. I texted and called him, but he hasn't responded. What if he no longer wants and loves me, Tasha?" Kyra's fears were evident as tears welled up in her eyes.

Tasha squeezed her shoulder. "He will always want and love you. Rick loves you to death. You just have to give him some time. I mean, think about it. He thought you were dead, Kyra," Tasha reminded her.

"Maybe I should've stayed that way," she remarked sourly.

Tasha grabbed her by the shoulder and looked her in the eyes. "Kyra! Don't ever let me hear you say that! Ain't no nigga worth feelin' like that! Aisha needs you. Your family needs you. Bitch, shit, *I* need you! Now, snap out of this bullshit funk you're in. Frankly, I'm getting sick of it!"

Kyra gave Tasha a big hug. "Thanks for saying that. It's just things are so crazy right now, you know?"

"Girl, please, you're like a sister to me," Tasha replied, returning her hug.

～

RHODES KEPT a safe distance as he followed Rinaldo and Rochelle. She told him where they were meeting Houser, but he wanted to see the approach for himself. If he could prove that Houser had helped Rinaldo by purposely botching the case, he could put them both in jail side by side. Nothing would make him happier. His camera was poised and ready to get proof.

They drove up to a small, rundown motel on the seedier side of town. This was a motel for crackheads and prostitutes, the perfect out-of-the-way place for the type of meeting they planned on having. When Rinaldo and Rochelle pulled up, it appeared as if they had arrived first, but when they walked up to the door, Houser opened it and ushered them inside. Rhodes looked around but didn't spot Houser's car, concluding that he'd probably parked a few blocks away or drove a different vehicle. Rhodes barely got the opportunity to snap a picture.

Smart.

Because Rochelle hadn't worn a wire, all Rhodes could do was sit and wait. *Oh, to be a fly on the wall inside that room,* he thought frustratedly.

Houser shut the door, saying, "Hello, Rinaldo. You've gotten fat," he chuckled, then turned to Rinaldo and shook his hand.

"What can I tell you? Prison food tends to sit on you," Rinaldo smirked, patting his stomach.

"I think it looks good on you, baby." Rochelle winked.

Rinaldo and Rochelle sat at the small table while Houser sat on the bed.

"So," Houser began rubbing his hands together greedily, "what's our next move?"

Rinaldo smiled. "To thank you for your...assistance," he replied, then looked at Rochelle. "Baby, I need you to show our friend my appreciation."

Rochelle knew this was coming, which was why she'd told Rhodes she couldn't wear a wire. Rinaldo never did major deals without taking precautions. He wanted Houser to strip, but he knew it was unlikely he would do it on his own accord. He also knew that if Houser did try to record their conversation, the evidence would be inadmissible because agents can't indulge in sex acts with the target of an investigation. Rinaldo tried always to be one step ahead of the game.

Rochelle stood up slowly, undoing the spaghetti straps of

her dress. It fell to the floor, revealing her totally naked curves underneath. She crossed the room wearing only her stilettos and took Houser by the hand. He stood up. She began kissing him on his neck as she unbuttoned his shirt.

Houser smiled to himself. He knew what Rinaldo was doing and didn't mind his methods.

"This is a hell of a thank-you, Rinaldo. I would've settled for a card," Houser joked. His breathing grew heavy with lust and anticipation.

Rinaldo pulled out a cigar, bit off the tip, lit it, and puffed it to life.

"Believe me, Houser, you earned it."

Rochelle took off his shirt, then dropped to her knees and lowered his trousers around his ankles. She took his repugnant dick into her mouth and began to suck him off while her hands gripped the back of his thighs. He grabbed Rochelle by the hair and began to roll his hips, fucking her face. Then feeling himself about to cum, he grunted, "Wait, turn around."

Rochelle didn't hesitate. She spun her body, then grabbed her ankles, her full, phat camel toe visible from the back. Houser ran his dick along the wetness of her opening.

"Mmmmm, don't tease me," she begged.

Houser used the wetness of her pussy to lubricate the head of his dick. He then spread her ass cheeks and penetrated her tight hole.

"Oooh," she gasped, trying to back away from him.

He grabbed her by the waist and began pumping himself deeper. Rochelle stuck her tongue out at Rinaldo as he smirked through the cigar smoke.

He tapped the ashes in the motel's little tin ashtray, then got up. Clenching the cigar between his teeth, he unbuckled his pants and pulled out his dick.

Rinaldo rubbed his dick across Rochelle's lips.

"This what you want?"

Rochelle answered by running her tongue over the head of his dick, then opened her mouth and took his whole length into her throat. She caught a glimpse of herself in the motel mirror. Her deep chocolate complexion between the two pale white bodies turned her on. She imagined that she was making a porn flick.

Houser couldn't take anymore. Her matching thrusts caused him to shoot his cum all in her ass. Rinaldo pulled out of her mouth and jerked his dick until he came on her face.

"Go clean yourself up," Rinaldo told her nonchalantly, then sat back down.

Rochelle scooped up her dress and went into the restroom.

Houser stood there butt naked. He opened his arms and asked, "Seen enough?"

"Can't be too careful, Houser," Rinaldo replied.

Houser chuckled as he got dressed, then sat down. "That's why I like you, Rinaldo. You're a smart guy and don't have a problem spreading the wealth."

"We have a problem. The guy who robbed me is dead," Rinaldo informed him.

"How is that *our* problem?"

"He was our only link to the girl, Nina Coles. We believe she has the money," Rinaldo explained.

Houser rubbed his chin. "Yeah...that is a problem. Look, give me all you have on this girl. Social Security Number, residential history...does she have an arrest record?"

"Besides the federal indictment, which, by the way, got dropped, I don't have anything else."

"Dropped? Who worked that out?"

"I was hoping you could tell me," Rinaldo said snidely.

Rochelle came out of the bathroom and sat down.

"I think I can," Houser smirked, thinking of Korn. "Give me a couple of days."

"Every day we waste is another day we risk losing the bitch," Rinaldo concluded.

"Don't you think I know that? I'm on it."

Rinaldo nodded, smoothed out his pants, then got up. "Then this meeting is over. Call Rochelle when you know something."

"Will do."

Rochelle and Rinaldo approached the door. Rinaldo turned back around to face him. "And, Houser?"

"Yeah."

"Don't keep me waiting," Rinaldo warned, then walked out without another word.

Rhodes perked up when he saw Rinaldo and Rochelle come out, get into the Escalade, and pull off. Several minutes later, Houser came out looking around. Rhodes ducked in his seat. Satisfied that all was clear, Houser started walking away from the motel. Rhodes followed him by sight until he disappeared from view. He knew if he tried to follow him in the car, Houser would spot him, so he let him go. He had all the proof he needed to know that Houser was behind Rinaldo's release. The photos did that. Now, he needed evidence. After a few minutes of deep thought, he knew just how to get it.

～

"Baby, I'm so glad to see you," Nurse Wright remarked.

Kyra was sitting on her couch in Nurse Wright's house in Phoenix. Nurse Wright sat in the armchair diagonal from her.

"It's good to see you too," Kyra beamed, taking a sip of coffee. "So much has happened since I saw you that I don't know where to begin," she gushed excitedly.

Nurse Wright giggled. "You got me excited already. Did you find your husband and daughter?"

*Husband...Marvin...*Her thoughts turned to what Trae had told her when she asked, *"Did you kill him?"*

"I went for him, but he was already got," Trae had told her, but she knew he was lying.

Nurse Wright watched the shadow pass over Kyra's face. But it was gone in an instant. Then Kyra pulled out her phone and showed her the screen saver. It was a current picture of Aisha.

Nurse Wright's eyes began to water. "Oh Lord! She is beautiful! She looks like you just spit her out," she remarked, and they both laughed.

"Oh, Nurse Wright, I was sooo happy when I saw her. They took such good care of her. I-I don't even have the words for it. I want to thank you for encouraging me to take this step," Kyra explained.

"We all need a little nudge now and then."

"I-umm-I—" Kyra stammered, looking down in her lap. "I even found an old...friend."

"Oh? How old, Kyra? You're blushing."

Kyra looked up at her. "Please don't judge me, but at the time I was going through so much, and he was there for me... when Marvin wasn't," Kyra told her, her mind flashing back to the night Marvin left her for dead.

"Only God can judge, child."

Kyra nodded. "I love him...I really do. It's just that now... He's with someone else, and I don't know what to do."

"I see. Is he married?"

"No, nothing like that."

Nurse Wright exhaled and replied, "That's a relief. Well, baby, if you truly love him, tell him that and let him know it. The Lord will make a way."

Kyra felt encouraged, and her smile said it all. "I will," she replied, standing up.

Nurse Wright stood, and then they hugged.

"Don't be a stranger," Nurse Wright smiled.

"Oh, I won't. As a matter of fact, if everything works out, I may be moving out of there. The guy I was telling you about lives here in Phoenix."

"Oh wow, small world. What's his name?"

"Rick Brown."

RICK WALKED the kids to the neighborhood rec center as if he were in a daze. It wasn't because of the federal dragnet steadily closing in or the Armenian death threats hanging over his head, or even the fifty million. It was his feelings for Nina and Kyra. He was torn in two.

On the one hand, Nina had been there for him. She had been the perfect woman. And now, she was the perfect fiancée and the mother of his first child. There was no question he loved her immensely.

But on the other hand, Kyra was the woman of his dreams. Always had been. Ever since he first laid eyes on her, he knew he had to have her. His love for her was timeless, defying the test of perpetuity—even in death.

After dropping off the kids at school, he noticed the Suburban slowly creeping up his block. His instincts kicked as he reached for his pistol under his shirt. The SUV stopped, then several seconds later, Kyra jumped out. He couldn't believe his eyes.

"Kyra! What are you doing out here? How did you know where—"

"Trae, okay? I snuck the address from Trae! Anyway, shut up...Stop right there. You could've at least returned my calls, Rick."

"Return them and say what, Kyra? That I want to be with both of you?" he spat, grabbing her arm and walking in the opposite direction of the house. All Nina had to do was look out the kitchen window, and she would've seen them.

"Is that what you would have said?" she asked.

"At this moment, yes. I have feelings for Nina, and she's carrying my baby."

"So, what about me?"

"I've always loved you, Kyra."

Kyra rolled her eyes and spazzed. "That's all bullshit, Rick! You have feelings for her, but you love me? That's some bullshit! You need to go to her and tell her what you just told me. And you know what she's going to say? Pack your shit, Rick! Matter of fact, go do that now, and I'll wait for you. Let's settle this shit once and for all."

Rick took her arm more firmly.

"Kyra, you ain't gonna do shit but get in that car and take your ass back to Tasha's. Let me handle the situation the way I see fit," he snapped.

"I got your address now, Rick. You need to handle your business...and if you don't, *I* will," Kyra threatened before snatching her arm away and heading toward the SUV.

The driver jumped out, ran around to the back passenger side, and opened the door,

"Thank you," Kyra said.

"Kyra, you know I love you more than anything, right?" Rick said, approaching her from behind.

She nodded.

"Then let me do this my way."

"Rick, I'm in love with you. Don't keep me waiting."

⟿

"How are you, Charley?"

"Rinaldo?"

He could hear the cocksucker smiling over the phone.

"The one and only," Rinaldo replied.

"You son of a bitch! You got the nerve to fuckin'—" Charley ranted, but Rinaldo pulled the phone away from his ear.

He was sitting by his pool, watching Rochelle and his son play in the water. When he heard the phone go silent, he put it back to his ear. "Finished?"

"No, but you are!" Charley roared.

"Charley...listen. Will you hear me out?"

"You've got five minutes!"

Rinaldo crossed his feet at the ankles as he kicked back on the patio chair.

"I just wanted to say...I fucked up. I got greedy, and I went too far. I just want to make it right."

"Yeah? Then take a gun, put it in your mouth, and blow your own goddamn brains out," Charley growled.

Rinaldo laughed. "But if I do that, I won't be able to give you the money."

Charley remained silent. Rinaldo knew he had his attention.

"My share of the money is a little less than twenty, give or take. You can have ten. Just leave me the change," Rinaldo offered, giving him the same spiel he gave Brandon.

Charley didn't speak for a minute. "You're gonna just *give* me your share?"

"No. I'm going to give you *all* of it except eight or nine mil. Consider it my sincerest apology. Brandon doesn't know. He thinks I took the money. That leaves you free and clear, and I'll take the wrap," Rinaldo proposed.

"What are you up to, Rinaldo?"

The challenge, Rinaldo mused in his mind, but he replied, "I want to live, Charley, and to do that, I know I have to get square with you. Brandon's no threat. I can handle him. It's you I'm coming to for a pass," he explained.

Charley's ego was appeased. In his mind, Rinaldo was simply coming to his senses.

"So, you're payin' me forty-plus in exchange for your life?"

"Exactly."

"No problem. My people will be in touch."

"But there's a catch," Rinaldo added.

"Don't fuckin' play with me, Rinaldo!"

"No games. I just need you to help me find the money. I think Nina has it, but I'm not sure. I need you to put the word out. See who's been trying to spend big. You and I both know that kind of money doesn't just disappear," Rinaldo replied.

Charley understood...or at least thought he did. Rinaldo needed his help to find the money. That's why he was coming to him. That, and he didn't want to die. Charley would find the money, but he was sure to keep it all. Just like Rinaldo knew he would.

"Sure...you got a deal. I'll find it. You better not be bullshittin' me, Rinaldo," Charley warned.

"How can I bullshit a bullshitter?" Rinaldo chuckled.

Charley hung up.

"Idiot!" Rinaldo remarked dismissively.

He dialed one more number. Deanna's. After this final step, his plan would be complete.

"Hello, Rinaldo?"

"Of course, it's me, baby. Who else would it be? Where's Brandon?"

"In his office. Do you want me to get him?"

"No. I'm just calling to make sure I can still count on you. You still got him on a short leash?" Rinaldo questioned, checking his nails.

"You know you can count on me, Rinaldo. What do you want me to do?"

"Nothing. Just watch him. I'm about to play him for every dime. The same deal I made with him, I made with Charley too!" Rinaldo laughed. "Except *we're* the ones that's gonna walk away with it all! You ready to be a rich bitch?"

"Yes, definitely," she replied eagerly.

"Then stick with the master. And don't breathe a word of this, okay?"

"My lips are sealed," she giggled.

Rinaldo hung up and remarked, "Dumb bitch." He was confident his plan was coming together.

Deanna hung up. "Stupid motherfucker." She got up and went straight to Brandon's office.

"Rinaldo's playing you and Charley against each other. He offered you and Charley the same deal," she tattled.

"Son of a bitch!" Brandon spat. "That slimy motherfucker!"

Brandon bought it, hook, line, and sinker. He couldn't see Rinaldo purposely telling him he was trying to play both sides of the fence. But his greed continued to make him overlook the obvious. He patted himself on the back for turning Deanna's ugly ass out. Rinaldo really did trust her.

"Good job, baby. Just keep that bastard on a short leash."

"I got him, daddy," she winked and walked out.

9

The whole community seemed to be flamed out. The color red covered the immediate area around Canada and her son's grave site because the Kings had come out in full force. Everywhere you looked, you saw a King flamed up. Some were even openly carrying pistols because they wanted to be on point just in case the Jamaicans tried to come through. That was who B-Murder thought was responsible for the massacre. He just didn't know the man responsible was the man standing right next to him.

Reese.

Reese stood there crying his eyes out. The sentiment may have been fake, but the tears were real. He was crying for his newborn son. The tears were even more painful because he knew he was to blame.

When T.J. first told him, he spazzed.

"You what?" he barked, snatching the gun from his waist and throwing it in T.J.'s face. T.J. put up his hands.

"I swear I didn't mean to! I didn't see him, I swear! The bullets went right through her!"

The bullets went right through. The bullets. The ones he

had himself authorized. He had given the order, so who could he blame but himself? However, he wasn't about to let his son die in vain. If he lost a son, he was determined to gain the top position. In Reese's greedy, twisted mind, that was ample compensation.

B-Murder put his arm around him.

"Believe me, homie, them fuckin' Jamaicans are gonna pay for this!" B-Murder cried, tears streaming down his cheeks. First his mother, now his sister and nephew. He felt like he was cursed. Like the old folk always say, *you reap what you sow*. Maybe he should have planted better seeds. But now, Wicked's people would reap a crop of revenge.

Reese wouldn't be so easily appeased. He shrugged B-Murder's arm off and turned to him. "Naw, homie, if they gonna pay, you puttin' in the work! This is *your* fuckin' fault!" Reese growled.

B-Murder eyed him hard but held back his rising anger.

"Ay, yo, Reese...I'ma let that go because I know you fucked up—"

"Naw, I ain't fucked up. This shit real! Nigga, you ain't handlin' your biz no more. The soldiers is starvin' while you get fat! How we 'posed to eat while we at war? But you sit back, push buttons, and count gwop? Fuck, no!" Reese spat.

B-Murder looked around. He could see the look of agreement on many of his soldiers' faces, which was no surprise to Reese because he had already sowed the seed in many of their heads.

"Reese...You stand at my sister's grave and think you can disrespect me like this?"

"Nigga, fuck—" was all Reese got out before B-Murder slapped the shit out of him.

Reese lunged at B-Murder, but one of the Kings got between them.

"Y'all niggas chill! Show some respect!" the King barked.

B-Murder and Reese glared at each other.

"Nigga...You know what it is now, don't you?" B-Murder hissed while wearing a crazy smile on his face.

"It is what it is...homie," Reese expressed with a sneer, then walked away.

B-Murder watched Reese with murderous intent in his eyes. He was definitely going to put Reese on the plate. Reese left alone. Meanwhile, several of his coconspirators stayed behind to play their positions in the plot.

The funeral concluded, and B-Murder made his way to his car. Two of his main shooters rode with him, and behind him in a red Escalade were three more of his most trusted lieutenants. As they emerged from the cemetery onto Scotland Road, a black Honda MPV minivan swerved up and blocked their path. B-Murder recognized what it was instantly.

"Oh, that's how he wanna play?"

The MPV's sliding door flew open, and automatic gunfire rang out. The windshield of B-Murder's car shattered into pieces as B-Murder ducked. His passenger wasn't so lucky.

"Yo—" B-Murder started to yell out until he saw his man's chest being riddled with bullets. The impact pinned him to the seat in an electrified dance. B-Murder aimed his pistol and returned fire blindly. He didn't dare raise his head to aim since the MPV had him nailed down with suppressive fire. If it hadn't been for the three shooters in the Escalade, B-Murder would've been a dead man.

The driver of the Escalade and the passenger jumped out, using the door for cover, and let two AR-15s blaze, killing one of the gunmen in the MPV instantly. B-Murder and his man in the backseat bailed out and began to army crawl on the ground, heading for the Escalade as bullets hummed like angry hornets overhead. Suddenly, fire erupted from behind the Escalade as several other Kings joined the shootout, aiming a barrage of shots at the MPV.

One of the shooters in the MPV hit the Escalade driver in the shoulder, hurling him back against the doorjamb.

"Fuck!" he bellowed, grabbing his lead-savaged shoulder.

"Get in! Get in!" B-Murder barked, dragging him into the truck. *This muh'fucka Reese thought shit was going down like this...nah.*

The driver scrambled into the back while B-Murder got behind the wheel. The MPV skidded off just as B-Murder came barreling into the intersection. Behind him, the sounds of gunfire resounded. It was King against King. He would bet it all that Reese was behind this. There could only be one ruler. One captain of the ship. They were set tripping, and the war was on.

~

AGENT RHODES WALKED into Houser's favorite bar. He knew he would find him there. Houser was sitting at the bar, nursing a drink. He looked up and saw Rhodes approaching. He smirked and raised his glass as Rhodes walked up.

"Houser."

"Rhodes."

"Mind if I join you?"

Houser shrugged. "Why not?"

Rhodes sat on the stool, then signaled the bartender. "Bring me a Heineken and bring him whatever he wants."

The bartender nodded, then brought them their drinks.

"I guess you'll be happy to know the Haywood case cost me my job. I'm going back to Washington to be reassigned," Rhodes lied.

Houser shrugged and downed his drink. "Why would that make me happy?"

Rhodes laughed. "Come on, Houser. You and I both know how you feel about me. So, for once, let's just be as honest as enemies," Rhodes proposed, waving for the bartender to bring Houser another drink.

"Honest as enemies, huh? You sure you can handle the truth?" Houser asked, doing a bad Jack Nicholson impression.

"Try me," Rhodes replied, drinking his beer.

"Okay...I think you're an arrogant son of a bitch who ain't half the cop you think you are, and my sister shouldn't have married you," Houser stated.

"Wow," Rhodes chuckled. "I didn't know you cared," he remarked sarcastically, then added, "but is that worth sacrificing justice?"

"Meaning?"

"Meaning you'd sabotage a case just to see me with mud on my face?"

"Hey!" Houser barked, banging his glass. "I didn't sabotage anything! The case was mine until you tried to steal it from me! If it wasn't for you, Haywood would have been in Camp Fed!"

The two men eyed each other evenly. Rhodes broke the glare with a smile.

"Look, Houser, I didn't come to argue with you. I just wanted...closure, to buy you a drink, and show you there's no hard feelings, okay? So, hey, how about one more? What do you say?"

"Yeah, sure. Just let me go drain the weasel," Houser replied, then headed for the bathroom.

As soon as he was gone, Rhodes made a move for what he came for. Houser's glass. He quickly reached in his pocket, pulled out a plastic bag, and dropped the glass in the bag using a napkin.

"Hey!" the bartender called out.

Rhodes flashed his badge on his way out. "Federal agent."

Meanwhile, Houser had entered the bathroom. He couldn't believe the nerve of Rhodes. To come all the way over to his favorite spot just to buy him a couple of drinks and accuse him of fucking up the Haywood case.

He—

Then his cop mind kicked in—*his favorite spot. Buy a drink. Another drink...*Houser cut his piss midstream and jetted out of the bathroom. He approached his spot at the bar and counted the glasses. He'd had four drinks. Only three glasses remained, and Rhodes was gone.

DNA!

Houser panicked and ran straight for the front door just in time to see Rhodes racing out of the parking lot.

"Shit!" he spat.

~

WICKED SAT with hands tented as he leered at Reese. He had proven that he wanted to take over the Kings and make a deal with the Jamaicans. Wicked wanted the King war to escalate. This way, whoever won would be weakened.

If B-Murder won, Wicked could throw all his forces at him before he had a chance to recover, finishing the Kings in Trenton once and for all. If Reese won, then not only would Wicked inherit half of Trenton, but he'd also supply all of Trenton and Reese's set in Atlanta. For Wicked, it was a win-win.

"You missed, eh?" Wicked remarked with a sinister snicker.

"Trust me, them niggas finished. Too many Kings been wanting somebody to make a move. Not that I'm that some-body, but it's only a matter of time."

"Time is a ting we no 'ave, star. You let the bumbaclot recoup," Wicked warned. He was annoyed that B-Murder survived. You don't kill a snake by chopping off a few bits of its tail.

"Let me handle that. You just make sure you handle your

end. If I'm the hand feedin' niggas, they won't bite me," Reese replied.

Wicked nodded, taking in the point. He knew Reese was in a good position to come out on top. Reese had already explained how his team of Kings in Atlanta controlled the flow of guns and combined with the fact that Wicked would now be his steady supplier, Reese was holding all the cards. Drugs were good, but guns were better.

"Me tinks you 'ave the upper hand. Don't lose it," Wicked said.

"I won't."

"One more ting, star. A favor for the Dread."

"No problem. What is it?"

"There's a likkle gal the Dread need to 'ave. Naughty gal, seen? The Dread need to teach 'er a lesson. So, I need you to use your network to see if you can find 'er for me, seen?" Wicked explained.

"I need a name and a picture."

Wicked clicked through his phone and landed on a picture of Nina from when he held her captive. Payment for a debt that had been sweeter than money. She was butt naked, laid on her back, and spread eagle. He slid his phone across the table to Reese. As soon as Reese saw her, he couldn't stop his jaw from dropping.

Wicked caught the expression. "You know dis gal?"

Reese couldn't believe his eyes. Wicked knew from his hesitation that he definitely knew her.

"Once...a long time ago," Reese replied, trying to control his flood of emotions.

Is everyone in the world looking for Nina? he thought.

"Good. Den you know her name. Easier to find de gal."

From the look in his eyes, Reese knew Wicked intended on killing her. And Reese wasn't about to let *that* happen, but to ensure that, he had to find her first.

"I'll find her," Reese replied.

LIVING with Nina lately was like driving in a hazy winter storm for Rick. His environment was cold and uncertain. He knew it was his fault, but he didn't know how to change it. Rick wished he could just split himself in half. That would be more feasible than loving both women at the same time. He was distracted, and things were getting to the wire.

He walked into the bedroom and found Nina lying on the bed watching TV.

"We have to talk," he announced.

"I don't have nothing to say to you right now, Rick," she replied, never taking her eyes off the screen.

"Well, I do," he returned, then flicked off the TV with the remote.

Nina glared at him.

"Baby, we can't keep living like this," Rick began, searching for the words to convey how he felt. The doomsday clock Vladimir had him under was constantly ticking. Rick could feel it fraying his nerves and thinning his patience like acid.

"You should've thought about that before you stuck your dick in that dead bitch," Nina huffed.

She got off the bed and started to walk out, but Rick took her by the arm. She quickly snatched it away from him. "Don't touch me, Rick."

"Then don't walk away when I'm talking to you," he answered.

"Why not? You ain't talkin' about shit," she spat and started to walk off again.

Once more, he grabbed her. "Nina."

Again, she snatched away, but this time, she tried to slap

him. When she missed, it only made her madder. She swung both hands like a windmill trying to hit him.

"I hate you! I hate you! You make me fuckin' sick!" she yelled. "You hurt me, Rick. You hurt me bad."

Rick deflected her blows, then wrapped his arms around her like a straitjacket. They ended up in front of the mirror with him standing behind her.

"Stop it, Nina! I love you!" Rick confessed. "You know that."

Nina gazed in the mirror at their reflection. Then a strong feeling of déjà vu made her shudder as if a cold breeze had passed through. The warmth of his body was the only thing separating her dream from this reality.

"Are you okay?" he asked.

"I got...cold. I'm freezing."

He wrapped his arms around her and began rubbing her stomach. "Baby, I promise we're gonna work this out. I love you too much not to," he whispered in her ear.

Nina barely heard him. She was remembering her dream. The one where Rick was standing with a mirror image that wasn't her. However, the comfort she felt as he held her reminded her he was right there with her. Tears of confusion began to roll down her cheeks.

"Tell me you love me more than her, Rick," Nina pleaded.

He turned her to face him.

"I love you more," he told her, but deep down, he wasn't sure if that was true.

The words released the dam holding back her emotions, and she sobbed in his arms. "I love you, Rick! I love you sooo much! Please make her go away! Don't end us like this, Rick."

He answered with his embrace and a sensual kiss, a kiss that began on her lips as he enveloped her tongue, then traveled down to her chin along her neck and into the cleavage of her oversized tee shirt.

"I love you, Rick. Promise you won't walk away from what

we've built together." Nina's tone was laced with hope and fear. They were so close. Nina had finally gotten what she had wanted for so long. She was far away from Jersey and the gang-bangin', Georgia, WMM, and Rinaldo's madness. Her family was finally back together, and she and Rick were adding a new member. *His first child*, Nina thought with a flutter of excitement. Now, everything felt uncertain, but she would be damned if she just let it slip through her fingers without a fight.

"I won't," he said, still not sure of his words.

HOUSER KNEW he had to get out of town. He had fucked up. If Rhodes had gone through all that to get his DNA, he must've had something on him. Whatever it was, he wasn't about to wait around and find out.

"Are you sure?" Rinaldo probed on the other end of the phone.

"Of course, I'm fuckin' sure! I know the trick 'cause I've used it myself!" Houser barked as he raced around, packing everything he needed.

Rinaldo sighed. "I don't just have one hundred grand lying around the house."

Houser stopped.

"Look, you little maggot piece of shit! You better *find* it, and I mean *now*! Because if I go down, *you* go down with me!"

"Okay, okay. Hit me back in twenty minutes, and I'll tell you where to meet me."

"Ten minutes, and I'll tell you where to meet *me*!" Houser shot back, then hung up.

He packed a small duffle bag and stuffed his briefcase haphazardly with paperwork. It was so full he couldn't get the latch closed so he just held it together. He deleted everything from his computer, then doused the hard drive with bleach.

Houser was a man on a mission. He grabbed his keys and headed out the door. As he neared his car, federal vehicles began to appear from everywhere.

"Fuck fuck fuck!" he spat and ran back into the house.

He glanced out the window and saw the Black Suburbans, Crown Victorias, and squad cars taking their positions. He hurried to the back of the house and ran out the back door. The SWAT team was setting up to take aim.

He was trapped.

"I'll be damned if I go out like a sittin' duck!" he roared.

He ran down into his basement and flipped the light. Mounted on the wall was a small arsenal. He had several assault weapons, sniper rifles, and large-caliber handguns. He grabbed two fully automatic M-16s, snatched up a couple of high-capacity magazines, and raced back up the stairs.

When he entered the living room, he could see shadows on the porch. He let loose a deadly barrage of gunfire.

"It ain't gonna be that easy!" he shouted as he watched some shadows fall while others ran off to take cover. He ran to the back, gun held chest high like he was back in Desert Storm, and emptied a clip at the SWAT team. They returned fire, but Houser knew evasive maneuvers, firing controlled bursts as he sought cover.

"Hold your fire! Hold your fire!" Rhodes screamed into his walkie-talkie. "Everyone, stay calm!"

He looked at Korn, who looked back at him. She was regretting ever getting involved with Houser. She knew she shouldn't have, but she got sucked in by the sweet talk and the sweet dick. Now, she was glad he was trapped because dead men could tell no tales.

"Should we move in with the gas, Chief?" she asked.

"No...it'll only make him mad," he replied, then got on the PA system hooked up in his car.

"Houser, calm down. We don't have to do this, okay? You're surrounded. Just come out with your hands up!"

"Hell no! You want to play? Let's play!" Houser bellowed as he broke two front windows with the butt of his gun and let it spit fire, riddling vehicles with so much force they rocked on their axles as sparks shot off their metallic bodies.

Rhodes took cover instantly, still squatting behind the car door. He shouted through the PA, "Houser, what are you trying to prove? It doesn't have to end this way. You've already got two bodies on your hands; don't make it any worse!"

"Two bodies on my hands?" Houser cackled. "Oh, so you think my hands are the *only* dirty ones, huh? You Fed bastards ain't so squeaky clean! Ask Korn! Tell him, Melissa! Tell him how I fucked your brains out, and you told me where they were hiding Armand!"

Korn's whole face turned beet red. She couldn't believe her ears. Every Fed in the immediate vicinity turned their heads in her direction, including Rhodes.

"He's lying! He's fucking lying! You piece of shit!" she yelled and fired several shots at the house in frustration.

"No...I don't think he is. Now, lower your weapon, Korn," Rhodes instructed her coldly.

He had been wondering how the killer had found Armand. His instincts told him there had to be a dirty agent behind it, but his mind wouldn't allow him to accept it. Now, he had no choice but to believe it as he stared her dead in the face.

"Agent Summers, escort Agent Korn back to my office...and stay with her."

Korn dropped her head as she was led away. Meanwhile, inside the house, Houser sat on the floor with the M-16 standing on its butt between his legs like a hard dick. He thought about his long career. He had been a good cop. He had cut a couple of corners from time to time, but for the most part, he had stayed on the straight and narrow. It's hard work being straight in a crooked world. Other assholes had won off the blood and sweat of men like him. He arrested scum that blew more money in ten days than he earned in ten years. Making collars for a different brand of asshole that wore his annual salary on their wrists, all while the real monsters, the bloody hands that drove the industry, never had to worry about guys like Houser bringing them to justice. The job took a lot. It ebbed at the soul. *Even in an unjust system, justice was a harsh mistress, and for what reward?* It was the fifty million that pushed him over the edge; that, and the intense rivalry with Rhodes did him in.

He knew it was over, but he wasn't about to go to jail. That was out of the question. He was too old to contend with being an ex-cop in prison. Houser knew there was only one choice left.

"Hey, Rhodes!"

"Yeah, Houser."

"Tell my sister...I love her."

As soon as Rhodes heard the words, he knew what was coming.

"Houser, no!" he yelled, dropping the bullhorn and racing across the lawn.

Before he even reached the steps, they heard the single blast. *Boom!*

The 5.56-caliber round ripped through the soft tissue of Houser's chin and his skull, splattering his brains across the walls and ceiling.

Rhodes knew it was over. He stopped and shut his eyes tight, shaking his head as SWAT moved in.

"Subject is down! Subject is down!" he heard being squawked over the walkie-talkies.

He didn't even go inside. He already knew what he would find.

"*Subject is nonresponsive. Apparent gunshot wound to the head, presumably self-inflicted.*"

Rhodes got in his car. Houser was a piece of shit, but he deserved a better end. He felt tired, sick of it all. The lies. The blood. It was all a waste. He headed back to his office with one thing in mind: *Korn.*

~

B-MURDER PACED the floor like a caged panther itching to rip ass while his two lieutenants, Tink and Justice, looked on.

"I can't believe that faggot-ass nigga fuckin' tried me like that—Me!" B-Murder barked, hitting his chest for emphasis.

"Yo, B, it ain't just him. The nigga got half the hood on his back. They planned that shit." Tink had already figured it all out.

"Whoever fucks with this nigga is on the plate just like him. I don't give a fuck who it is!" B-Murder growled. "Spread the word because it's SOS!"

Tink nodded. He knew SOS meant shoot on sight. "Only fucked-up thing is the homies down in ATL are mostly rollin' with him too because of T.J., yo," Tink told him.

B-Murder didn't respond right away. He knew that could be a major problem because Atlanta was where the Kings in Trenton got their supply of guns from. They had an army connect that always hit them big. Now, Reese would control that pipeline.

"We ain't got nobody down there we can trust?" B-Murder asked Tink.

Tink shook his head. "Them niggas respect T.J. It's gonna be hard as fuck to get somebody from the ATL set to go against him."

B-Murder stroked his chin in deep thought. He needed a straight killer from outside of the King organization. Somebody he could count on to go to Atlanta and regulate things for him. Someone who would move for the dollar, no questions asked, and handle business.

Supreme.

The name suddenly popped in his head. When he'd sent word to the Kings in NJ State Prison, no one had heard of any Teflon, but the description he was given fit Supreme to a T. He looked up the name they gave him online. When he saw his picture, he knew he had the right man. Especially after the Kings at NJ State Prison told him what Supreme was about. He was definitely a straight killer. He had terrorized the streets of Trenton for years before he got arrested for a body. Then, when he hit the yard, he carried on with his nefarious ways, keeping several dudes under pressure who were scoring packages for extortion fees.

He was just the type of dude B-Murder needed. He clicked through his phone until he got to Charlese's number, a.k.a. Lala the Hood Hacker. Then he dialed her number.

"Who you callin'?" Tink asked.

B-Murder held up his finger, instructing her silently to wait a minute because Charlese had answered on the second ring.

"What's good, baby?" she greeted.

"You already know. Check it, where you cousin, Teflon?"

"Around," Lala responded vaguely. "Why, what's good?"

"I got a proposal for him. Five figures if I can reach him in the next few minutes," B-Murder offered.

There was a pause on her end. Then she asked, "Can he reach you on this number?"

"Indeed."

"Lemme call him."

"A'ight. I'll be waitin'," B-Murder replied.

He didn't have to wait long. Five minutes later, he got a call from an unknown number.

"Yo, what's good? This Teflon."

B-Murder smirked. "No, it ain't."

"What?" Supreme grunted.

"This Supreme. But it's cool because you the man I need to see."

Supreme frowned up. He knew it wouldn't have been hard to find out who he really was, but he was curious to know why B-Murder would go through the trouble to do so.

"Yeah, a'ight, I'm listenin'."

"This ain't somethin' I wanna discuss on the phone. Where can we meet?"

"We can't. I'm out of town."

"Shit!" B-Murder cursed under his breath. "How long before you back? I'm tryin' to get at you wit' ten stacks."

"Wit' numbers like that it ain't hard to tell what you askin'," Supreme assumed, adding, "Who is it that's a problem?"

B-Murder liked dealing with smart people, and he could tell Supreme was bright because of how quickly he read between the lines.

"Reese."

Supreme smiled. "Word? I thought that was your man."

"Yeah, well, things change. You wit' it or what?" B-Murder shot back.

"I'll handle it."

"When?"

"Like I said, I'll handle it," Supreme replied and hung up.

Killing Reese would be a pleasure, but at that moment, Supreme was concentrating on business. He and Lala had made their way to Arizona and were already on their way to the hospital Lala had tracked Nina to. They had just arrived. But they didn't even stop to get a room. They drove straight to the hospital.

When they walked in, they went directly to the information desk.

"Excuse me. Nina Coles's room, please," Lala requested, wearing a polite smile.

The Asian girl behind the counter entered the name, then replied, "I'm sorry, but we don't have a Nina Coles admitted."

"Are you sure? Could you check again? We just drove here all the way from Atlanta. She's my cousin, and I'm really worried about her." Lala ran it down convincingly, like the con she was.

The Asian girl checked the computer again. "Well, we had a Nina Coles, but she checked out a while ago."

"Was she...okay?"

"It doesn't say. But her physician was Doctor Rupta. I can see if he'll speak to you if you'd like," she offered.

"Would you? We'd really appreciate that," Lala smiled.

Half an hour later, a short Indian doctor came out to speak to them.

"I'm sorry to bother you, Doctor, but my husband and I are looking for my cousin, Nina. We were under the impression that she was still here," Lala explained.

"No, she checked out some time ago. But not to worry, she's fine," the doctor assured her.

Lala sighed like she was relieved. "That's good to know. We drove all the way out here from Atlanta when we heard she was in the hospital...I know this is unusual to ask, but do you know how to get in contact with her?"

"Sorry, can't help you there, but perhaps Nurse Wright can. She seemed to know Miss Coles very well," the doctor answered.

Lala smiled, thinking, *Jackpot!* "Great. Is Nurse Wright on duty now? Can I speak to her?" she eagerly asked.

From the moment she saw them, her spirit said something wasn't right. She had listened to Lala's story about coming from Atlanta, thinking how long ago it'd been since Nina was released. *If they were so close, why didn't they know that?*

Nurse Wright stepped toward the pair slowly as Lala finished, then replied, "No, I'm sorry. I can't help you. I only met her once. Now, if you'll excuse me, I have patients to attend to."

She left without waiting on a reply. Lala and Supreme turned and watched her walk off.

"She knows something," Lala whispered.

"Yeah, and I know just how to make that old bird sing," Supreme scowled.

"No. Our faces are all over the cameras," Lala reminded him.

"Fuck it. We'll lay on her and follow her home," Supreme said, already scheming.

They waited until Nurse Wright got off and followed her. When she made a right, Supreme made a right. When she turned left, he turned with her, staying back a reasonable distance. But after the next left, Nurse Wright drove right up to the police station, got out of the car, then turned and looked at them.

Supreme drove on by. Lala couldn't help but giggle. "She may be old, but she ain't dumb," she told him.

"Yeah, well, neither am I. She know Nina, and she gonna tell me somethin'!" Supreme vowed.

He was so close, he could smell the fifty million dollars and his daughter in the air. There was no way he was going to lose the scent.

10

"Hey, Mama, how are you?" Kyra gushed joyfully, embracing her mother, the only mother she had ever known.

They hugged each other in the doorway for almost five minutes because they missed each other so much. Kyra was back on Hoffman Avenue in Trenton, NJ, the house she grew up in. The familiar smell of her mother's cooking brought back so many memories, and Kyra welcomed them all.

"I'm fine, baby! Look at you! I missed you so much! Where's that gorgeous grandbaby of mine?" her mother asked.

"Still in California. I promise I'll bring her next time," Kyra answered, walking into the living room.

Everything was still the same. It was almost like stepping back in time.

"You better," her mother chuckled.

They played catch-up, with her mother telling her about various family members and asking about Angel, Jaz, and Tasha. Kyra decided not to tell her mother about everything she'd personally been through. But after some time, she finally spit out, "Marvin and I are no longer together."

"Oh?" her mother responded.

Kyra nodded. "We had some...problems that we just couldn't work out. But I've met someone else," Kyra beamed. "And I just found out that I'm pregnant!"

The words felt good coming out of her mouth. She'd told Rick recently when he snuck into L.A. to see Trae about some business. He was surprised, but she could also tell that he was pleased by the news.

"Oh, that's wonderful!" her mother gushed, hugging her. "Baby number two. I'm so happy for you!"

"Me too! I'm really looking forward to giving Aisha a baby brother. At least, I hope it's a boy."

"Being a mother is the best feeling in the world."

"I know...and that's something else I wanted to talk to you about." Kyra began getting down to the real reason she had come. She looked down at her hands in her lap, fiddling with her fingers.

Her mother put her hand on Kyra's and gave her a reassuring smile. "Baby...it's okay. Whatever it is, you can talk to me."

Kyra didn't know how to say it, so she just blurted out, "Ma, how come you never talk about my father?"

Her mother's jaw dropped, and her bottom lip quivered. It took her a minute before she was able to respond.

"What...What do you want to know?"

Tears welled up in Kyra's eyes. "Marvin...He's dead, Ma. And I just don't know what to tell Aisha."

Her mother took a deep breath, then slowly nodded.

"Growing up, you didn't talk about my father much, but his absence didn't go unnoticed. What happened to him?" Kyra questioned intently, not knowing how to feel. She was really hoping for insight on how to handle telling Aisha about her father.

"I didn't know how to tell you, baby...your brother. It was

your brother. There was an incident between him and your father. And...honestly...I only recall what I was told. One thing led to another...and your brother killed him," her mother said, choked up.

Her mother's tears melted Kyra's heart. How could she be mad at her? She knew that must've been hard for her.

"Mama, don't cry," Kyra said, looking at her mother. She had the same caramel tone and full lips. She had aged into the sixties with the grace of a beautiful Black woman. She couldn't have asked for a better role model growing up.

"No, baby...you're right. It's something I should've made time to tell you about. I mean, how could you not wonder about your father," her mother explained.

"No, Mama. It's okay. Really. I understand. Plus, you provided me with all the love I needed," she reassured her. "I just have to figure out what I'm going to tell Aisha about Marvin."

Her mother nodded. "I can help you with that whenever you're ready, okay?"

Kyra took a deep breath and nodded. "Yes, thank you, Mama."

～

KORN KNEW Rhodes was deliberately leaving her in his office alone. It was a tactic they had used on suspects. He was letting her stew. She never really knew how effective it was until that very moment because she was *certainly* stressing. Houser had put her on front street, and now, not only was her job at stake, so was her freedom.

Rhodes walked in and closed the door behind him. He slowly walked around her, then rounded his desk. Before sitting down, he glared at her. She wilted under his stare.

"Tell me everything," he said calmly—too calmly—as she sat down.

"Chief, I have nothing to tell. He's—"

Rhodes cut her off by slamming his hand on the desk. The sound made her jump.

"Goddamn you, Korn. Don't lie to me!"

"I'm telling the truth!"

Rhodes let a sinister smile play across his face. "So, that's how you want to play it? Huh? You're sure?"

"Chief, bring me face-to-face with Houser, and I'll prove him a liar."

"I can't do that."

"Why not?"

"Because Houser's dead. He killed himself," he informed her.

Korn was speechless.

"Do you know what that means, Korn? It's a deathbed testimony. You, of all people, should know how juries view deathbed testimonies. It's over for you. Now, you either give me everything, or I'll charge you with conspiracy to commit murder," Rhodes threatened.

"Murder?! I-I didn't know he would kill the CI!"

"Do I have to remind you that doesn't matter? Talk, Korn. It's your only chance. Tell me what Rinaldo offered."

"I can't tell you about Rinaldo. I had nothing to do with that. But I can give you Brown."

Rhodes couldn't believe his ears. "You *what*?!"

Korn took a deep breath. She had strong feelings for Rick, but once she heard "murder," it took her no time to throw him under the bus. *Ain't no dick worth a life sentence.*

"It was me that helped him escape the L.A. dragnet...I-I smuggled him out in the truck," she admitted.

Rhodes wanted to slap the shit out of her. "You bitch! You

crooked bitch! Do you *know* how much you've damaged this department?"

"Chief, I swear I'll cooperate! Rick's in Arizona. I can get him. Please," she pleaded.

Rhodes glared at her. "Look...you *better* get me the son of a bitch! Do you understand me?"

Korn nodded vigorously. "I promise I won't let you down, Chief," she vowed.

Rhodes stormed out and slammed the door.

~

"NINA...ARE you in some kind of trouble?" Nurse Wright questioned.

The words resonated in her mind then bounced around and echoed like a stone in a bottomless well. Nina was stuck. She took the phone away from her ear, then stammered, "Wh-why do you ask?"

Nurse Wright sighed. "Baby, I'm not trying to pry in your business, but I remember when we first met, you were so...frazzled. You just seemed to be running from something...or someone."

Nina didn't respond, so Nurse Wright continued.

"And then when you passed out and went to the hospital... Baby, I've dealt with a lot of pregnant women, and the only ones that pass out are usually under a mountain of stress."

"I can't lie. I *am* stressed," Nina admitted. "Moving, being pregnant, and—"

"But that's not it, is it, Nina?" Nurse Wright interrupted. "Baby, I don't know what this means, and I don't know if you'll tell me, but two people came by the hospital looking for you. A man and a woman. The man was brown-skinned and very muscular, and the woman was light-skinned, slim, and had a short haircut. They claimed to be your cousins," Nurse Wright explained.

Nina's breath caught in her throat. An invisible hand grabbed her heart. When she heard Nurse Wright say the man had a tattoo of two overlapping crowns, she knew exactly who it was. Supreme.

He had found her! *But how?* her mind frantically inquired. She thought about the moment she heard her mother being killed and Supreme's final words to her. *"Trust me, I will find you!"*

He had made good on his threat.

"Nina...Nina!" Nurse Wright called out.

Nina snapped out of her daze. "I'm sorry, Nurse Wright. What did you say?"

"I asked if you knew who they were, and by how long it took for you to answer, I can only assume that you do, right?"

Nina was silent, not knowing what to say. Nurse Wright picked up on her hesitancy.

"Baby, whoever it was, if you need a place to go—"

"No, no," Nina cut her off. "It's...he's...my ex."

"Should I call the police?"

They're looking for me too, she thought bitterly, but "no," was all she said.

"Nina, what about your children? Please, just—"

"They're fine," Nina snapped, taking offense to the implications that she couldn't protect her kids. "Nurse Wright, I thank you for your concern, but believe me, I'm good."

She hung up before the nurse could respond. Nurse Wright looked at the phone, then started to dial another number but hesitated after dialing the first three digits. Her spirit told her to call Dion, but did she *really* want to get her nephew mixed up in Nina's messy life? Why did she always attract the most troublesome patients? Was it her calling? She knew her nephew had strong feelings for Nina, and knowing his past, he was well equipped to intervene. She decided to call because she knew Dion would be crushed if anything happened to Nina.

She called.

"Hey, Auntie."

"Hey, baby. Listen, I'm calling because...I think Nina's in trouble."

She explained everything to him about Supreme at the hospital, how they followed her, and her conversation with Nina. By the time she finished, Dion was ready for war.

"I'll handle it, Auntie," he assured her, then hung up.

He shook his head. This situation was calling for the old Dion. The Dion he no longer wanted to be. He had fallen back from Nina since his confrontation with Rick. He knew he could crush Rick, but that wasn't his decision to make. It was Nina's. Now, it seemed like destiny was pushing them together, and he fully embraced the force. He dialed Nina's number, but when she didn't answer, he texted her.

Call me.

Nina looked at the ringing phone in her hand. The caller ID read "Dion." Reluctantly, she sent him to voicemail. Then the text came in.

Call Me. She wanted to, but she fought the urge and headed out to the patio.

Rick was in the pool teaching Jermichael how to swim. She smiled, enjoying the moment. She loved Rick and what they had, but she wasn't a fool. She knew he had gone back to L.A. and doubtlessly saw Kyra while he was there. But her heart wouldn't let him go, and at the moment, she needed him more than ever.

"Rick," she called out, "I need to speak to you."

Rick helped Jermichael doggy-paddle to the edge, then climbed out of the pool. He pecked her on the lips.

"What's up, baby?"

"Supreme is here," she told him, feeling the queasiness in her stomach again.

Rick frowned and gritted his teeth. "Yeah, well, that's good. We can finally put an end to this bullshit," he hissed.

She had told Rick how Supreme abused her, and he knew all about the Jatana situation, so he had long wanted to get at Supreme. Now, here was his chance.

"But, baby, we can't afford the heat right now. I really think we should just...move on," Nina suggested. "Pack up and go —now!"

Rick thought of the wisdom in her words. As bad as he wanted to put a bullet in Supreme, he knew she was right. It *was* time to move on. Then he could pay off the Armenians and finally start living their lives without fear of being tracked down. If Rinaldo had tracers on the money or tracked the bills, it wouldn't lead to Rick and Nina. If he was lucky, that would be a beef that removed Zev from the equation. He had told Nina about his plans and explained why he had moved the money.

"Okay. Let's make it happen," he told her.

Nina turned to walk away but stopped short and grabbed her stomach.

"Nina...You okay?"

"Yeah, I just—" she started to say. Then it hit her like a sledgehammer to the gut. The stress had triggered Braxton Hicks contractions. "Shit! Rick!"

He cradled her body and helped her into one of the patio chairs.

"Is it the baby?"

She couldn't speak, so she just nodded hard. The kids noticed what was going on and ran over.

"Mommy!"

In the midst of the madness, Rick's phone rang. He looked and saw it was Korn. He sent it to voicemail.

"We've got to get to the hospital!" he exclaimed.

Rick started to call 911, but Nina grabbed his arm.

"Not Banner-University Medical Center...Supreme," she gasped, unable to stand the pain.

His phone rang again. It was Korn again. He started to send her to voicemail once more, but since she was the Feds and it could be important, he answered.

"Yeah?"

"Baby, where are you? Rhodes is on a rampage—"

"Melissa, slow down! What's up?"

"Where are you? I have to see you now. It's an emergency!" Korn emphasized.

"Look, I'll call you back in—"

"Rick!"

"Goddamn it! I'll call you back. I think Nina's about to have her baby!" he barked, then hung up.

Korn glanced up at Rhodes. He had heard every word because they had her phone patched through the tracking system. Rhodes hoped she would be able to keep him on the line long enough to track him, but he had something just as good.

"Okay, people, you heard him! Coles is about to have her baby. If we're lucky, she won't do it on the bathroom floor! I want every fuckin' hospital in Arizona on the line! Any Black woman coming in to give birth anywhere in Arizona, I want to know about it before the baby does!" he barked, and the whole team scattered like roaches, heading to the phones.

"What do you want me to do, Chief?" Korn asked eagerly.

He looked her in the eyes and hissed, "Pray." Then he walked away to do the same.

～

DEAD.

Kyra stood before the grave site feeling the soft drizzle

sprinkle her face like tears from heaven. She read the headstone:

Marvin Blackshear

1952–2013

Once again, her conversation with Trae came to mind. She would put money on him and Rick being the ones responsible for Marvin's death after he left her for dead. *I can't let Aisha find out her baby brother's father, and basically, her uncle were the ones responsible for her father's death. It would ruin their entire relationship!*

She took a deep breath and started to walk away when a man walked up. He was carrying flowers and was dressed in a greasy jumpsuit that bespoke his profession. A mechanic. Kyra followed his every movement.

"How are you?" he greeted politely, then laid the flowers on the grave.

"I'm fine, and you?" Kyra responded.

He shrugged. "Could be better, but then again, could be worse." He chuckled. "How did you know my Marvin?"

"It's...complicated," she hesitated.

She looked at the man again. She couldn't exactly recall his face, and she wondered if it was because her memory hadn't returned one hundred percent or because this was her first time meeting him.

"Oh, okay. Well, I'm Jabaar. He was my big cousin. I used to want to be just like him."

Kyra shook his hand and smiled. "And I'm Kyra...Brown," she said, unsure if she'd just made a huge mistake. *Maybe I should have told him Blackshear,* she wondered. But Brown was a popular enough last name. She figured it was fine.

"Yeah, man," he sighed. "I can't believe he's gone. I wish I could catch the son of a..." He let his voice trail off but not his anger. "The person who did this."

"I-I understand. Well, I'll let you have some time here

alone," Kyra said, questioning if Trae had actually been telling the truth.

"Thank you. I came on my lunch break."

"Well...Nice meeting you."

"You too." Jabaar tried to shake the strangest feeling of déjà vu. This Kyra looked an awful lot like Nina. It had been so long since he had seen her or any of his siblings that he felt his eyes burn with unshed tears. After Derrick had gotten killed and Peedie was maimed, his mother had forced him to stay away. It was as if his family was cursed. So Jabaar tried to beat it with distance. He had been away for so long. He couldn't help but see the gaps his loved ones once occupied. It was just him and Nina now. *Maybe even just me.* With his mother gone, he had no way of knowing if Nina were alive or dead. His mind turned back to Kyra's uncanny resemblance to his sister as Kyra walked away.

Part of her wanted to go back and tell him the truth. She just didn't know how. She headed back to her cab, but before she could get in, a red Charger skidded up, and a masked gunman jumped out.

B-Murder had been visiting his sister's and nephew's grave site. Despite the citywide King beef, he preferred to roll solo when visiting his family.

"I'm all alone now, sis...So I ain't got nothin' to lose," B-Murder remarked, allowing the tears to flow freely because they were hidden in the rain. "I swear that nigga gonna pay! He took my family and broke up my set. I'ma make that nigga *beg* me to kill him!"

As he spoke, he looked up, and that's when he saw her. Across the cemetery a few yards away. *Nina.* His adrenaline kicked in. B-Murder couldn't believe his eyes as he squinted across the graveyard. "I know that ain't that bitch!" he hissed.

There was no way he was about to let her get away. But he

knew he couldn't just kill her. She was worth more alive. *I got you, bitch!*

B-Murder raced to his Charger and grabbed his red bandana. He tied it around his face and headed for that grave site. As Kyra neared the cab, he accelerated, blocking the cab's path, and hopped out.

"Oh shit!" Kyra gasped.

"Bitch, shut up!" B-Murder based and struck her in the head with the pistol, knocking her out instantly.

At that moment when he hit her with the gun, he realized that she wasn't Nina. But he couldn't stop his momentum. Besides, they looked so much alike. *Her sister?* his mind questioned.

"Hey!" Jabaar called out when he saw B-Murder hit her and her body slump.

He started to run toward them, but B-Murder let off several shots that made Jabaar jump to the ground and stay there. The cabby had ducked below the dashboard before pulling off.

"I ain't see shit!" he yelled.

B-Murder threw Kyra in the passenger seat, jumped in over her, and skidded off. As soon as he was off, Jabaar jumped up, filming the back of the car to get a picture of the license plate as B-Murder disappeared. *What was that all about?*

❧

CHARLEY DIDN'T FEEL comfortable being a free man. He still owed some very powerful people. His name may have carried weight, but theirs carried more. So, he was on pins and needles waiting for Rinaldo to call about the money. Instead, he got a call from the Armenians.

"Charley The Ace Adams?"

"Who wants to know, and how the fuck did you get this number?" Charley barked.

Vladimir chuckled. "I can assure you that it wasn't from Angelo Borcelli."

Charley stiffened just hearing the name. "Who the fuck is this?"

"Just call me Vladimir, or your savior, whichever you prefer. How I got the number is irrelevant. I have a deal that you better not refuse," Vladimir stated firmly.

"Fuck you. I'm hanging up."

"I can get your money for you."

Charley didn't speak, but he didn't hang up either.

"I assume you're still there."

"I'm listening."

"I know who has your money. I know where he is; you don't. He and I have a deal for twenty million. If you can come up with a better deal than his, it would be *my* turn to listen," Vladimir propositioned.

"How do I know you are who you say you are?" Charley questioned.

"You don't. But you know you can't afford *not* to take me at my word," Vladimir replied.

"Twenty-five. But I wanna be there when you pick it up."

"That can be arranged. How quickly can you be in Arizona?"

"Arizona's a big state," Charley said.

"Pick a city, and I'll have you taken to the destination. Do we have a deal?"

"I guess I don't have a choice, huh?"

Vladimir chuckled. "No, Charley, in this situation...you don't."

～

"THIS IS WHERE IT GETS INTERESTING," Rinaldo chuckled as he sipped his drink.

Deanna asked, "Who was that?"

Rinaldo hung up the phone. He knew this was the crucial part of the plan. The part where the mark thought they were the ones running game. But if he moved too fast, they'd see right through him.

He looked at her, then rose from his seat and crossed the room to where she sat.

"Deanna...Remember when your mother was sick and desperately needed that operation? Who paid all the medical expenses?" he questioned her.

Her mouth was silently agape, and she began to feel guilty about the role she was playing.

"You did," she answered, lowering her eyes, not being able to meet his gaze.

Rinaldo squatted down in front of her, then lifted her head by putting his hand under her chin. "And when your father lost his job, and they were about to foreclose on the house, who paid the mortgage until he got back on his feet?" Rinaldo probed, voice smooth and nonthreatening.

Tears creased her cheeks. "Why are you bringing all this up, Rinaldo?" she sobbed.

He smiled sweetly, the smile of a vampire right before he sucks you dry and replied, "Because you've been untrue to me, Deanna. When I needed you the most, you jumped the fence on me."

"No, Rinaldo! I would never do that!" she protested through her tears.

He kept his smile sweet and his voice calm. "Yes, Deanna...I know everything. You can't lie to me, baby. Why did you do it? What did Brandon offer you to betray the man who cared for your family?"

She broke down, covering her face with both hands. "A million dollars! I told you he wanted me to spy on you!"

"I know that much, but while you were supposedly double-crossing him, you were triple-crossing me."

She nodded her head. Rinaldo smiled to himself. Brandon would never see this coming.

"But now, Deanna, you have to choose: him or me. Brandon's going down. Charley is going to kill him. I can't protect you if you choose him," Rinaldo explained.

She threw her arms around his neck. "I'm sorry, Rinaldo. I swear I choose you! I choose you!" she lied.

Why do the students always think they can play the master's game? he mused to himself as he untangled her arms from around his neck, looked her in the eyes, and replied, "Are you sure?"

She nodded vigorously.

Rinaldo stood up and paced the floor. "Charley...He's got the money. Or I mean, he knows where it is. That bitch Nina and some guy named Rick...an ex-Fed. Can you believe it? The Feds set me up to rob me!" He laughed, then added, "But I can't go pick up my share of the money."

"Why not?" she questioned.

He looked at her like she was the dumbest bitch in the world. "Because the son of a bitch would kill me. But he won't kill the person I send because then he knows I'll tell Brandon he has the money. He has to play fair as long as I don't show up. Which is why I'm sending you," he explained.

"Me?" she echoed.

He nodded. The look in her eyes said she was taking it all in. "He'll give you my cut. You won't be in any danger. He has to pay. Then you meet me in Louisiana with the ten million. You keep two, and we ride off into the sunset," he proposed.

"I'll take care of it, Rinaldo. You can trust me."

"I know I can, baby," he answered, simultaneously thinking, *Trust you to play yourself out of position.*

She couldn't wait to get on the phone with Brandon to tell

him everything. As soon as she left, Rinaldo was on the phone with Rochelle. "Get little man packed up and meet me in Miami. I'm taking a little trip."

~

LALA AND SUPREME sat down the street from Nurse Wright's front door, waiting for her to come out. Getting her address had been easy. Once Lala hacked into the hospital's human resources files, she quickly found all she needed to know.

"This time, I don't care what you say. I'm snatchin' the old bitch up," Supreme vowed.

Before she could respond, Nurse Wright came rushing out of the house and jumped in her car. When she pulled out, Supreme wasn't far behind.

Nurse Wright had just gotten a call that Nina was in labor. She was worried because the baby was early. She knew it was from stress.

"Oh, my Lord, Nina...I tried to tell that girl," she said, reciting a quick prayer in her head. Too focused on what was in front of her to concern herself with what was behind her, she headed straight to Nina's house.

She reached Nina's house just as the ambulance did. Supreme fell back when he saw the lights. He went around the block, then parked a few houses down when he was back on her street. He noticed a black sedan slowly drive by filled with three white boys, but he didn't think anything of it. He was focused on the EMT's and the big Black guy bringing Nina out. He caught a glimpse of her before they loaded her into the van and his blood boiled. He was so close.

In the ambulance, Rick tried to comfort Nina.

"Don't worry, baby, I'm right here," he said, squeezing her hand, but he had a funny feeling in the back of his mind.

He had seen the black sedan, too, out of the corner of his

eye. But when he looked again, he could only see the backs of the occupants' heads. His mind said he was bugging, but his street senses screamed, *Be on point!* His gut was resting on Vlad's people, the Armenians.

Supreme followed the ambulance to HonorHealth Sonoran Crossing Medical Center.

"So, they were gonna try to duck us, huh?" He chuckled, taking in the fact that they had chosen a hospital different from the one where Nurse Wright worked.

"That means the nurse told her we're here. Be on point," Lala cautioned.

"Always," he replied cockily.

The EMT's rushed Nina inside.

"My babies? Where are my—" Nina huffed between contractions, but Rick cut her off.

"Nurse Wright, baby. She's with the kids."

His words and presence comforted Nina, but the pain seemed unbearable. The contractions with this baby were stronger than any of her other births.

"Oh God!" she cried in anguish. "I'm not even eight months."

"I'm here, baby! Just breathe!"

Supreme and Lala went into the hospital through the lobby. They knew they would have to wait until the baby was born.

But Rhodes wasn't prepared to wait.

It took twenty minutes after Nina arrived at the hospital before one of the agents came rushing into the room.

"Chief, we got her! She's at HonorHealth Sonoran Crossing Medical Center in Phoenix!"

"Get Phoenix on the phone! Forward them pictures of both Rick and Nina and tell them to approach with extreme caution! We'll be there within an hour!" Rhodes instructed, then shot out the door with Korn on his heels.

~

FOUR AND A HALF HOURS LATER, Nina gave birth to a beautiful baby boy. Rick's first child. He was premature, so he had to go into an incubator. Nina and Rick looked through the glass at him.

"Rick?"

"Huh?"

"No...That's what I want to name him. Rick," Nina remarked, looking up into Rick's eyes.

He smiled and replied, "I love you, baby," before kissing the mother of his firstborn child.

"As soon as the baby's strong enough, can we just...go?" Nina asked.

"No doubt," he assured her, his mind saying fuck the Armenians.

Rick had decided to make his move solo. He hoped Trae would hold up his end of the bargain. If so, the Armenians wouldn't be able to make a move on them anyway.

He wheeled Nina to her room and got her comfortable in the bed. Then he walked over to the window and looked out, contemplating their future, but thought, *What about Kyra?*

Even if he did leave, he wasn't about to just walk away from Kyra. He started to look away, but then he saw the police lights and federal vehicles speeding into the hospital parking lot.

"Oh fuck!" he spat, then spun and quickly approached Nina, "Baby, the Feds! We gotta go!"

"How did they know?" she panicked.

Rick didn't have time to think about it. They had checked in using fake IDs that Rick had just gotten from California, so he was baffled, not realizing his own words did him in.

"Can you walk?"

"I-I can...yes," Nina answered.

He helped her off the bed, but he scooped her off her feet

and carried her from the room when he saw the baby steps she was taking. They couldn't take their son, not yet, but Rick resolved to come back for his firstborn later. They would have to trust Nurse Wright to help with this one.

"Excuse me, sir," a nurse called out.

"Newlyweds," Rick smiled, trying to appear carefree.

Before the nurse could object, they disappeared out of the exit door to the steps.

When Supreme and Lala saw the federal convoy march in, he was worried that they were for them. But when he heard one ask for Dolores Miller's room, his gut told them that Dolores was Nina's alias.

"Let's go," he mumbled to Lala before they calmly headed to the exit.

Once they were outside and saw how deep the police were, he knew they were there for Nina.

"Goddamn, yo!" he barked, knowing that the fifty million was as good as gone if Nina got arrested.

"Go get the car and call me. Stay close just in case we gotta move," he instructed Lala.

She nodded and walked off.

Meanwhile, inside the hospital, Rick could feel the Feds getting close. But he wasn't giving up. They found him at the hospital, but he knew they didn't have a drop on the house. On the other hand, Vlad did. But he already figured out how he would use that to his advantage.

His only hope was the ambulance bay. He took Nina out the side door just as several officers ran by. Then, quickly, he opened the back of an ambulance.

"Stay low," he ordered.

Checking over his shoulder, he walked between two ambulances to the driver's side. An EMT was smoking a cigarette in the ambulance with the engine running. *My lucky day.* Rick tapped on the window. The guy looked.

"Got a light?" Rick asked.

"Sure," the guy replied.

He opened the door to give Rick a light, but Rick hit him with a vicious right twice. The man slumped so quickly Rick had to catch him. Rick yanked him out of the vehicle, laying him on the ground. Now he could make his getaway without worrying about a witness to his escape.

Rick jumped behind the wheel. In seconds, the ambulance was on the move.

"Our son, Rick!" Nina murmured fervently, coming up behind him.

"Get down, Nina! This is our only chance. We either stay with the baby and get caught or go now," Rick said.

Baby Rick! The thought still rippled through him with a shock. A cold part of his mind asserted the fact that if they were caught, he and Nina would lose him anyway. He had to take this chance.

Supreme was onto them.

He put himself in Rick's shoes. How would he get out of a hospital surrounded by the Feds and police? You couldn't just walk away. So, unless you could hide out inside, the best bet was an ambulance.

As soon as he saw the ambulance pull out with Rick behind the wheel, he ran to get Lala.

"They're in that ambulance! Drive!" he said as he jumped in.

"What ambulance?" she screamed. There were four of them.

"Bitch, right there! Don't let them get away!" he barked.

Rick drove cautiously back to the house.

"Rick, what about my baby? We can't just leave him!" Nina cried. "Jatana...Oh my God, Rick. How are we getting out of this mess?"

Rick had been thinking of that the whole drive. He had to

grab their exit bag at the house. He had looked at every angle, and as painful as it was, there wasn't anything he could do. There was no going back to the hospital. Even though he told Nina he'd come back and steal the baby after a few days, he knew he couldn't, but he didn't want to get Nina all hysterical with the truth.

"I'll take care of it. I promise," he said.

$\approx$

WHEN KYRA BOUGHT a ticket to Phoenix, the Armenians knew she was headed to see Rick. After Rick's visit, Vladimir had eyes on him. The woman seemed important to Rick, and that made her interesting. With fifty million on the line, everyone was a target.

When she rented a limo at the airport and was driven to Rick's house, the Armenians had known about it. They knew because they tracked her credit card and the limo company's log. Armenians were not only cold-blooded killers, but they were also expert hackers. They excelled at cybercrimes.

Kyra had led them right to Rick.

The first time Vladimir, Zev, and their driver drove by in the black sedan, their plans were interrupted by the ambulance, so they drove on by. But when they saw the ambulance return with Rick behind the wheel, they knew their patience had paid off. As soon as he turned into the driveway and helped Nina out of the ambulance, the black sedan skidded up behind them.

Zev and the driver jumped out with their guns drawn.

"Fuck," Rick mumbled to himself, raising his hands.

They had caught him without a gun. Zev approached, wearing a crooked smile.

"Hey, my friend, no hard feelings, right?" Rick smirked.

"None," Zev croaked. Then he hit Rick with a hook to the gut that knocked the wind out of him.

"Oh my God!" Nina gasped.

"You want your money, right?"

"Damn right."

"Then let me get my bag. It's right by the front door, already packed. We don't even have to go in." His bag had cash and IDs for both of them.

"Shut up and get in the car," Zev based, taking Nina by the arm while the driver took Rick.

As they put her in the car, Supreme and Lala drove by. Supreme's eyes met Nina's. Supreme was scowling. Nina was pleading. An invisible line of tension stretched between them, freezing the moment in time.

"That's them crackas from earlier," Supreme remembered as they drove by.

"What you want me to do, 'Preme?" Lala questioned.

"Pull over. Once they pass, follow 'em," he ordered.

Supreme wasn't the only one who saw the abduction.

Nurse Wright saw it too. "Lord, protect that child," she prayed.

As soon as they left, she called out, "Children, come on! We gotta go!" She then called Dion.

"Baby...She's in *real* trouble now!"

∽

ZEV TOSSED Nina into his sedan, followed by Rick, putting her in between Rick and Vladimir. Vladimir looked at Nina approvingly. "Rick, where have you been hiding this one? She do tricks too, or is she personal?"

Rick ignored his taunt. "I was going to give you your money. All this is unnecessary."

"Put yourself in my position, Rick. You ambushed Zev, ruining a beautiful relationship in the process. Then you don't return my calls. What would you have done?" Vladimir questioned. Rick knew this would come up.

"I'm fuckin' wanted by the goddamn Feds, Vlad, so you'll excuse me if I don't pick up on the first fuckin' ring!" Rick shot back sarcastically.

Vladimir laughed. "I see your point...Well, you know since you didn't pick up, we decided to pick you up, eh? Now, let's cut to the chase. Where's the money?"

Rick looked at Nina, and she looked at him. He knew he was stuck. If he didn't show Vladimir where the money was stashed, he'd kill him. But if he showed him, would he take it all? Hopefully, at least he and Nina would have time to make their escape from the Feds free and alive.

"How do I know you won't take it all?" Rick asked.

Vladimir shrugged. "I won't...but he will," he answered, pointing at a parked Benz they were approaching.

It was parked in a motel parking lot. When the Armenians pulled up beside it, Rick saw Charley Adams and Deanna in the backseat, with Charley's bodyguard behind the wheel. Nina looked at Deanna, who gave her a triumphant smirk and a curt nod. *I know this 'bama bitch ain't in cahoots with Charley Adams!* Nina thought.

When Rick saw Charley, he knew it was all over.

"Goddamn, Vlad, like this?! You cross me like *this*?" Rick seethed.

"What can I say, my friend? He offered me a bigger cut," Vladimir shrugged. "I know you would've done the same, eh?"

Charley glared at Rick, cigar clenched tightly between his teeth.

"You sorry son of a bitch! You thought you could rob Charley Ace? Give me my fuckin' money, and I *might* let you keep one testicle!"

Rick ground his teeth so hard the tension gave him an instant headache. After all he'd been through, to lose it all like this was mind-numbing. But there was nothing he could do. He sighed and said, "Okay...I'll take you there."

"I *know* you will!" Charley barked.

Rhodes was in a rage when he found out Rick and Nina had escaped the hospital dragnet. The federal plane was just about to land when the news reached him.

"They *what*? How the fuck did you let them get away?"

"They took an ambulance," the special agent in charge in Phoenix replied like it was no big deal. This was Rhodes's case, not his, so he knew Rhodes would take the heat. Besides, they had the same rank, so Rhodes couldn't throw his weight around.

"I can't believe this shit! What kind of fucking show are you people in Phoenix running?" Rhodes spazzed.

"Look, Rhodes, I told you I'd give you all the help you needed, okay? But hell, you didn't give us much to fuckin' go on in a matter of hours."

"Hell, I didn't *have* much to go on! Okay, listen, trace back to the original 911 call. I want the house the ambulance was sent to covered, from the sewer to the chimney! Can you at least handle *that*?!" Rhodes barked. "For crying out loud, I thought you were the Feds!"

"Don't be a wiseass, Rhodes," the special agent replied, then hung up.

~

RICK TOOK them to an old refinery warehouse on the outskirts of Phoenix. The place reeked of gas. The ground outside was gooey with the runoff sludge.

"You picked a helluva stash spot," Charley remarked, pissed the goo was gumming up his gators.

They all went inside—Charley, his bodyguard, Deanna, Zev, Vladimir, the driver, Rick, and Nina. But none of them realized they weren't alone.

Brandon and two of his gunmen had been following Charley. Deanna had secretly left her phone on so Brandon and his team could track them.

"Don't make a move until we see the money, got me?" Brandon ordered as he loaded his Mini-14.

Both gunmen nodded as they loaded up their submachine guns. Supreme and Lala were still following the Armenians.

"This gotta be where the fuckin' money is!" Supreme exclaimed.

"Yeah, 'Preme, but look at all these other mutha'fuckas. How we gonna get to it?" Lala questioned.

"Whateva it takes, yo. We ain't leavin' here empty-handed! Besides, we got the element of surprise on our side!" he surmised, as they got out to make their way inside.

In the warehouse, the smell of toxic fumes was even stronger. Rusted out steel barrels leaked all types of industrial fluid everywhere, leaving trails of rainbows when the light hit it right. The floor was a little slick in certain places, places Rick was familiar with. He had chosen this place for exactly that reason. He may have been unarmed, but he was the only one who knew the lay of the land in the darkened warehouse, and he planned on using that to his advantage.

They weaved along the rows and rows of empty oil barrels, making their way to a stack of crates. Rick stopped in front of them, all eyes glued on him. Greed winning. Fifty million dancing in all eyeballs.

"Do I also get a finder's fee?" Rick joked, looking at Charley.

Charley shoved him aside and cracked one of the crates. Inside were the five suitcases. Charley tried to pull one out, but it was too heavy.

"Damn. What's in here besides bills? Gimme a hand, would ya?" Charley grunted at his bodyguard.

The bodyguard lifted it out by himself and laid it on the ground.

He cracked the lid and looked inside. Everyone feasted their eyes on the money. A smile spread across Charley and Vladimir's faces while Nina and Deanna's pussies simultaneously throbbed. Rick damn near cried; he was so sick—sick to his stomach thinking of all the money they were about to lose.

And then all hell broke loose.

~

SUPREME'S DICK got hard as a rock when he saw the money. He and Lala had climbed a staircase that hugged the back wall of the warehouse that led to a small office. From where they were positioned, they could see the entire warehouse, while everyone else was nearly blind to all that was happening in the shadows.

When the bodyguard opened the suitcase, Supreme made the fatal mistake of thinking he could catch them all by surprise, shoot them all, and make off with the case. His plan may have worked if he'd been a better shot. Instead, his shot missed the bodyguard's head and grazed Vladimir's stomach.

"It's a setup!" Vladimir yelled, cupping a hand to his bleeding gut, pissed he hadn't worn a vest.

Guns came out from everywhere, but before they could get a shot off, Brandon's team was already letting their barrels blaze.

After Supreme had set it off with the first shot, Brandon figured Charley had a backup team in place. The trap was sprung for him. He stood up from his hiding place and opened fire, walking a line of bullet holes through Vladimir's driver's back. Like the killer he was, Zev didn't flinch. He spun and returned fire. The next to go down was Charley The Ace Adams. Vladimir took the opportunity to press the barrel of his

Sig Sauer to Charley's ear and blow his brains out at point-blank range. With bullets flying everywhere, he had plans of keeping all the money.

One of Brandon's gunmen saw the bursts of fire in the dark, revealing Supreme and Lala's location. He couldn't see them, so he just aimed at the muzzle flash. The first shot caught Lala in the throat, jerking her head back as though she had been snatched by an invisible hand.

"Laaaaaaaa!" Supreme screamed, his grief-stricken mind fueling a desperate urge to save her.

The second shot hit her in the chest, pitching her lifeless body headfirst over the rail to land with a bloody splat on the concrete below.

Forlorn and angry, Supreme squeezed off bullets, killing Brandon's gunman as he ran down the steps to Lala's body. It was apparent she was dead, empty eyes staring up at the ceiling. "Sorry, cuz," Supreme said, tenderly kissing her, then closing her eyes.

Gunfire filled the air. The moment Vladimir had blown Charley Adams's brains out, Rick made his move. He dipped low and caught Vladimir square in the nuts, bending him double and finishing him with an uppercut that dropped him. Zev saw his boss fall, lurching with a shout at Rick. Charging like an angry bear, he zeroed in on Rick. Unmindful of his footing, Zev stepped in the slippery sludge, skidding wildly on the oily surface of the warehouse. One little push from Rick sent him flying. Wasting no time, Rick grabbed Vladimir's gun and put three in Zev's chest, killing him instantly. He then put the barrel between Vladimir's eyes.

Vladimir looked at him. "Sorry, old friend. It was just business," Vladimir smirked, fully prepared to die.

"So is this," Rick replied before turning Vladimir's brains into a puddle under the ruin of his head.

Rick tried to grab the suitcase and Nina at the same time.

There was no way he could do both. Without hesitation, he let the suitcase go and grabbed Nina with both hands. He hadn't hesitated to choose her over the money. This wasn't lost on Nina, and her love for him swelled.

"Flames! Come on!" he urged her.

They were making their way out just in time. All the gunfire had set several oil slicks ablaze at various places around the warehouse. One slick ran along the ground, carrying the roaring flames right to the trailing hem of Deanna's dress. It caught with a small *whomp* and burned merrily.

"Oh no! Help, someone!" she cried, trying to beat out the flames. But it had spread too quickly and totally engulfed her in seconds. She screamed in pure agony as the fire burned her alive.

Flames leaped all around Brandon. Desperation beat at his thoughts as survival began to trump greed. He knew he had to get out. Both of his gunmen were dead. The smoke alone was becoming unbearable. Still, he saw the money burning inside the open suitcase and wanted to run over and grab one of the others. But he knew he would never make it. Just as he turned to exit, a wall of fire leaped up and blocked him in. There was nowhere he could go. He was trapped.

Outside, Rick and Nina hopped in Vladimir's black sedan. Thankfully, the driver had left the key in the ignition in the event they needed to make a quick getaway. They sped off, not realizing Supreme was right behind them. Rick watched the warehouse burn, but in his mind, it was fifty million dollars that were burning. Nina read his expression. She reached over and took his hand, then squeezed it.

"Thank you, baby," she said, her heart full.

"Believe me, Nina, you're worth way more to me than fifty million," he replied. Then his phone rang.

～

B-Murder took Kyra back to one of the apartments he owned. It was a run-down little spot in East Trenton that he used to stash guns. They wouldn't be there long. He figured he could stash her at a motel if need be. The only furniture was a table in the kitchen and a couch in the living room. As soon as they entered the apartment, he slung Kyra onto the sofa.

"Why are you doing this?" Kyra sobbed. "Who are you?"

"Bitch, shut the fuck up!" B-Murder spat, backslapping her so hard blood spurted from Kyra's mouth. "Just know I'm your worst nightmare!"

"What did I do to you?"

"It ain't what you did. It's what that bitch Nina did! Who is she to you? Your sister? Might as well be because you gonna suffer for what she did to my mother!" B-Murder threatened. It was hard to care at this point. Even if she wasn't Nina, she had to be related. Blood would answer for blood.

"Nina? I don't know who you're talking about," Kyra sobbed, her mind too frazzled to think. Her heart was racing, and she wanted to go home. She wanted to be anywhere but here with this raving lunatic. She wanted Rick.

B-Murder laughed in her face. "Don't know her? Bitch, you think I'm stupid?" B-Murder gritted, grabbing Kyra by her throat and squeezing hard. "You look just like her, and I saw you talkin' to her cousin, Jabaar! How the fuck you don't know her?"

You look just like her...You look just like her...you look...

B-Murder was in a murderous rage. All he could think of was his mother and how Nina had set them up. In his mind, it was all Nina's fault, and looking at Kyra's face made him madder that he still hadn't caught Nina. He kept choking her, watching Kyra gasp and struggle. It was Nina's fault he was choking whoever this lookalike bitch was. *Close enough, though*, he thought as his fingers gripped her throat.

"I can...get...her," Kyra gagged.

"What?"

"Ni...na."

B-Murder let her go, and the oxygen rushed to her head, giving her an instant migraine. She slumped on the couch, trying to clear her dizzy head.

"Bitch, you better talk!"

"I...said," Kyra panted, "I...can...get you...Nina."

"Oh, so *now* you know her!" B-Murder laughed.

Kyra glared at him. "I hate that bitch...probably more than you do," she hissed, adding, "I'll gladly tell you how to get at her."

B-Murder could tell by the look in her eyes that she was dead ass. He wondered what Nina had done to her.

"How?"

"She's with...my man. If you let me go, I can lead you right to her."

B-Murder laughed. "Let you go? Fuck outta here! You go free when I got her, or you die in her place!"

"I can't get her from here."

B-Murder smiled because an idea had just popped into his head. "Yes, you can. You said she's with your man?"

Kyra nodded.

"Does your man love you?"

"Of course."

"You better hope so," B-Murder warned. Then he handed her his phone. "Now call him."

She took the phone, and with trembling fingers, dialed Rick's number.

~

RICK DIDN'T RECOGNIZE the number.

"Who is it?" Nina asked.

"I don't know," he answered, adding, "but the area code is 609."

Nina looked frozen because 609 was Trenton's area code, and to her, Trenton meant *Supreme*. "It's Supreme. I-I saw him when they put us in the car! He knows where we live!" Nina exclaimed.

Rick gritted his teeth and flexed his jaw. He was vexed. "How the fuck this nigga get my number?" he asked aloud but really was talking to himself.

"Are you going to answer?" Nina questioned.

Rick looked at her, then answered.

"Yo, who this?" he barked. But what he heard took all the bite out of him.

"Rick!" Kyra screamed with such anguish it almost brought tears to his eyes.

"Kyra?!"

"Kyra?" Nina echoed, totally confused. *Why is that bitch calling him, and why the fuck is he picking up?*

B-Murder snatched the phone from Kyra and hissed, "You don't know me, and I don't know you, but if you care anything about this bitch, you better listen real goddamn close!"

Rick's pulse hammered. Something sane and vital broke in his soul. His chest constricted, and his breaths became labored and erratic. Rick thought about how broken he had been after Kyra died. He'd lost himself to a darkness so deep he had forgotten light existed. He couldn't be broken like that again. He had a child to think about now, and Nina—on top of losing the money. *I need to put an end to this shit, once and for all.*

Rick wanted to jump through the phone. "Nigga, who the fuck is this?" Rick growled.

"Rick, who is that? Kyra?" Nina probed.

Rick couldn't even hear Nina. All his attention was focused on his conversation.

"Fuck you. *I'm* asking the questions, yo! Now...Do you want this bitch to live? Yes or no?" B-Murder barked.

Rick's head was spinning. There was no way he would let Kyra die, so he quickly replied, "Yeah, man."

"Yeah, what? Speak, nigga! Do you want her to live? Say it! Say 'I want her to *live!*'" B-Murder ordered.

"I want her to live!"

"Want who to live, Rick? What's going on?" Nina wanted to know, the fear and anxiety building in her voice. Her intuition told her something terrible was about to happen.

"That's more like it," B-Murder sneered. "Now, I want to know...is that Nina with you?"

Reluctantly, Rick answered, "Yeah."

B-Murder laughed like a crazed demon. "Then we can trade. I'll let this one live if you bring me Nina," B-Murder proposed.

This nigga is fuckin' crazy! Sacrifice Nina? He couldn't wrap his mind around it, so he stammered weakly, "What...are you talking about?"

"Nigga, you heard me! As a matter of fact, you don't even have to bring her to me...I just want confirmation she's dead. So, what's it gonna be? This bitch or Nina?" B-Murder threatened. Then put his phone on speaker as he put a gun to Kyra's head.

"Rick, he's going to kill me! Please, baby, don't let me die!" Kyra pleaded, feeling the cold steel to her temple for the second time in her life. "My baby."

Hearing Kyra beg him to save her gripped Rick's heart and wouldn't let go. He couldn't let Kyra die. But killing Nina? He couldn't see that happening either. However, it was clear that B-Murder wasn't playing games.

Somebody would die, and it was up to Rick to decide who.

"Rick, where are we going?" Nina questioned.

"What's it gonna be, Rick?" B-Murder taunted.

"Oh my God, Rick, don't let me die!" Kyra cried.

He stopped the car and put his head on the steering wheel. *What to do?*

"How...how do I know—" Rick started to say, but B-Murder finished his sentence for him.

"That I won't kill this one anyway? I 'on't even know this bitch! You can have her! But Nina? That bitch killed my mother, so it's nonnegotiable! You got ten seconds. Ten..."

Rick could see Nina out of the corner of his eye.

"Nine..."

He gripped the pistol in his lap and looked over at her.

"Eight..."

"Rick?" Nina asked, her tone so soft and loving, Rick felt sick.

"Five..."

"Nina...get out of the car," Rick mumbled.

"Huh?" Nina replied, confused.

"Three...Rick, you're disappointing Kyra. Say goodbye. Two...one..."

"Okay! Okay! I'll do it!" Rick yelled.

"I thought you'd see it my way!" B-Murder cackled. "And just so ain't no funny shit, leave her body where it can be found. If it ain't on the news tonight, this bitch is dead!"

Rick looked at Nina.

"Nina, I said...get out of the car!" Rick barked. Pointing the gun in her face. "Please, Nina. Just get out," he ordered.

She willed herself to wake up because this had to be a nightmare. There was no way the man she loved—the man that had just chosen her over fifty million dollars—would put a gun in her face. But the crazed look in his eyes told Nina he was dead serious. She got out, and he was right behind her.

"Baby, what's going on? Please tell me—" Nina pleaded, but his guilt couldn't take the sound of her voice.

"Shut the fuck up!" he told her. Then into the phone, he

said, "Nigga, you betta keep your word, or I promise I *will* find you and kill you!"

"Fuck that big-boy talk! Put the phone on speaker so Nina can hear me," B-Murder spat.

He was so close to getting his revenge his dick was bone-hard. Rick put his phone on speaker.

"Surprise, bitch! Remember me? Remember my mama and what your punk-ass brother did, huh?"

Nina didn't know B-Murder's voice, but she knew who he was by his words. The world had come full circle, and she was looking down the barrel of her death.

"Rick, please, don't do this!" Nina begged. "I love you!"

"Rick, he's going to kill me! Please, baby, I love you!" Kyra urged him. Then the line went dead.

"What the fuck!" B-Murder yelled into the phone. Then he turned to Kyra. "Looks like your boyfriend just jetted on you."

"No, no! You-you heard the shots! She's dead!" Kyra exclaimed.

"I don't think so...but *you* are, bitch," he replied. Then he raised the gun to Kyra's head just as his phone rang.

∽

THE FLAME from the barrel lit up the darkness like a flare. *Boom! Boom-boom-boom!* Four shots. Each one tore into Nina's flesh, flinging her body around like a rag doll. Each bullet made her cry out in painful agony.

Her blood-soaked hand left a bloody streak down the side of the car as she slumped to the ground. The sound of her own heartbeat filled her ears. The pain was so great she welcomed death with open arms. The last thing she saw was the gun aimed at her one final time.

"Nina!"

She heard a familiar voice call out her name and then one last gunshot that ended it all—*Boom!*

~

RICK DIDN'T HEAR Supreme approaching until it was too late. "Nina!" he yelled.

Supreme had followed them from the warehouse, thinking Rick had spotted him when he abruptly turned into the woods. He drove a few more yards, then pulled over before jogging into the woods. He stayed low and tried to make as little noise as possible. He didn't know what was going on until he heard the gunshots. When he saw Nina's body jerk from the impact, his anger and bitterness left him.

"Nina!" He couldn't believe the love of his life had just been killed right in front of him. Supreme listened to the words and recognized the voice. He wondered what made Rick shoot Nina and what B-Murder had to do with it. But he couldn't dwell on that. He knew he had to get Nina to a hospital. *Fuck!* Then he remembered the Feds were looking for her. He hadn't seen Rick raise the chrome Desert Eagle. Then Rick pulled the trigger, and the bullet tore through Supreme's skull.

I'm sorry, Rick thought, his mind on his son and his three siblings that had yet to meet him.

Rick ran over to Nina and cradled her in his arms.

"Nina! Nina, can you hear me?!" he questioned, hating himself.

~

WICKED AND REESE backed their tinted-out, black-on-black Escalade away from the scene. Tracking Nina had been fruitless, so he did the next best thing. He and Reese followed

Supreme. But neither of them were expecting what they'd just witnessed.

The money was gone, and the warehouse they had tracked everyone to was surrounded by the Feds and engulfed in flames. Then, to see Nina die. *It was all for nothing*, Reese thought as they drove away from the forest. Suddenly, in the rearview mirror, Reese saw Rick come into view. Wicked was too busy cursing, but he noticed Rick loading Nina into the car with more care than a dead body usually got and felt a glimmer of hope.

Reese's phone buzzed. He looked down and saw that his spy was calling. B-Murder had him guarding a woman who, from the picture, looked just like Nina. Reese felt the stirrings of a plan.

"Yo, peep this," he said, handing the phone to Wicked.

"Rasclaat, who dis den? Can't be Nina," Wicked crooned, his single eye glittering with lust and something darker. Something he could use.

"B-Murder has her. He thinks she's related to Nina somehow. It's crazy how much they look alike, right?" Wicked's tongue flicked across his lips like the tail of one of his rats. Reese retrieved his phone before Wicked could lick the screen. Wicked's eyes met his own.

"Let's go back to Jersey, Star."

11

By the time the fire department put out the fire, the warehouse had almost been totally consumed. Rescue workers and uniformed officers ran to and fro as Rhodes and Korn stepped through the charred wreckage. One of his agents walked up to update them.

"Any survivors?" Rhodes asked.

"Most of them were either shot, or the fire got them. But two are half-alive. They're burned up pretty badly. We can't even ID them until the dental records come back. But we know for sure one is male and the other is female. They probably won't survive the night," the agent informed him.

Rhodes nodded. Then he and Korn walked away. They stepped over two bodies to reach the crate. Scattered all around was half-burnt money and the charred remains of the other suitcases. Only one suitcase remained unburned.

Rhodes lifted it out of the crate and opened it up. It was full of money.

"The root of all evil," he remarked, shaking his head.

"Chief, maybe this isn't a good time to ask, but...what are you going to do with me? I know I fucked up bad, but...What's wrong?" Korn inquired when she saw Rhodes looking at the money with a weird expression on his face.

He squatted down and took out a band of bills and fanned through them. Then he pulled out a single bill and felt it.

"Well, I'll be..." he chuckled.

"What?"

He stood up, still looking at the bill.

"I wondered why we didn't find Rinaldo's body here," he remarked.

"Chief, I don't understand."

He looked at her with a crazy smile. "You know what they do with old money once they take it out of circulation?" he asked, reminiscing about his old gig. Compared to the filth he currently found himself in, that was just a mild layer of dust.

"Burn it, right?" she answered.

He nodded.

"Exactly...Burn it. I used to work for the Department of Treasury. I was the one who burned it. I used to say, 'Look at all that money going up in smoke.' I'll never forget that smell. Korn...I don't smell it now," he explained.

"But all this money! Look at it. It's burnt!"

"I *am* looking at it."

He snickered, then held up the bill. "Got a light?" She handed him a lighter. Before he flicked it, he said, "It's not money. Money isn't made of paper. It's made of cotton and polyester. A very special blend that has a very distinct smell. In fact —" he added, igniting the bill, "when it burns, it burns orange." He had seen a lot of things on the job, come across some genuinely brilliant criminals. Rhodes had seen all types of crimes: robbery, blackmail, extortion, and more than one scheme worthy of making it to the big screen. This, however, took the cake. Rinaldo was indeed a master.

She looked at the burning bill. It wasn't orange. It was bright red.

Her eyes got big as Rhodes laughed long and hard. "Are you saying..." Korn began but couldn't finish her statement. She was now sick to her stomach. How many lives were ruined? How many careers? People had sold their souls for just a whiff of money they could never spend—even if they got their hands on it! It was absurd. Korn wondered if Houser was laughing at them from hell. In a way, Korn envied him.

"I'm saying all of these people died for nothing. I'm saying you fucked up your career for a *lie*. I'm saying Rinaldo fucking hustled us all! This money is *counterfeit*!" Rhodes cackled as his bitter laughter filled the burnt-out shell of the warehouse.

12

Rinaldo tucked his sleeping son into bed and kissed him. "Sleep tight, my little prince. Tomorrow's a new day," he whispered.

"Night, night, Daddy."

He took one last look, then cut off the light as he headed out the door. He could feel the gentle sway of the boat as he made his way topside. Rinaldo was on this twenty-eight-foot yacht. He'd copped it for 4.6 million. It was expensive, but he wasn't truly spending his money anyway. He had appropriately named the boat the *GOLDEN HUSTLA*.

Once topside, he gazed out over the dark blue sea and the big, fat full moon in the distance. The moon always seemed bigger in the Gulf of Mexico. He had decided to visit the Caribbean for a while. Then maybe Brazil. He'd take his time, though. There would be no more rushing. He was set for life.

Rinaldo walked along the aft to the stern of the ship. Rochelle was stretched out in a patio chair, looking delicious in a white, two-piece Gucci bathing suit.

"You look scrumptious, baby. Good enough to eat," he

smiled. They had won. Out of all the people that had taken a run for the fifty million, they were the last standing. He was glad Rochelle had survived when so many didn't. He had to admit, she was a survivor. He was proud of her, and he really did love her. Not unconditionally, the way he loved his son perhaps, but in his own twisted way, it was indeed love. Rinaldo felt a fondness for Rochelle that he hadn't felt in years. It surprised even him, and he was truly happy to see her.

"I still can't get over you, baby," she snickered. "How did you manage to pull it off?"

Rinaldo shrugged as he opened a cooler on the deck. He was more than brilliant; he was a god.

"The switch was nothing." Rinaldo leaned forward, smiling. His eyes sparkled.

"Counterfeit money so good a bank manager would never be able to tell the difference...Every time I went to the original stash, I'd swap the real money with an equal amount of the phony stuff. I knew I could always count on Charley to be nosy enough to check. But people see what they expect to see until you give them a reason not to."

Rinaldo was genuinely enjoying himself. To him, this was better than sex. To most people, everything came back to sex. Except sex was never actually about the sex...was it? *Sex was about power.* Rinaldo had fucked them all, long and hard, and his self-satisfied smirk said it all.

Rochelle thought about all the trips he'd made to Florida. Her brain worked through the implications. Exactly how much money had he moved? He'd never said a word.

"I always made sure the top layer was real. Just enough to satisfy. Maybe five million altogether in the old stash," he said. His smirk transformed into the smile of a man who knew he was the smartest person in any room he walked in. It was a predator's smile—the grin of a monster that liked to play with his food more than he enjoyed eating it. Rochelle didn't know whether to be disgusted or impressed. "Five million, that's all the thieves got. The rest is safe and sound where only I can touch it."

"That's a far cry from fifty." Rochelle was stunned. All that mayhem, all the blood for five million cash and forty-five million in *counterfeit money!*

He chuckled.

"Tell that to Charley and Brandon. I played them both perfectly. Brandon knew Charley and I had a lucrative partnership. Charley knew Brandon was greedy and trying to be the next me. So, I'm willing to bet my life that the guns blazed as soon as they laid eyes on each other," he surmised correctly.

"But what if they didn't? What if they're looking for you right now?" she challenged.

"Then I guess I'll be like the gingerbread man...Catch me if you can. Besides, how would they know the money is fake?" he replied as he tossed chunks of bloody meat into the water.

"What are you doing, baby?"

"Feeding the fish," he replied.

Rochelle looked at him admiringly. A false stash was perfect. *They would be insanely anonymously rich.* "I love you so much right now. You played all them fools!" she snickered. "You're such a genius!"

Rinaldo held out his hand. "Then why not dance with the devil in the pale moonlight?"

"But there's no music," she remarked.

"Then we'll make our own," he flirted.

"I like the sound of that," she replied.

Rochelle got up and embraced Rinaldo. Then they moved to their own rhythm.

"The world is ours," she whispered in his ear, glad that she was his last man standing.

"So says the blimp," he mocked, referring to the Scarface scene. "Did I tell you, you look delicious?"

"Mm-mmm."

He inhaled her scent. "You even smell delicious. I bet you taste delicious too," he said, twirling her around.

"You want to find out?"

"No...but *they* do." Rinaldo smiled with genuine warmth.

Before she could ask who, Rinaldo had gripped her by the waist and shoved her over the edge of the boat.

Splash!

"Oh my God, Rinaldo!" She frantically tried to stay afloat. "No! Please, baby, whatever I did, I'm sorry! Why, Rinaldo?" she screamed, trying to grab hold of the boat.

Rinaldo leaned on the rail. "Your services are no longer needed. You've been dismissed."

"Rinaldo!"

He could hear her desperation. All that calm, cool shit had gone out the window when she hit the water. Rochelle had wanted to swim with the sharks. Now, she would see what that was really like. She screamed again as the fins cut the water like knives. Finally, they zeroed on her thrashing form.

Rinaldo calmly headed up the short ladder to the yacht's wheelhouse.

"Oh, I almost forgot the music!" he yelled, adding, "*Dun-dun-dun-dun-dun-dun.*"

It was evident to Rochelle now. She saw the fins emerge from the depths of shadowy water. They were coming at her from three different angles. Rinaldo already knew what he would say to his son. *Mommy didn't listen. She played close to the edge where Daddy says never to play, and she slipped.*

Rinaldo sailed off into the night. The moon shimmered on the water in front of him with Rochelle's bloodcurdling screams behind him. Theirs was a marriage of convenience. It had been good, even fun for a while. It had worked well for its purpose, but they were never *in* love with each other. Rochelle wasn't made to go the distance with him, he concluded. When shit got hot, her cage got rattled, and Rinaldo had seen the truth of it. She wasn't really the ride-or-die type, which made her a liability, and liabilities and loose ends never sat well with him. Well, he hoped the sharks enjoyed their meal.

EPILOGUE

Rick landed at Newark Liberty International Airport and caught an Uber to the address. While still an FBI agent, Rick had procured his FFL dealer's license, enabling him to legally transport his Hi-Point 9mm rifle, Sig Sauer, and his now-lucky chrome Desert Eagle. His heart sang a song of revenge against the man that kidnapped Kyra and forced him to shoot Nina. He still couldn't believe what he had done. She had given him a son, and he repaid her with gunfire. Rick had agonized, dissecting his decisions. But at the moment, it was the only solution, the only way he could free Kyra and throw the hunters off of Nina's trail altogether. *It was the smart play, the right play*, Rick told himself over and over. *Even if I had let them kill Kyra, they would still be coming for Nina.* He knew it was the truth, but it didn't stop his guts from churning with anxiety.

Nurse Wright sent Rick a text, relaying the news that Nina and baby Rick were alive and well. However, Nina's coma troubled him. Medically induced or not, Rick knew how tricky head injuries could be. Nurse Wright had also said something about memory loss. Part of Rick hoped Nina wouldn't remember what he had done. But even if she did, she'd either understand or kill him.

Come what may, Rick made a vow to himself. He would love, protect, and cherish the women in his life. He had failed, but he wouldn't fail again. He had all his eggs in two separate baskets, and the results had been disastrous. Being distracted had almost cost him both Nina and Kyra. The shit must stop. Rick's mind sprouted the seeds of a plan. Both women were a part of him, and nobody could be complete or function with their parts in different places.

When he arrived at the motel, Rick paused only long enough to tuck his handguns and strap into his body armor. Next, he put a shower cap on his head, slipped a medical mask over his face, and booties over his shoes. Then he slung the rifle over his right shoulder and draped his coat over himself. Fully prepared, he stormed through the establishment headed straight for the room number he received via text.

The door exploded inward with a mighty kick, and Rick was steady with years of practice. Raids were nothing new to him, and the government had trained him well to do like Biggie said, except he was toting a carbine rifle instead of the infamous four-four. The room looked much as he'd expected. Cheap motel furniture, a lamp that was accidentally antique, and two full-size mattresses that looked as though they were made of lice and bedbugs holding hands. Two red-wearing goons stood, drawing guns. One had been sitting on the bed, the other seated in the rickety chair next to the room's cheap desk. Rick didn't hesitate—no questions were asked. Instead, he shouldered the Hi-Point rifle fast and fired, taking the quicker of the two goons with a headshot. Kyra emitted a muffled scream as the bullet ripped through her captor's temple, spraying bloody brain matter against the wall.

"Yo...yo...chill!" the second goon screamed as Rick took aim and silenced him with two in his throat.

Rick was already moving to free Kyra from the duct tape binding her hands before the body dropped.

"Rick, Rick, oh my God, you came." Kyra, visibly shaken, sobbed as they embraced, goose bumps swelling up and down her arms.

"I came? What the fuck, Kyra? You had no faith that I would come for you?" Rick snapped, unable to hide his disappointment.

"Baby, the only thing I could think about was that you didn't know where I was." She burst into tears. "This was fucking scary, Rick."

"I know, baby. But damn, I will always be there for you and won't stop until I get whoever causes you harm. Now, which one of these muthafuckas is B-Murder?"

Still shaken, she took a moment and examined both faces. "Neither one. These are the two he left to watch me." Rick nodded and retrieved a pair of nitrile gloves from his pocket and put them on.

Then he went to the dead thug with the biggest chain and fished an iPhone out of his pocket. *Flashy niggas love iPhones*, Rick smirked, using the dead man's thumb to unlock the phone. *Gotcha!* He went to the recent calls and found a contact labeled "Big Homie." *Gotchu, nigga!* Rick turned to Kyra with a predatory grin forming on his lips. "Time to end this," he said, dialing to reach "Big Homie."

B-Murder picked up almost instantly. "Yo, y'all gotta problem?"

"No, muh'fucka, but you do. Count your fucking days, pussy! Your boys think they got me pinned down." Rick popped a few rounds into one of the corpses. "They might need your help," Rick shouted into the phone with a mad cackle, then hung up. *Should have known this shit was too easy*, he grumbled, pissed one of the dead men wasn't B-Murder, but Rick had a plan B. *These niggas like red, so a little blood and mayhem shouldn't be a problem.* He hadn't booked a return flight, so he had time to exact some revenge.

Rick turned to Kyra, cupping her tear-stained face. She would always be absolutely beautiful to him no matter what. Her dark eyes drank him in as if it were her first time really seeing him. Rick put down the gun for the first time. He moved toward Kyra, and their lips met like stars colliding. Kyra seemed to melt into him, and Rick embraced her as the kiss broke.

"I can't believe you're here," she repeatedly murmured as her tears soaked his chest.

"Kyra..." Rick started, but the stress of the last twenty hours combined with the flood of emotion dried the words in his throat. He simply pulled her tighter, hoping his physicality translated the tumult his lips couldn't navigate. It had taken a lot of blood to get here, including that of a woman he loved.

His eyes strayed to the dead goons. Rick could feel Kyra's heart stuttering against her chest like a caged animal. Her body trembled against his. Rick felt regret, guilt, and with the scent and touch of the woman filling him who he'd loved—and lost —only to find again—he felt desire rise to swamp the tangled knot of emotions he had no hope of unpicking. Rick kissed Kyra again, feeling himself stiffen and a feral growl emanate from his lover as his hard on poking against her. He effortlessly lifted Kyra in his arms, and she wrapped her legs around him. His next thought was to carry her to the bed. He took one step, then another, until his bootie-covered foot squelched in blood. *This has to end.*

With a sigh, Rick put Kyra down. The soft lines of her nut-brown face registered confusion and a hint of frustration.

"Rick, if we not about to have a morbidly tender moment, what are we doing?" she said, showing the feisty edge he loved. Rick smiled.

"Business before pleasure."

Kyra rolled her eyes, but Rick was already moving.

She watched as he went to the other dead goon and ran his pockets until he found his phone. Rick clicked the side button, and the home screen opened immediately. *What kind of nigga don't lock his phone?* he muttered to himself as he sent out a group text using a few of the names he found in the inbox. *Time to start a party.*

Rick began to type quickly, as close to the dead man's text style as possible. He had to move fast in case anybody came to check the hotel.

Pussy-ass nigga snatched up the li'l bitch and Quan's phone and bounced. Said if we followed him, he would give the phone to 12 niggaz. I Got this nigga pinned down by Jesse Allen Park. He can't see us, and we can't see him. Nigga stuck but Idk for how long. He's hit, but he's strapped up heavy. With enough heat, we can burn this nigga. K's up

Kyra watched him work, a wry look on her beautiful face. "So, this is what they teach in the FBI?"

Rick smirked and muttered, "You have no idea."

Half an hour later, Rick waited in a spot that offered decent cover, keeping the group chat on the dead thugs' phones buzzing, hyping up B-Murder and his goons. He had sparked a shit storm by saying that Quan had shit in the phone that would see them all in a cell. Rick smiled. Nothing motivated niggas like fear of indictment. Vows of vengeance and blood-shed fueled more plans to link up and move on the park. *Too easy*, Rick thought.

Then a black Infiniti full of red-wearing goons circled until a similarly full black Suburban pulled up. A few moments later, two groups of men exited the vehicles and converged on Rick's location. They started to split up until Rick called out, "Aagh, fuck! I can't believe this nigga shot me!"

Soon, the two groups came running in a single clump toward Rick's position. He opened fire. The rich tang of gunpowder filled his nostrils as he emptied his clip. The light semiautomatic rifle had barely any recoil, and the 9mm rounds hurled themselves at his targets, striking any he could reach, center mass. Of the eight men that had approached, none were standing. Every time he pulled the trigger, all he could see was Nina's petite frame tossed like trash by his Desert Eagle. He thought about closing on his stricken enemies. Rick felt the burning desire to bring his enemies the same suffering he had felt. Overcome with the need to see B-Murder bleeding at his feet, Rick started to storm through the trees but changed his mind when he heard sirens blare.

Rick scurried in the opposite direction. Dipping into a random yard of a dilapidated house that might have been green a decade ago, he used a K-tool shovel to bury the Hi-Point rifle behind some overgrown bushes. When he finished, Kyra appeared, having watched from the window of the abandoned house.

"Did you book the reservation?" he asked.

Kyra nodded. "The Uber should be here soon." Rick moved in, kissing her again. Even if B-Murder wasn't dead or dying in the park, he'd have bigger problems than tracking them down.

B-Murder waited for somebody—anybody—to pick up. All of them soldiers for one man seemed a waste of resources, but that bitch and that phone could bury them all.

Tired of waiting, he decided to take a ride. When he got to the scene, he smelled the powder in the air before he saw the bodies. The luckiest had died in a clump. Some had clawed bloody trails across the pavement before their lives expired to pool in sticky, red puddles on the ground.

B-Murder was angry, but deep down, he was afraid too. The loss of so many soldiers would hurt him on the street. Product would move slow; rivals would get bold. It was time to make some different moves.

∼

RICK LOOKED at Kyra as they rode. It had been three hours since his encounter with the clowns in red, and they were on their way to a new life. Rick wanted better for his children, and recent events had reminded him that he had talents that could be put to legal and lucrative uses. Plenty of guys went private sector security. Rick would too. He was hoping Dion would pan out. Rick had checked in regularly and was impressed with his initiative, and Dion promised him one hell of a story when they were off the phone.

Kyra had been asleep for most of the ride. Her eyes told him that she was overwhelmed by the whole ordeal. He had let her sleep, knowing that they would need to have the first of several long talks when she got up.

They crossed the Pennsylvania line, and Rick pulled over at a rest stop for gas. He tapped Kyra's shoulder and winced at her startled expression. It took her a moment to realize where she was.

"You hungry?"

"Yes!" Kyra replied emphatically. "And I've gotta pee!" So, hand in hand, they went inside.

∼

AS THEY SAT CHOWING down on Big Macs and fries, Rick asked Kyra the question that had been plaguing his mind.

"Kyra, why were you at a graveyard?"

Her eyes got distant, and for a moment, he thought she wouldn't answer.

"Since I was in town, I wanted to visit Marvin's grave. I needed the closure."

Rick choked on his food, eyes smoldering with anger he had almost forgotten. *I know she not pining for no dead nigga*, he thought peevishly. *Even dead, this nigga still almost getting you killed. Damn.*

~

KYRA LIVED in an apartment a few blocks away from the office he rented for his security business. He had started hiring and even had a few small contracts. He was getting his feet wet, and it felt good. Kyra, Nina, and the children were his main priorities *and* the biggest source of his stress. Rick had spent the whole ride home from the office trying to figure out the best way to force Kyra and Nina to talk. It had to happen.

Kyra's intransigence was typical, but the selfishness of it hurt Rick. *You can't just come back from the dead and demand shit.* He regretted ever going to California. The plan to off-load Rinaldo's hot money for drugs had been solid, but he didn't really have to go back to Cali for that. Something had drawn him, a magnetism that he didn't understand, and when he had seen Kyra, he knew it was fate. He just didn't understand why fate wanted to complicate his life.

Rick shook his head with a deep sigh. *Nina.* He had coordinated his return to Arizona with Nurse Wright. Thanks to her help, he had been there when Nina woke up and showed up as often as he could for her recovery. Nina had healed well, and other than a couple of scars and some memory loss, she was back to her usual self. The fact that she didn't remember a damn thing after the fire at the warehouse was a blessing. Rick had been gifted a miracle. Now, he just had to cook up another one.

READING GROUP DISCUSSION QUESTIONS

1. Nina and Rick stole from Cream and Shawn, who originally stole from Rinaldo. Is it wrong to steal from other thieves?
2. Do you think Supreme is justified in his anger toward Nina, especially when it comes to having custody of his daughter?
3. Rick's connect, Agent Korn, never trusted Nina. Why do you think Korn doesn't trust Nina and do you think her distrust is valid?
4. Do you think Rick truly loves Nina, considering he shot her, which could have potentially killed her?
5. What did you think of Nurse Wright's character?
6. Is Nina to blame for the deaths of her brothers and mother? Is she totally responsible or are there other factors that played a part in their murders?
7. Should Nina and Kyra be more understanding of Rick's predicament? Can a person be in love two people at once or should Rick choose one woman over the other?
8. What do you think about Reese's plot to overthrow

B-Murder? Was he motivated by his lust for Nina or by his genuine concern for lower level Kings?

9. Why do you think Deanna chose Brandon over Rinaldo? If she had stayed loyal to Rinaldo, do you think he would have let her live?

10. The rivalry between Rhodes and Houser ends with Houser's suicide. Do you think this proves Houser feels guilty for what he's done? If the roles had been reversed, do you think Rhodes would've killed himself to avoid incarceration?

11. What did you think of the ending? Did you expect Rinaldo would be capable of pulling off such a complicated heist? Why or why not?

ABOUT THE AUTHOR

Wahida Clark is also known as the Official Queen of Street Literature. She is a Celebrity Book Writing Coach, Celebrity Ghostwriter and author of 26 titles, including 4 New York Times Best-Sellers. She is the Business Development Officer of W. Clark Book Distribution and Executive Producer of the Queen of Street Lit Docuseries and is a lover of anything books...Writing, Publishing and Promoting.

BESTSELLING TITLES BY WAHIDA CLARK

Thugs and the Women Who Love Them

Every Thug Needs a Lady

Thug Matrimony

Thug Lovin'

Justify My Thug

Honor Thy Thug

Thug Seven

Lucky Seven

The Golden Hustla

The Golden Hustla 2

Payback Is A Mutha

Payback Ain't Enough

Payback With Ya Life

Blood, Sweat, & Payback

Sleeping With The Enemy

What's Really Hood

Thuggz Valentine

Covid, Mayhem, and Murder: A Headhunters Christmas

The Virus Brought Me My First Love

Thug Letters

Meet The Macklins

Emperors & Assassins

The Clubhouse Power Journal

The Queen of Street Lit Autobiography

How to Turn Your Message or Expertise into a Profitable Best-Selling Book

How to Turn Your Message or Expertise into a Profitable Best-Selling Book 2.0

#1 Best-Seller Training: Why Every Author Needs the Status of Best-Seller

Start to Finish: An Author's How-to Boxset

CLASSIC
STREET LIT
SERIES

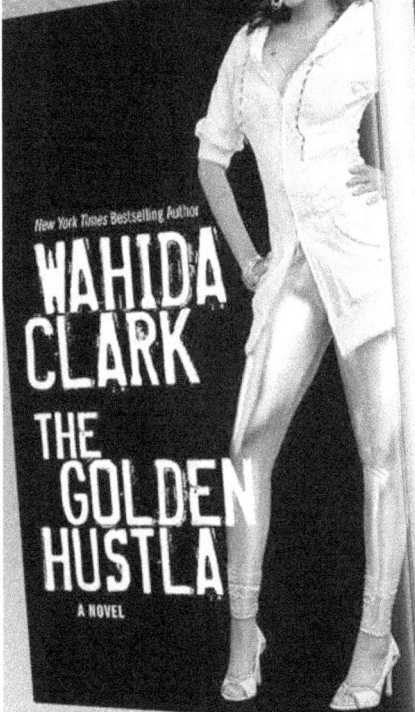

WAHIDA CLARK
PRESENTS
INNOVATIVE PUBLISHING

NEW SCI-FI FANTASY

FROM WAHIDA CLARK PRESENTS INNOVATIVE PUBLISHING

#1 INFLUENCER PUBLISHING & WRITING COACH, CELEBRITY GHOSTWRITER
WAHIDA CLARK
OWN YOUR COPY TODAY!!
HOW TO TURN YOUR MESSAGE OR EXPERTISE INTO A PROFITABLE BEST-SELLING BOOK
By 4X's New York Times Bestseller
WAHIDA CLARK
BOOK 2.0
By 4X's New York Times Bestseller
WAHIDA CLARK
WAHIDA CLARK
PRESENTS
INNOVATIVE PUBLISHING

READ THIS 1973 ORIGINAL CLASSIC

UNCLE YAH YAH
THE 21ST CENTURY
MAN OF WISDOM

BY AL DICKENS

UNCLE
Yah Yah
21st Century Man of Wisdom

Al Dickens

UNCLE
Yah Yah
21st Century Man of Wisdom
PART II

Al Dickens

WAHIDA CLARK
PRESENTS
INNOVATIVE PUBLISHING